ZANE PRESENTS

THE
BAD SEED

Dear Reader:

Lee Hayes has done a remarkable job, once again, of bringing vivid, powerful characters to life in *The Bad Seed*. Two powerful novellas will take you, the reader, on a roller-coaster ride that is too invigorating to walk away from until the final line. In "I Guess That's Why They Call It The Blues," a young, handsome gold digger is married to a man that he would much rather bury than engage in intimacy with. Ultimately, he discovers that money cannot define happiness in the face of evil. In "Crazy in Love," a male student becomes infatuated with a teacher and will stop at nothing, even violence, to gain his love in return. *The Bad Seed* serves as a wakeup call for those who get involved and fall in love too quickly with people that they really do not even know. The storylines are so real that the characters jump off the pages.

Lee Hayes is a wonderful novelist. His previous titles (*Passion Marks, A Deeper Blue: Passion Marks 2, The Messiah,* and *Flesh to Flesh*) have established his prolific voice in an industry that tends to be plagued with redundancy. Each work is significant and compelling within itself.

Thanks for giving *The Bad Seed* support and I am confident that you will enjoy reading it as much as I enjoyed editing it. Thanks also for supporting the dozens of other authors that I publish under Strebor Books. We truly appreciate the love. For more information on our titles, please visit www.zanestore.com and you can find me on my personal website: www.eroticanoir.com. You can also join my online social network at www.planetzane.org.

Blessings,

Zane

Publisher
Strebor Books
www.simonsays.com/streborbooks

ZANE PRESENTS

THE BADSEED

LEE HAYES

STREBOR BOOKS

NEW YORK LONDON TORONTO SYDNEY

Strebor Books
P.O. Box 6505
Largo, MD 20792
http://www.streborbooks.com

ISBN 978-1-59309-263-4
ISBN 978-1-4391-2791-9 (ebook)
LCCN 2011926496

First Strebor Books trade paperback edition May 2011

Cover design: www.mariondesigns.com
Cover photograph: © Keith Saunders/Marion Designs

10 9 8 7 6 5 4 3 2 1

Manufactured in the United States of America

For information regarding special discounts for bulk purchases, please contact Simon & Schuster Special Sales at 1-866-506-1949 or business@simonandschuster.com

The Simon & Schuster Speakers Bureau can bring authors to your live event. For more information or to book an event, contact the Simon & Schuster Speakers Bureau at 1-866-248-3049 or visit our website at www.simonspeakers.com.

To my father, John Andrew Hayes,
October 18, 1936 – September 30, 2010.
You are missed each day. Rest in Peace.

Dedicated to anyone who has ever been…misunderstood.

CHAPTER 1

East Texas
April 2002

I gritted my teeth and with all the force I could command, I hurled my body into the solid frame of my adolescent lover and sent his body flying off the rooftop. Jabari's body plunged seven stories and crashed into the jagged rocks that jutted up from the ground like the fangs of an enormous primordial beast.

I heard his body crack on the rough stones below.

Crack.

Crack.

Crack. Crack.

The unmistakable sound of death spun swiftly around my ears, causing me to become disoriented. I was dizzied and dismayed by what I had done. I stumbled clumsily backwards as a flood of emotions swelled within me. I tripped over a rusted pipe that lay diagonally across the commercial rooftop, but regained my balance by anchoring myself against the air conditioning unit that rose from the rooftop.

I shook my head from side to side in wild disbelief and screamed silently into the night; horror stole my voice, but I could not free myself from the sound of his screams and the cracking sound of his body splitting the rocks below. The chilling sound of death would echo in my ears long after this night had passed.

Crack.

Crack.

Crack. Crack.

The breaking sound of Jabari's body felt sharp and cut into my skin like a scalpel. I doubled over in pain and expelled a hot puff of breath when I felt a splinter of pain in my heart; it was as if my body had been deeply penetrated by one of the pointed stones below. Jabari's pain was my pain, too, as if we were the Corsican brothers.

I swallowed hard and steeled my disposition. With carefully measured steps, I moved closer to the edge of the building and stopped several feet from the ledge. I tried to propel myself farther, but my feet were held in place by a thousand pounds of guilt... and shame.

Crack.

Crack.

Crack. Crack.

I covered my ears with my hands.

Crack.

Crack.

Crack. Crack.

I could not free myself from the sound. It reminded me of the snapping sound the branches made when a strong summer storm violently tore them from the tree in my front yard and sent them crashing through my bedroom window. This cracking sound was not made by breaking branches, but breaking bones; yet, the sounds of both events were eerily similar.

I stepped closer.

I had to see, even as my heartbeat pounded ferociously in my chest.

I wasn't sure how I would react to the sight of my dead lover. My mind raced and a litany of unpleasant thoughts threatened to topple me. What would I see when I looked down?

Oh my God! What have I done? Please God, let him be alive.

In spite of my anemic pleading, I already knew the truth. No one could survive that fall. Not even Jabari.

Crack.

Crack.

Crack. Crack.

I teetered and tottered slowly to the edge of the building. My breathing was labored and dug deeply into my chest. In the distance, a thousand points of light punctuated the peaceful sky, in severe contrast to the night's discord.

When I mustered up the nerve, I peered downward, toward the ground in search of Jabari. Despite the darkness, I could see far better than I had expected. My senses were acute, sharpened by the adrenaline racing through my veins. From atop the building, I could clearly see the labels of broken beer bottles that were strewn across the landscape; an old tire, whose tread was worn and abused, was halfway buried near an old stump. Cigarette butts were so common they looked as if they were sprouting from the ground. The landscape itself was dotted with nappy patches of dry grass, tangled, coarse and uneven.

Then, my eyes locked onto the twisted and mangled body of Jabari. His body was broken in ways I never realized a body could be broken.

Blood flowed from his body, as if he had an endless reservoir of it. I had never seen so much blood; it seeped from the corners of his mouth and flowed from his chest, aided by a crooked piece of wood that shot up through his sternum like a jagged monument to our failed love affair.

In my heightened state of awareness, I could even smell the blood.

A frightening thought assaulted me even more than the sight of the body below—the animals. Out here in the country, they would come to claim what lay beneath me. The creatures that lived in the night would smell the blood and would soon search for its source. I shuddered. It pained me to imagine Jabari's body being ravaged by some wild thing, torn to pieces in a ravenous display of savagery.

In my heart, I knew that Jabari's body had already been ravaged by a wild thing.

I continued to eye my dead lover. This was no proper end for our love, with Jabari lying twisted below me. I thought, albeit briefly, about moving the body, but my inclination to do so diminished the more I looked at him. I wouldn't be able to stomach the stench of death so up close. Even if my thoughts were more sincere, I certainly would fail in my quest to carry the body to hallowed ground; I barely remained in command of my own limbs.

Still, I longed for a final touch from him.

I longed to feel his warmth once more, before his body went cold.

Only days ago, we had been locked in a passionate embrace on this very rooftop, making love like it was our first time. Only days ago, our lips had locked in a fiery kiss that set every cell in my body ablaze. I remembered how my skin sizzled when Jabari grazed his fingers across the arch in my back. Even now, with Jabari splayed unnaturally across the earth below me, I could feel the weight of his body on top of mine, pressing down with perfect force. We panted in a unified rhythm, as our bodies sang together in harmony; that night, I thought our union had been blessed by heaven, instead of cursed by tonight's hell.

Now, Jabari was dead at my hands.

Crack.

Crack.

Crack. Crack.

I cocked my head to the side and eyed the lifeless body, almost expecting him to rise before my eyes, but Jabari was no Lazarus.

Even from my distance, I could see the pleading in Jabari's eyes; his eyes were wide, held open by shock. His mouth was agape, as if terror had been ripped from this throat. One of his arms was folded artificially behind his back and his left leg seemed to point in multiple directions at the same time.

Dear God. What have I done?

I wanted to scream, but I could not find my voice; it was lost in the madness of the moment. In the still of the night, I would have settled for any sound, regardless of how infinitesimal. I would have settled for the flutter of insect wings or the annoying blaring of a car horn in the distance; instead, a haunting silence suffocated all sound, locking it inside this awful dread. The silence taunted me, reminding me of death's finality. As I stood motionless, awash in my worst nightmare, the irony of it all was not lost: I had always known, even from our first kiss, that he and I were destined to say goodbye.

The breathtaking silence stood in measured contradiction to the chorus of chaotic thoughts that powered through my mind.

Flee.

Scream.

Cry.

Call 9-1-1.

Hide any evidence.

Run. Run. Run.

Instead of taking action, I remained motionless, almost catatonic.

My mind wildly spun, replaying the moments leading to this terrible turn of events.

✪ ✪ ✪

"Thanks for meeting me," Jabari said in a voice that struck my ears as unusually rough.

"Hey, baby." In spite of his lackluster greeting, I was more than happy to see him, even though something was off; I could feel it in the air. An uneasy breeze chilled the air, not enough to cause alarm, but enough to make me take notice of the goosebumps that speckled my bare arms. I was wearing a thin pullover shirt—something I could easily slip in and out of in case things got heated. In spite of the trepidation in my spirit, I had come prepared to light up the night in our usual carnal way.

Earlier, when Jabari phoned and asked me to meet him in our special place, I recognized the uneasiness in his tone, but I didn't press the issue with him over the phone. Instead, I agreed to meet him and prayed that tonight was not the night I'd been dreading for months.

We named our special meeting place "heaven" because there was no place in the city that we could claim as ours. The isolated and dilapidated building that sat atop Mount Royale, a very large hill overlooking the city, kept a watchful eye over the town below. The building, an old schoolhouse, had been condemned years ago and had been cut off from the world by an intimidating barbed wire fence, but we were able to sneak through a narrow opening near the back. From the rooftop, Jabari had crowned himself emperor and claimed the world below as his kingdom; a kingdom he would lay at my feet.

Looking out, the colorful city lights decorated the horizon and the sound and fury of a world furiously spinning beneath our feet did not register at our height. This was the one place Jabari could be himself without fear of rejection or reprisal. Here, he didn't have to worry about being an athlete or a favored son; here, he didn't have to entertain thoughts of going to Harvard or Yale or wherever his father would send him; here, he was a lover—my lover—and that was all that mattered.

Jabari stood on the edge of the building, with his hands in his pockets. He smiled uncomfortably and shifted his weight as I approached.

"What's wrong?" I moved closer to him and kissed him, but Jabari didn't kiss me back. His lips were cold and void of passion.

Then, I hugged him.

Jabari's embrace was empty.

Have I done something wrong? Is he mad at me?

A sick feeling grew in my stomach as Jabari turned away from me.

"It's a lovely night, isn't it?" Jabari spoke, but his voice was low.

"Yeah, it is, but what's going on? Are you okay?" I felt panicked, like I couldn't catch my breath, but Jabari didn't respond. I looked at him and his eyes confirmed my greatest fear—this was the end. Our love affair had run its course. Jabari needn't speak the words for me to know. I realized that when we started this affair that we had an expiration date—Jabari was clear in stating that in the beginning. There would be no happy ending for us, no warm Christmas days with the family or moving into an off-campus apartment together for college. Jabari told me that he could never fall in love with a man and what we had couldn't last. He said he was experimenting, and despite the fact that he had a girlfriend, he allowed himself this experience to get it out of his system.

But, the last year had been magical. He couldn't deny that. We loved in ways that resisted definition; in ways that made it difficult for him to shake off. Even as our love grew, I carried worry in my heart; worry, that on a night very much like this night, he'd break my heart.

Jabari turned to face me. "I can't do this anymore."

His words felt like hot bullets.

"What are you talking about, baby? Can't do what?" I knew what he was talking about.

"I'm talking about us—this *thing* we're doing. I can't…anymore."

"Why? Has something happened?" I stepped closer and he

backed away. "I love you. You love me. What's the problem?"

"The problem is I'm not a fag." The careless and hateful word leapt from his mouth, but it had undoubtedly been placed there by someone else, probably his father; the same father who demanded perfection, and the same father that I was certain Jabari would spend a lifetime trying to please.

"I'm not a fag either," I said with some irritation. "I just happen to love you."

"I'm not like you. I…I don't want this life. I want a normal life."

"Normal? What's normal? Look around you, Jabari. Think about all the people we know who are divorced or alone or miserable and you tell me what normal is. What we have is as normal as anything else."

"If it was normal, we wouldn't be sneaking around, meeting on the rooftop of some raggedy-ass building. If it was normal, I'd take you to the prom or home to meet my father, but I can't, now can I? What we're doin' ain't normal. My family would never accept this in me."

"Stop worrying about your family and think about us." The growing desperation in my spirit shook my voice. "We could move…we could run away and be together."

"And do what, Blues? We're in high school. We don't have any money. How would we live?"

"We can get money."

"How? You gonna rob a bank?" Jabari exhaled in frustration. "Don't be so fuckin' naïve."

I gritted my teeth. I hated when Jabari cussed at me.

"Jabari—"

"Stop saying my fuckin' name!" For some reason that remained a mystery to me, Jabari started to get angry, as if he was placing the blame of his homosexuality at my feet. Jabari's face twisted and his voice sounded final, as if there could be no compromise, but I was not ready to let him go. I had to convince him to stay.

"Baby," I said in a pleading whisper, "please don't do this. Okay, so we won't run away. We can keep seeing each other. I don't care about Nia—you can keep seeing her and I won't give you shit about it anymore."

"You don't get it, do you? This will never work. I don't want to be like you!" Jabari screamed.

I felt Jabari's thunder in my chest.

"You don't want to be like me?"

"You know what I mean."

"You're more like me than you want to admit."

"Fuck you, Blues!"

We stood in silence as seconds stretched into minutes. The empty space between us grew and I struggled to find words to close the gap. The wounded sky, although speckled with flickers of starlight, seemed to feel my pain. I felt small and insignificant, crushed by the weight of Jabari's pronouncement. The air was still and the night silent; all that could be heard was the breaking of my heart.

Jabari's decision had stolen my voice. There were so many things I wanted to say, so many things I had rehearsed in case this day ever came, but I couldn't find the words that I had practiced over and over again. All I could think was *don't leave me, don't leave me, don't leave me, don't leave me…*

Suddenly, it became hard to breathe and the world started spinning around me. I doubled over as if I had been hit in the stomach. Such pain was dealt to me by five small words: 'I can't do this anymore.' Everything collapsed around me. My head hurt. My chest hurt. Hell, even my feet hurt. As I looked up into the sky, I saw the stars tilting out of orbit. Any second, one would hit the earth and destroy everything I knew and loved.

"Baby…" I said as I wiped tears away from my face. Jabari looked away again, avoiding eye contact. "Whatever you're looking for out there, you won't find. Everything you need, everything you want, and everything that you are is right here with me." I spoke with outstretched arms as tears streamed down my face. I laid it all on the line.

Finally, Jabari looked at me. I expected some emotional response to my emotional plea, but the expression on Jabari's face wasn't love—it was mockery. He looked at me with such disdain, as if I was some rabid stranger on the street begging him for loose change.

That was the moment that everything in me changed.

My tears stopped falling. My heart stopped beating. I stopped breathing.

I looked at Jabari through newly formed eyes. This wasn't a man that loved me; this was a man that despised me and used me for months to satisfy his temporary pleasure.

His vacant eyes taunted me.

His callous words mocked me.

Five words eviscerated the love we shared and left me a cold, empty shell.

I felt many things in that horrifying moment, but the most pronounced thing I felt was rage. Something inside me broke and the popping sound of whatever it was rang so loudly in my ears that I heard nothing else. I could see Jabari's lips moving, but the words remained indecipherable through it all. In a quick-fire blind impulse, I lunged at him. I lunged at him with a strength I didn't realized that I possessed. I sent his body reeling over the edge of the building to the rocky earth below.

As Jabari plummeted to the ground, I heard his screams. I would always hear those screams and the sound of breaking bones.

Crack.

Crack.

Crack. Crack.

That wasn't the first time I had killed.

I had been born a killer. My father had told me so.

I burst into the world on a sweltering July afternoon, with the merciless force of a pounding sledgehammer.

I tore my mother apart.

I violently pushed my way out of my mother's belly, using my head like a battering ram. I would not be stopped, but when I was free of her womb, I struggled to breathe on my own. My mother panicked, but before any proactive measure could be taken to save my life, she gasped, stretched out her arms, and drew in her last breath. The moment she drew in her last breath, I drew in my first—a circle of life in the truest sense. She died, never having seen my face.

When she drifted into that eternal night, she released her secret shame; the secret she kept tucked away into the recesses of her mind died with her. No one would ever know that she had been raped and I was the result of that unholy union. My father would never know that his son belonged to another man, a nameless and faceless being who forced himself into his wife on a very ordinary October afternoon.

She had been jogging along a familiar trail when she was snatched and forced deeper into the woods. When it was over, she steeled her disposition, went home, showered and pretended that it had never happened. She pretended that she didn't wince with pain with each step she took; she pretended that she could no longer feel the stranger's coarse hands rubbing against her inner thigh or the smell of beer on his hot breath.

Later that night, she cooked her husband's favorite meal, set the table and stuffed herself into the pantry and cried while the meatloaf baked; her tears were not pretentious. When it was time to eat, she fixed his plate and served it to him, as she usually did. Then, she pretended that she wasn't feeling well, excused herself, and went to bed early. The pillows muted her sobs and drew in her tears, but the horror did not diminish—even in her dreams.

She pretended for nine months, but she could never forget. Her pregnancy was difficult, full of highs and lows. She alternated between mania and moods so sullen it appeared that someone had stolen her life force. The fire in her belly was constant, never relenting or dulling. When she died, a part of my father died, too. When I was placed in his arms and my father held me for the first time, he looked at the immutable blackness of my sublime skin and my exquisite features. He thought about all the misery this beautiful child had already caused, even before his first breath. He thought about the constant morning sickness and the severe mood swings my mother had faced; he remembered how this child had transformed her into something he hardly recognized. He remembered her constant tears.

This child had given her the blues.

He tried to feel love toward me but, he couldn't. He simply didn't feel it. Deep inside his heart, he blamed me for her death.

And so I was aptly named.

CHAPTER 2

Washington, D.C.
Summer 2011

I*'m going to kill you*, I thought with all the seriousness I could muster as I peered across the table into the aging face of my curmudgeonly husband. I had never had a more sincere thought. I wanted him dead, like yesterday. His beady black eyes, razor-thin mustache, and shiny bald head gave him a macabre appearance, as if he was an over-the-top clichéd villain from some ancient black-and-white movie.

Die, you miserable old bag of bones.

I smiled lovingly at him and sipped champagne while pretending to actually enjoy his company. I had become an expert at pretending and hiding my true intentions in plain sight.

I'm going to bury you and salt the earth so that nothing will ever grow from your wretched remains.

I watched his wrinkled, peanut-colored hand reach for his champagne flute. I hated Robert's hands because those hands pawed at me daily like he was a wild animal in heat.

Maybe I'll hack them off with an axe and then slap him across the face with them.

With an almost choking disgust, I watched Robert grab the glass with exaggerated effort. He sometimes feigned feebleness for effect or to make light of our significant age difference, much to my chagrin. I didn't need a constant reminder that Robert was old. All I had to do was look at his weathered face to see that he was aged.

Robert raised his glass and smiled the way only an old fool would. *A fool and his money would soon part.*

"Here's to you, my love," Robert said in that sappy tone that I despised. "You are everything an old man could want and more." *There's that word again—old.*

I offered a tepid smile and raised my glass in mock celebration. While Robert was toasting our relationship, I secretly prayed for death. When the time was right, like a thief in the night, I would strike; or, at least Marquis would.

"Here's to us, baby," he said. I tried not to choke on my words. "We need to start thinking about a vacation. Where should we go? Paris? Monaco? Milan? Durban?"

"Robert," a wispy voice called out from behind us. Before I could fully turn around, the figure had moved closer to the table and was facing Robert with outstretched arms and a wide grin plastered across his plastic face. It was Bernard, one of my least favorite people in the world. "Robert, I'm so happy that you stopped by on a day when we are all celebrating your generosity to our community."

Robert stood slowly and was pulled into the embrace of this sloppy giant, and they kissed on both cheeks. Bernard's thick French accent made his sentences choppy and almost unintelligible, not that he was saying anything of any importance. I hated most of Robert's gay-faced, pompous friends, but I especially loathed this piece of Euro trash. Every time we dined here, Bernard fawned over Robert like he was royalty.

As much as I hated Bernard, I hated this terrible little canteen more. Bernard was the owner and proprietor and it was supposed to be the trendy *it* spot, but this quaint little cafeteria was nothing more than a cramped box with a few garish velvet curtains strewn about; it looked like it had been decorated by a one-eyed gypsy.

For me, the food didn't fare any better. The overpriced faux French food tasted more like it was out of Paris, Texas, rather than Paris, France; yet, for some reason that remained incomprehensible to me, Robert insisted on coming here and it remained one of his favorite places in the Georgetown area of D.C., in spite of its myriad of shortcomings.

We were celebrating because Robert was featured on the cover of *Washington Metro*, a local magazine, and had been honored earlier in the day by the mayor at a ceremony because he had donated a million dollars to some shelter for gay homeless teens. *Big deal*, I thought as the award was being presented. Now, the whole city was acting like Robert's shit didn't stink, but I knew better—I knew the real Robert Douglas. It annoyed me that the city was treating him like royalty.

It annoyed me more that Robert spent all that—money that would've been mine—for a *local* headline.

"Where else would I be besides my favorite place in the city? We had to stop by for one of your decadent desserts. Bernard, you remember my husband, Blues."

"Oh yes," he said with a hint of shade in his voice, "so nice to see you again."

"Likewise." I smiled, picked up my glass and turned so that I could mumble *bitch* under my breath.

"I am so happy for you. You looked so handsome and debonair on the magazine cover. You are a treasure to the community."

He's a treasure alright and I'm ready to bury him.

"I do want I can. There is so much need out there." Robert's false modesty sent a wave of nausea to my stomach. He may have had the whole city eating out of the palm of his hands right then, but Robert didn't give a damn about those kids. What he cared about was money, fame, and his reputation. Every good deed he did was done with a self-serving purpose. I seriously doubted that he had ever done a good deed in his whole life without expecting something in return.

"Well, I'll let you get back to your dessert," Bernard said with his back turned toward me. "Order whatever you like. I'll take care of the bill."

"Bernard, I couldn't let you do that."

"I insist. You've done so much, the least I can do is pick up your check," he replied.

"Well, if you insist," I inserted. Robert had spent enough money already, and I was not about to let him pay for anything in this place. Bernard smiled delicately at him and flitted away.

"Now, back to us." Robert picked up his glass again and started babbling about love and happiness, but I tuned most of it out; I simply sipped.

As the cool, bubbly champagne coated my throat, I watched him closely. I prayed that the next bite of food Robert stuffed into his mouth would lodge in his throat and choke him to death— that would at least spare me the process of murdering him. Plus, if he choked to death now, that would remove me from the god-awful position of having to sex him when we got back to the mansion. If I had to look at Robert's flabby, naked ass one more time, I might have vomited.

I watched with keen interest as Robert picked up a chocolate-covered strawberry from the silver serving tray and took a bite. *Choke! Just die, you miserable old bastard! Just die!*

I thought that if I prayed hard enough, my wish might come true.

I watched as Robert chewed the strawberry and reached for another without hesitation. Clearly, I wouldn't get my wish—at least not yet. He was going to die; of that, I was sure.

I took another sip of champagne and tried to mask my disappointment. It was all I could do to prevent myself from grabbing the knife from the tray, jumping across the table, and plunging the cold, hard steel into Robert's chest. The thought of thrusting the knife into his chest repeatedly made me smile. I reveled at the thought of hearing the gasping sound Robert would make when the blade first dug into his chest. I imagined the look of shock that would consume Robert's vacant eyes when he saw me above him, bloody knife in my hand. I imagined Robert's limp body falling to the floor with a great thud. Robert would struggle for his last breath as blood filled his lungs and I would smile.

Reality crept in as I took a deep breath and looked around the restaurant at the perfectly poised patrons. I decided that stabbing Robert in front of a room full of tightly wound, upscale society types wouldn't be prudent. I wanted him dead, but I certainly wasn't going to prison for his murder.

"What are you smiling at?" Robert asked in his usual rasping voice that snatched me out of my daydream. Robert leaned in closer and continued speaking before I had a chance to respond. "You ready for tonight? I bought some new toys for us," he said in a wicked whisper that sent a wave of nausea to my stomach. The grating sound of Robert's voice felt like sandpaper on my skin. I downed the rest of my champagne like it was a shot of tequila.

I didn't know how much longer I'd be able to put up with Robert's clammy hands clawing my body; nor, did I know how much longer I'd be able to indulge Robert's silly fantasies of school boys and priests. If I had to wear one more costume, thong, pair of ass-out pants, or leather straps with protruding metal parts across my chest, I was likely to suffocate him in his sleep. In spite of his seemingly frail demeanor, for an old man, Robert was cockstrong and his penchant for the perverse bordered on pornographic.

"Baby, you will excuse me, won't you?" I pushed away from the table. I had to get away; get some air.

"Where are you going?"

Why is this fool questioning me?

"I have to pee. Is that alright with you?" My tone was stronger than I intended. For a brief second, I could see shock brush across Robert's face—he wasn't used to people speaking to him like that. Then, his shock gave way to something else.

"Can I watch?" he asked with a licentious smile. He then started laughing, which morphed into a hacking smoker's cough that almost sent him hurling to the floor. I dropped my napkin into my chair and walked away in a huff. I didn't even wait for Robert's cough to dissipate. I dashed away without looking back, even as I heard his cough digging deeply into his chest.

Just die.

As I walked down the hallway and turned the corner, I slipped outside of the restaurant instead of going to the restroom. I walked a few steps and took a turn around the building to the side parking lot. The lot was full of parked expensive foreign vehicles, and a few cars were lined up waiting for the owners to give their keys to the valet attendant.

I pulled my cell phone out of my pocket, scrolled through to find the entries, and dialed Nigel's number, which I stored under the name Jill, in case Robert felt the need to peruse the contacts in my phone. It rang a few times before he answered.

"Wassup, sexy?" he said in a voice so rich and deep that I felt it in my bones. With the sound of his voice, I forgot all about Robert sitting at the table, hacking himself into a coma; I forgot about having to go home and fuck him for the next few hours. "You okay, baby?"

"Yeah…no. Not really."

"What's the matter?"

I paused. "I can't do this anymore. That old fucker is driving me crazy, and I'm about to lose it."

"Now, baby, I'm working on a way to get you out of this marriage with some money. Give me a couple more months."

"Months? Are you fucking kidding me? I'm not sure I'll last the next couple of days." I reached into my pocket and pulled out my pack of cigarettes.

"You know as well as I do that if you leave him, you'll walk away with exactly what you came into the marriage with…nothing. Your pre-nup is airtight."

"Yeah, thanks to you," I said sarcastically.

"I was only doing my job. As Robert's attorney, I had to protect my client. I can't help that I'm good at my job." Nigel chuckled, but I didn't find anything funny.

"Eh, huh."

"You can't leave him or you'll end up waiting tables at some greasy diner, and I don't want that for you. Living with Robert can't be that bad."

"Excuse me? You ain't the one that's gotta fuck his old ass every day. You ain't the one that's gotta listen to that voice of his. You ain't the one he's constantly grabbing. You ain't the one that got to suck—"

"Okay, okay. I get it. You're right," Nigel interjected. "All I'm asking is that you hang in there a little longer and trust me. I'm working on it." I rolled my eyes and looked up into the night sky. Little dots of light blinged out the sky like diamonds. "I don't wanna lie to you. This pre-nup is tight, but I'll find a way to get you what you need and then we can be together."

"I'm not asking for half of what he's got; just a nice chunk of change. I won't go back to being poor. Been there, done that."

I listened to Nigel's words, but they offered little solace. My haste in signing the pre-nup without an attorney was coming back to haunt me. I signed away any claims to any money upon divorce. At the time, I was under severe duress and Robert was not going to marry me without the pre-nup. Robert gave me an ultimatum. I had to marry him and sign the agreement or he'd end our relationship completely. I thought about walking away, starting over with someone else, but when I checked my bank account balance and my source of income, the numbers didn't add up. So, I did what I had to. Now, a year later, I wanted out of this marriage, but I refused to walk away empty-handed—not after all Robert had put me through. So, I stayed.

His death was the only way I could inherit.

From the moment I said "I do," I felt that Robert treated me as a possession, like something that existed only to please him and something that he could show off to his ridiculous friends. Robert never said it explicitly; he didn't need to. He made it perfectly clear with his disapproving glares that cut with the sharpness of a blade. Robert's heavy expectation that I become the perfect husband weighed heavily on me from the time I opened my eyes in the morning until I laid head to pillow at night. I had to maintain a certain weight, keep a certain appearance, speak with the proper words, smile when I didn't feel like it, and laugh when nothing was funny. I had to organize little parties and be cordial to Robert's annoying friends. I had to tend to his every need, be at his beck and call, and perform vulgar sexual acts that would make experienced hookers blush. Sex with Robert made me feel dirty, like a little whore with porn star aspirations.

"Shit, I'm beginning to think the only way for me to get out of this is for him to die." I spoke with a light bounce in my voice, as if I were joking; even still, a heavy silence wedged its way into the conversation. I chose the words carefully to gauge Nigel's reaction to the idea of Robert's death.

"Well," Nigel said after pause, "that is one way. As of now, you are his major benefactor."

I chuckled. "Isn't that interesting?"

"Blues," he said with some concern rising in his voice, "what are you thinking?"

"Oh, nothing. Merely fantasizing."

"If I'm reading your thoughts correctly, and I'm sure I am, I don't want you to entertain those thoughts. Fantasies can be dangerous."

I remained silent.

"Blues, do you hear me? Blues?"

"Yeah, baby. Don't worry. I was only joking."

"I don't want you doing anything crazy," he said.

Nigel's loyalty to Robert was strong, even though we were fucking. Sex is a long way from murder, and I doubted that homicide ever figured into Nigel's career advancement plans. He was ambitious, but not murderous. He wasn't like me. So, I kept him in the dark. If things went according to my plan, Robert would be dead in a matter of weeks and I would be rich beyond my wildest imagination. Then, there would be no need to wiggle my way out of a tight pre-nup.

"Trust me, I won't." I took a long drag off the cigarette and expelled smoke into the night air. "I've started smoking again," I said, trying to change the subject. I wanted him to know what the stress of living with my lawfully wedded husband, Mr. Robert P. Douglas, had done to me; it had driven me to a pack and a half a day of nicotine. I hoped my rising levels of stress would make Nigel work harder at finding a way out of this marriage. I wasn't completely heartless and my ideal solution was not homicide. If Nigel could find a way for me to walk away with at least five million dollars, I'd consider letting Robert live, but Nigel had a small window of opportunity to make it happen. For Robert's sake, Nigel needed to get me a divorce and a seven-figure settlement quick, fast, and in a hurry.

I inhaled deeply. My vice had once again found a place in my life; even my vanity couldn't keep the cigarettes away from me. Robert smoked and now so did I, along with regular puffs of marijuana and an occasional bump of cocaine—anything to make living with Robert more tolerable.

I often thought about what smoking and other drugs would do to my looks if I kept up the habit. I imagined that my dark, smooth skin would begin to resemble worn leather, and lines would begin to snake across my face from the corners of my mouth when I smiled; lines would stretch out in all directions from the corner of my eyes like a spider's web.

I was blessed with a strong bone structure, full lips, and deep, almond-shaped eyes. My looks were unique, like a proud African warrior. The immutable blackness of my perfect skin was sublime. People often mistook me for a model, but I always believed that most models would look ordinary standing next to me. I had always been envied and despised for being extraordinary. My looks wouldn't last forever, and who would I be without my looks? For me, there was nothing sadder than the fading beauty of a fading fag still holding on to the glory of his faded youth. I could never live like that. I had a plan. Robert's money would help ensure that would never be my fate. The moment anything on me began to sag, I was going somewhere to get it jacked up.

At twenty-seven years young, I still had it going on; in fact, I had never been in better shape, but smoking had become a habit born out of necessity. It was the only thing keeping me from setting Robert on fire while he slept.

Nigel was speaking again, but his words didn't register; instead, I listened to the velvety voice of my paramour. His calming voice ushered in a wave of peace and quieted my discordant thoughts.

"Can we fuck tomorrow?" I interrupted. "I need you to meet me at our spot tomorrow during lunch. After tonight, I'll need the touch and feel of a *real* man."

"We can fuck whenever you like. I got you, baby." The rich baritone of his voice spun deeply into my ears and burned its way down to my loins like fire. I felt his heat, and the anticipation of his touch made my dick jump. "I love you. I really do."

"I love you, too." I said it, but I wasn't even sure I understood what love was. I just knew the words sounded nice. "Baby, one last thing. Is Robert planning on giving away any more money that I need to know about? This donation spree he's been on lately is going to send us to the homeless shelter."

"He hasn't mentioned anything to me. Why?"

"I wanna make sure he has something left to give me when you get me my settlement."

"Trust me; there's more than enough to go around."

"If you say so. Aight, baby. I'll see you tomorrow."

I took a last drag off my cigarette, let it fall to the asphalt, and crushed the bud underneath my foot.

When I was preparing to put the phone in my pocket, it made a sound to alert me that I had received a text message. I looked down at the screen and saw the message was from "Mama," the code name I had given Marquis. Truth be told, I hadn't spoken to my real "Mama" in years. I looked at the message on the screen.

WHEN CAN WE HOOK UP?

Marquis and I usually fucked a few times a month and it had

been almost two months since I had seen him. I tried to keep the business of killing Robert separate from the business of fucking Marquis, but sometimes, we'd lie in bed and talk about Robert's death as casually as we talked about a television program.

I liked Marquis; probably a little more than I should. He was a little thug, but he wasn't a killer without a conscience. He agreed to be the trigger man in this plot because, in part, he had fallen for me and I often told him about the many abuses I suffered at Robert's hands, including physical violence, which I made up to convince Marquis. Robert had never laid a hand on me, though I'm sure there were times he wanted to slap the shit out of me. My chicanery worked like a charm on Marquis—he believed every word I told him and his hatred for Robert built up in his system. He'd used that hatred, one day, to kill him.

I sent a reply text.

SOON. I'LL CALL YOU.

I took a deep breath, puffed out my chest, and walked back into the restaurant with my head held high.

I couldn't wait for Robert to die.

My day wasn't just coming—it had arrived.

CHAPTER 3

After Robert and I left the restaurant and arrived at our Georgetown mansion, he didn't waste any time trying to ravage my body. The coarse skin on his hands—hardened from years of cigar smoking—felt like sandpaper against my smooth skin. We barely made it to the staircase before Robert forced his forked tongue into my mouth. He pawed my ass and tried to force me down onto the staircase so that he could continue his gritty sexual assault.

"Baby, baby, calm down. We have all night." I pushed him away gently as he continued kissing me sloppily, his wet tongue darting across my face like a lizard. *Uggghhh*. I wanted to kick him in the nuts and toss him out of a window. "Tell you what, why don't you go upstairs while I make us a couple of drinks? I'll meet you in the bedroom and then we can do whatever you like," I said in a sing-song voice with a seductive wink and smile. He paused momentarily in contemplation, his thin top lip curling up in the corner.

Ugggghhh, just die.

"Just don't be too long. Daddy needs some attention," he said as he grabbed his puny penis through his pants. "While you're down here, put some food in Bailey's dish. I don't want her whining all night."

I watched him maneuver himself up the winding staircase. *Wouldn't it be a blessing if he lost his footing, tumbled down the stairs, and cracked his head open on the cold, marble floor?*

I made my way into the kitchen so that I could feed Robert's pussy. The only thing I hated more than Robert was that damned cat of his. She never liked me. The first time I came home with Robert, she arched her back and stared at me with those cold green eyes; she hissed as if she sensed real danger. I wanted to hiss back, but Robert would've thought I was crazy. Since then, she'd become slightly more cordial toward me; I guess she recognized I was there to stay. Now when she walked into the room where I was, she'd pause, glance at me for a second in a haughty manner, and keep it moving. She'd learned who was runnin' shit around there.

Robert had had Bailey for eight years and I'm not sure how long cats live, but it was time she took a dirt nap. Maybe when I killed Robert, I'd tie a brick around her neck and throw her into the swimming pool.

I made my way over to the bar in the den and poured myself a shot of whiskey. I took it to the head and poured another one, ignoring the burning in my throat. Plan B was that if I had to have sex with him, then I needed to be so drunk that I didn't vomit when he touched me. Plan A was to drug his old ass so that he'd pass out and think nothing more of having sex. I kept vials of GHB—the date rape drug—in the house because I never knew when the mood would strike him. Usually, his sexual aggression followed drinking so I'd learned how to nip it in the bud. When he asked for a drink—and he always asked for an evening cocktail—I'd slip him something special. Two teaspoons usually did the trick. It wasn't unusual for him to pass out after a night of drinking so when I drugged him and he didn't wake until the next morning, he never thought anything of it. I didn't drug him all the time; only those times when I didn't have the wherewithal to stomach his touch.

I moved over to the cabinet opposite the wall, opened the drawer, and reached way into the back. I pulled out a small vial that contained the drug. "Lady, please be my friend tonight," I said as if the clear liquid was a sentient being. I had to do something. I didn't have it in me, and I certainly didn't want *it* in me tonight. I could hear his hacking cough from upstairs as I poured the colorless, tasteless, and odorless liquid into his glass. Now, I had to buy some time for the concoction to take effect.

As I was about to leave the kitchen, a wicked thought dawned on me. I stopped dead in my tracks and looked carefully around the room, as if someone could have been in the room. Bailey hovered in the corner, with a smug look on her face.

"Get outta here," I said, trying to scare her away, but she didn't move. She stared at me and I swear that she twisted her top lip and shook her head, as if in disgust. "What are you looking at, bitch? Fuck you." I turned my back to her so that she wouldn't see the act. Quickly, I unzipped my jeans and pulled out my dick. Tonight, he'd have a special kind of Whiskey Sour made with my unique, organic ingredient. I lowered the glass to my dick and peed into in his drink, not enough to fill the glass, but more than a few drops. I shook the glass from side to side so that the pee mixed well with the whiskey.

I walked upstairs, trying to conceal my smile. When I opened the door to our master bedroom, Robert stood in the center of the room, naked, wearing a leather mask, black combat boots, and carrying a whip. I wanted to vomit.

Just die.

"You ready for this?" he asked as he grabbed his anemic dick engorged by the use of a cock ring.

"Now, you know I need some time to prepare myself. I'm going to go into the bathroom to get ready. You stay out here and enjoy this drink. I stirred it with my dick," I added, knowing the effect it would have on him. He cracked the leather as a sign of approval.

"You nasty little thing. Gimme that drink." He practically snatched the drink out of my hand.

"Give me a few minutes. When I come back, I'm going to rock your world."

"I'm counting on it." He brought the drink to his lips and stopped suddenly. "Well, hurry up. Daddy's ready now!" He slapped me on the ass—hard! My eyes grew big and I held my breath and watched as he took a hearty swig of his drink. I could tell that the first swig stung because his face puckered up like a prune. "This is strong; just like I like it," he said as he smacked his lips, "tastes different though."

Shug Avery's pee ain't got nothing on me!

I tried very hard not to laugh and prayed that by the time I got out of the shower, he would have passed out.

"Come here and give me a kiss."

Fuck that.

"Let's save that until I get out of the shower." I turned my back to him and burst into laughter as I entered the bathroom and closed the door.

✪ ✪ ✪

I emerged from the bathroom some forty-five minutes later and, to my delight, Robert was asleep lying across the bed, still wearing that damned mask and those boots, with that flea bag cat curled up next to him. The empty glass was on the nightstand. *Old fool.* Bailey raised her head and looked at me as I stood in the doorway.

"Fuck you, too," I said to her.

I happily strolled by him and his pussycat and stepped out onto the balcony. I couldn't have been happier that I didn't have to fuck him tonight.

I inhaled deeply. I stood out on the balcony and looked at the lights that dotted the landscape. Then, I looked back into our master bedroom at Robert, who lay naked across the bed, his peanut-colored flesh exposed to the world. I watched his chest rise with each inhalation and then deflate. *Which breath would be his last?*

In business, Robert was notorious for his mercilessness. The years of bloody fights with his enemies—battles he usually won— had hardened him. Building his huge real estate empire with properties that stretched from coast to coast required a certain viciousness. He had driven many of his enemies into bankruptcy or worse. I heard that one of them actually committed suicide when Robert seized control of his company and forced him out. When I buried Robert, I'm sure the line of people waiting to spit on his grave would snake through the cemetery.

I gazed into the night sky and lost myself in my thoughts. I had come a long way from East Texas. I had grown up a lot and experienced far too many things to recall. I thought about how rough my life was then compared to now. Growing up was no bed of roses for me. I learned at an early age that beautiful, blue-black boys with high cheekbones and deep-set almond-shaped eyes who grew up in the rural south with angry fathers and drunken stepmothers weren't supposed to be loved. Growing up, I was far too pretty for my father and far too black for my step-mother. In my house, the notion of love was a fallacy, and when the façade faded, it left us broken and bitter. I only knew love as a few well-chosen curse words hurled at me with such force that I felt it in my chest; the venom of those words entered my bloodstream and poisoned every inch of my body; that kind of love changes children—it changed me into something *fierce*.

In my experience, love wasn't something that was real, but I knew pain well—it had been a constant companion. In those dark and lonely moments as a child, I decided that one day I'd have a better life, a perfect life—by any means necessary.

As I grew up, I learned my worth.

I learned there are plenty of people in search of pretty young black men; more than enough to provide me with the comforts of life that eluded me as a child. Men, fascinated by my gifts, had always tried to own me; women beguiled by my charms, wanted to wed me. I used them all. In spite of growing up in a world that devalued the exquisiteness of my black skin, I learned to love myself and I harnessed the power of my physicality. Beauty is the ultimate commodity and can be traded in any market in the world; it is a universal currency and I possessed it in abundance. Suitors pursued me and many wanted to tame me, but like trying to catch lightning in a bottle, no one could ever possess me.

Over the years, my life ain't been no crystal stair. I had been used, abused, chewed up, lied to, hoodwinked, bamboozled, and led astray; I had been disowned, dishonored, and thoroughly dissed but, like the air, I rose. I always did. I stood tall in the face of adversity and I persevered. I became the master of my own fate. I decided that as soon as I could get away from my hard knock life, I would run and never look back.

And I hadn't.

Over the years, I learned to reveal only those parts of myself absolutely necessary. Everything else could be created. Nothing about me was real; I was an illusion, all smoke and mirrors. I was a fantasy, a chameleon who had mastered the art of remaining cloaked in plain sight. I had learned to bend perceptions at will, to fit any situation. No one knew me because I didn't exist, except for my manufactured image.

As soon as I graduated high school, I took what money I had saved up from waiting tables at the Whispering Hollow Country Club and from trickin' in backseats of old Chevys, and I caught the first thing smoking toward New York City—big city of dreams. I packed my few belongings and sparse memories and slipped out of the house in the dead of night to begin a new life. I refused to spend the rest of my life in misery in the backwoods of East Texas. I was destined for greatness and the only place that could contain the force of what I knew I was to become was New York City.

When I arrived in New York, I thought about calling home and letting them know where I was, but decided to let them wonder. I hoped that my disappearing act would cause worry and pain, but they didn't care. I'm sure they were happy there was one less mouth to feed. I often wondered how long it took for them to realize that I was gone.

The first thing I learned was that New York City is a cold mistress. She has no love for the loveless and offers little grace for the disgraced. When you meet her, you must be prepared to do battle. I spent years doing odd jobs, working in retail stores, waiting tables, freelance modeling and hustling, just to make ends meet. In my naivety, I imagined that as soon as I stepped off the bus at the Port Authority that I would instantly be discovered as the next big thing in modeling. I was certain that some model scout who was going about his very ordinary day would see me and immediately whisk me away to some fabulously fashionable photo shoot. I saw magazine covers, European runways, and television shows in my future, but evidently fate had other plans for me. Instead of modeling, I churned and burned and fucked my way through New York City as a means of surviving the concrete jungle; I drank and smoked and partied in excess as a way of blotting out the perils of my poisoned life.

My past deeds haunted my spirit, regardless of my attempts to forget.

The hardships I faced forced me to work harder at my dreams, but still things did not come together, and as I struggled at fame, the years passed. New York City was full of younger, model-types all competing fiercely to be the next face of Sean John, Tommy Hilfiger, or Gucci, but most ended up as poster children for shattered dreams. I was no different.

After years of fighting in the trenches to be noticed among the giant skyscrapers and glitter of the city, my fortunes barely improved. Then, on a very ordinary day, something extraordinary happened: Robert Douglas limped into the New York City café where I worked while trying to get my fledgling modeling career off the ground. The second he walked in, my head snapped in his direction. I immediately noticed his sharp, pinstriped Armani suit and his thousand-dollar shoes. I saw all of this across a crowded restaurant because I had skills. I could pick a rich man out of the middle of Times Square while blindfolded.

When he entered, I jockeyed for position to be his waiter—my no-talent, has-been, wannabe coworkers were not about to stand in the way of my next meal ticket. And, from the look of things, it was sure to be a feast. He wouldn't be the first old man I fucked for money. Times were hard back then and I was tired of the day-to-day struggles. I was a month and a half behind on my rent and my cell phone was about to be disconnected for lack of payment.

I sauntered up to Robert's table after he was seated, my beautiful smile in full effect and my chest protruding through my tight shirt. Robert looked up casually, as if he hadn't noticed me and turned away. I was confident that once my image etched itself to the lens of his retina and registered in his brain, he would take notice. All men did.

And, then it happened.

He looked in my direction again.

And smiled.

I had him on the hook. Now, I had to reel him in. He had no idea that he was about to be thoroughly fucked and fucked over. Robert immediately took a fancy to me—as I knew he would.

Over the next few months, he showered me with gifts and wined and dined me at the best restaurants all over the city. We attended Broadway plays, art openings, and parties of the fabulously wealthy. Robert lived in Washington, D.C. but did lots of business in New York. He flew me down to D.C. several times because he couldn't bear to be away from my side for too long for fear that someone else would steal my heart. He certainly knew how to romance a man.

After four months of seducing him, he proposed to me, as I knew he would. During our whirlwind courtship, I pulled out the big guns—no pun intended—and showed him the time of his life. I taught him how to live freely and recklessly. I pulled the old turtle out of his shell so that he could feel the sun on his naked skin. He was so wound up from the many years of being uptight that I thought he was going to pop.

I did all of this to reconnect him with life and his feelings for the sole purpose of getting him to fall hopelessly in love with me. He wasn't the first man that I had seduced into loving me, but if I played my cards right, he'd be the last. As gruff as his exterior was, deep down he longed for love, and I believed that he viewed me as his last chance at love. No one wants to die old and alone.

When I accepted Robert's proposal, I understood that I'd have to move with him to D.C. I'd have to leave the city I had come to love and loathe. Luckily, he owned a glorious penthouse in Tribeca, so I would have a place to stay when I missed the city. We married on March 9, 2010—the first day that gay marriage was allowed in D.C.—in a lavish ceremony attended by the city's elite, including the mayor. Our wedding was a sight to behold, but now, a year later, I wanted to behead my lawfully wedded husband.

CHAPTER 4

I woke up in the middle of the night in a cold sweat, my chest heaving.

Another nightmare.

The bad dreams had started coming more frequently, sometimes preventing me from sleeping through the night. I knew exactly what they were about, but I couldn't stop them.

I looked over at Robert, who stirred in the bed. I hoped he didn't wake because I didn't want to talk about what I had seen in my nightmare. Flashes from the past could haunt across space and time.

His face.

His voice.

The building.

The words.

The push.

The sounds of death.

Crack.

Crack.

Crack. Crack.

I didn't want to relive the nightmare, nor did I want to tell Robert what else I had dreamed. I didn't want to tell him about his mangled flesh or his funeral service. I looked at him. I wondered if he sensed his imminent death. Did he know how soon it would come? Did he feel a chill in the air on a beautiful summer night? Did he get an uneasy feeling in the pit of his stomach when

I looked at him? When he looked at me, was there a warning in his heart?

I didn't want him to suspect anything, so I went on pretending. Every day. I was the greatest pretender of them all. Each day I pretended to be in love with him. Every night I pretended to like his touch. I pretended the smile on my face reflected the joy I felt as his spouse, but behind every smile and every embrace, darkness lurked. Until the moment he expired and even beyond that, I had a part to play. For now, I had to be the doting spouse, but I longed to play the part of bereaved widower. Robert would die soon and a few bad dreams would not prevent me from doing what I had to do to secure my future.

There was a sliver of conscience that had caused me to delay, but I had to strike first before the truth was revealed. I wasn't arrogant enough to believe Nigel and I could keep doing what we were doing for much longer without consequence. My grandmother always said, "It would come out in the wash" and that "The truth would always be brought to light." So, I had to strike soon or all would be lost.

What would happen if he found out about my affair with Nigel?

Knowing Robert, his wrath would scorch the earth. Without hesitation, he'd toss me out onto the street with nothing more than a suitcase filled with a few cheap accessories; credit cards would be canceled and he'd take possession of my car because it was in his name; no more fancy manicures or pedicures; no more facials, massages, $200 lunches, or shopping sprees in Chevy Chase. I saw horrific reflections of my future life; visions of homeless shelters, tuna fish sandwiches, and bus passes shook me to my core.

Robert's revenge wouldn't simply stop with my ejection from his house—his vengeance would be much more thorough. He had destroyed his enemies in business, leaving them broken, mere shells of their former selves. He'd do far worse to me because the pain of my deceit would cut him much deeper than a business deal gone awry. I was certain he'd keep tabs on me for the rest of my life and each time I got close to picking myself up, he'd knock me back down for his own amusement—his relentless attacks would endure beyond time and distance because that's the kind of man I was married to. He believed in the total destruction of his enemies and if he found out I was cheating, that's exactly what I'd become—his enemy.

Who knew what he'd do to Nigel.

Ironically, outside of his millions, ruthlessness was one of the qualities that attracted me to him—if I had ever been attracted to him at all. In spite of his age, he felt…dangerous, like a serpent ready to strike with little provocation. He kept me on edge, like I could never quite catch my breath because I never knew how he would react. And I kind of liked that, along with some of his sadomasochistic sex games. While he wooed me before we were married, he kept his sexual inclinations hidden from me, but as soon as we were married, his perversions spilled from the closet.

At first, I was shocked that such a distinguished gentleman could be so uninhibited. When we dated, our sex life was cool—the way I wanted to keep it; however, once I became his husband, he turned up the heat and he quickly shot from lukewarm to blazing.

From his bag of tricks, he pulled out whips and chains and leather straps; he loved handcuffs and beads and things that vibrated. Some of the games turned me on because they played into my domination fantasies. His affection for erotic-asphyxiation provided the most ground-breaking orgasms I had ever had—danger titillated in ways that I had not imagined. I remembered the first time he put his hands around my neck and squeezed tightly while we were fucking; we rarely made love now, only fucked. I was on top of him moving my hips with a steady rhythm, pretending he was someone else, with my hand working my manhood. I liked being on top because it offered me greater control and it was the only time Robert let me take control. I closed my eyes and pretended he was a young lover and my moaning became more guttural, signaling to him that I was close to my peak. He sat up a bit and placed his hands around my neck, gently at first. I assumed he wanted to add in a few deep thrusts and placed his hands around my neck for greater leverage. As I rocked and rolled faster and harder, he began to apply pressure. Instinctively, I placed my hands on his wrists, in case I needed to forcibly remove them. "Shhh," he said when he sensed I was about to protest. "Trust me, baby," he said soothingly, trying to assuage my growing fear. Then, I looked into his eyes. His gaze filled me with fear, excitement, and apprehension, yet, I let him continue. He told me it would be okay and to trust him again and for some reason, I did. Slowly, I removed one of my hands from his wrist and resumed stroking myself.

I submitted to his will again.

The emotions—danger, fear, excitement—added to the fire growing in my loins and filled me with the strangest sensation. It was as if every cell in my body caught fire at the same time. The adrenaline pumping through my veins powered my increasingly aggressive rhythm. Robert knew I was close to release because my body began to shudder. Then he squeezed harder—so hard I could see the veins throbbing in his wrists. I could barely breathe and I grew lightheaded, but I continued to stroke myself. I wanted to pry his hands from around my neck, but I didn't. Finally, right before I felt like I was blacking out, I released with an unbelievable force that left me far beyond wobbly and weak. Burst after burst after burst expelled from my body. It was far more intense than I had ever imagined.

Even after I collapsed onto the bed, my body continued to jerk.

Robert simply kissed my lips and finished himself off, clearly pleased at his handiwork. I didn't know a word to describe a feeling so utterly consuming.

That was then. This is now. Now, if Robert found out I was cheating, when he placed his hands around my neck and squeezed, he would squeeze with force for an entirely different reason; he'd choke the life out of me.

So, I had to kill him first and claim the spoils of war.

When I started planning his death a few weeks ago, that's when the nightmares returned. A few times I had to get out of bed and go sit by the pool in the middle of the night; I hoped the gentle breezes and rolling waves would comfort me, but I found no such solace. In order to pull this off, I had to reconcile my past deeds with my future actions. I had to weigh the costs and not let my teenaged guilt prevent me from striking decisively.

As I sat up in the bed thinking, Robert stirred and his eyes slowly opened.

"Baby, what are you doing?" Robert asked when he opened his eyes and saw me sitting up in the bed.

"Nothing. I couldn't sleep."

"Is something wrong?" He sat up and wiped the sleep from his eyes. He looked at me oddly and moved closer. He put his arms around me in an effort to comfort me.

I cringed.

"You seem tense. What's on your mind?"

"Nothing. Just a bad dream."

"About what?"

About the death of a boy I once loved.

"I can't remember," I lied.

He looked at me again. "You sure?"

"Yeah, I'm sure. Now, go back to sleep. You have an early morning meeting," I urged.

"I know that and we have that party tomorrow evening, so I want you to get some rest, too. I want you to look your best."

I always look my best.

"You don't have to worry about that. You know how I do." I smiled.

"I know *what* you do, too," he said with a chuckle. I felt his hand slide between my thighs.

Dear God.

CHAPTER 5

By the time we made our appearance at the party, the place was packed with some of D.C.'s elite. Robert didn't have any real interest in politics unless it served him personally, but there were a few political figures sprinkled across the room, including the mayor. I recognized some of their faces, but since I didn't care about politics either, I didn't know most of their names.

We were in the executive wing of Robert Douglas Enterprises (RDE) on the Georgetown waterfront, a place Robert often used when he wanted to entertain and impress. The elaborate space was decorated with high-priced paintings and sculptures that made it feel like a museum and the room opened up to a rooftop patio that overlooked the Potomac River. From our view, you could see the Kennedy Center and the Wilson Bridge in the distance. The view was spectacular, particularly when the light from the setting sun reflected off calm waters.

Stationed strategically in the corner near the glass door to the terrace was a local jazz band led by a bluesy female soul-singer who wore a yellow flower in her natural hair. A form-fitting white dress clung tightly to her hourglass figure. She sang like an angel, her delicate and soulful voice hovered just above the meaningless chatter of the guests. I made a mental note to find out her name so I could catch her next performance in the city. Maybe I'd take a new date.

Robert threw this gala as a fundraiser for some charity I didn't care to remember; another one of his empty gestures to gain favor and improve his reputation in the city. I didn't want to be there because I didn't feel well at all. My sleepless night turned into a restless day, but Robert forced me to come; there was no way he'd let me stay at home. It was one of my many husbandly duties. I was hoping that I'd vomit on his shoes.

When we walked arm-in-arm into the room, the crowd parted as we made our way down the aisle. There was a collective sigh as people acknowledged our presence and smiled our way. Some people envied us. Some wanted to be us, while others wanted something from us. Either way, they looked on with awe.

That was another thing I loved about Robert—he commanded attention and respect in every room in which he entered. There was something innate about his presence that drew people's attention; however, as much as I usually enjoyed all eyes on us, tonight I wanted to be invisible. I didn't have enough energy to support a fake smile for the next few hours as Robert worked the room. When I looked out among the sea of strange and smiling faces, I didn't feel the usual rush I felt when people stared.

"Blues, are you okay?" Robert asked me. He must have sensed my nervousness.

"Yeah, I'm okay…just not feeling well."

He leaned in and whispered ever-so-sweetly. "Don't embarrass me. You've had all day to get it together. Maybe you should go have a ginger ale." The smile on his face camouflaged the shrillness of his words. I'm sure it looked as if he was whispering something romantic in my ear, but bitter words cut across my head. I offered a tiny smile and continued to walk with him, smiling.

Just die.

I separated from Robert and found my way to the bar, where I instructed the attractive, copper-colored bartender to pour me a glass of ginger ale. I watched him pour and he smiled at me, with a twinkle in his eyes. He watched me watching him and I smiled back at him. He was no older than twenty-three, probably in college at Howard University, earning a little spending money, and his beautifully puffy, red lips made me want to fuck him later. I winked at him and he smiled back, as I walked away.

After I finished the ginger ale, Robert saw me in a corner near the bar and beckoned me in his direction. In spite of the drink, I still didn't feel any better and Robert couldn't care less about my pain. It was always about him. *Always*.

Throughout the evening, he dragged me from one boring conversation to another, holding onto me like his most prized possession, while showing me off to his ridiculously egotistical friends. I played the role of the loving spouse, clinging to his arm as he regaled them with delicious stories of his business prowess and his philanthropy. I played along; I certainly didn't want him having a hissy fit when we got home because he thought I was being rude to his guests. He could be as rude as he wanted—and he usually was—but if I dared open my mouth to throw any kind of shade, he'd never let me forget it.

I knew how to play the game. I smiled, nodded, hugged, and air-kissed as if these people were my oldest and most beloved friends.

After some time and some gentle prodding on my part, Robert finally allowed me to excuse myself as he found another group to entertain. I faded into the background and tried my best to remain incognito.

Two drinks later, I felt a little better. I found a quiet place in the back by the bar to rest and observe the comings and goings of the crowd while avoiding Robert. I watched as Charles Rouge strolled through the room with his beautiful wife in tow. Charles, one of Robert's executives, had always been nice to me, unlike some of the others. When his wife saw me looking at him, she raised an inquisitive eyebrow and instinctively tightened her grasp around his arm, never once letting her fake smile diminish.

What was that about?

The upper echelon of D.C. high society had mastered the art of slitting your throat while smiling in your face. Maybe she felt threatened by me—my sex appeal had been known to break up marriages, even from across the room.

I stepped out onto the patio and claimed a quiet corner for myself. I needed some fresh air. I took a sip of my drink and gazed out across the skyline. The iridescent sun sat just beneath the horizon, making its last appearance for the evening. As beautiful as the view was from so high up, my mind drifted. Planning a murder was hard work. I'd talk to Marquis soon to go over the details.

"Hey, Blues," someone said after a few moments. When I turned my head, I saw Charles standing before me. Apparently he had slipped away from his barracuda of a wife. He looked dapper in a gray suit, but his face seemed tense. "I was wondering if I could talk to you for a minute."

"Uhh, sure, I guess." He stepped in a little closer. I held my breath. I hoped he wasn't about to proposition me. Usually that was the case with men; as soon as their wives or girlfriends or boyfriends were out of earshot, they'd make their move. I had no interest in Charles and I was gathering my words to cut down any hope he had of getting with me. He was fairly attractive, with sparkling green eyes and blond hair, but I wasn't about to take him up on any offer.

"This is awkward," he began nervously. "I need to ask a favor."

Here it comes.

"Okay. I'm listening." He shifted uneasily from side to side like a schoolboy about to ask a date to the prom. "What is it?"

"I need you to talk to Robert for me. Would you put in a good word?"

"Huh? I don't understand."

"Well, I sort of screwed up this deal the other day and I think he's planning on firing me. I can't lose my job...not in this economy. I have a wife and two kids and, if he fires me, I don't know what we'd do. I want him to give me another chance to make it right."

I exhaled. Crisis averted.

"I don't know, Charles. I don't usually get involved in Robert's business affairs."

"Please, at least try. He'll listen to you. Can you mention how loyal I am to him? How I work really hard; something to get him to reconsider. Anything would help."

"How do you know he's going to fire you?"

"I just know it. You know how he is when he doesn't get his way. I'm surprised he hasn't done it already. I can't lose my job right now. My family would never recover."

He spoke the truth about Robert. If anyone couldn't or didn't deliver, he had no issue with replacing them. Robert rarely gave second chances. A few words from me probably would not change anything, but the desperation that sparkled in Charles' eyes made me want to help him. He genuinely looked scared. I liked Charles and one day I might need a favor from him. It never hurts to have allies.

"Okay, I'll do it. I can't make any promises, though. Like you said, you know how Robert is."

"Thank you so much, Blues. I owe you big time." He smiled and lingered a few seconds longer than he needed. We didn't have anything else to talk about. "Well, let me get back to my wife."

I watched him walk away with his shoulders back, as if a weight had been lifted. I lit a cigarette and stared into the evening sky. I let the melodic sounds of the soul-singer tickle my ears; her voice helped to relax me. Finally, I felt somewhat at peace, if only for a moment. At any second, Robert could burst through the crowd like a bull in a china shop and snatch me out of my peace. Halfway through my cigarette, I heard another voice.

"Finally, we're alone," a soft and sweet voice said. I turned around and saw a beautiful but unfamiliar woman standing behind me, smiling.

Who is this bitch?

I didn't know her and I had no interest in getting to know her. If she was trying to pick me up, she was barking up the wrong tree.

"Excuse me?"

I took a moment and looked at the woman. There was something vaguely familiar about her, but I didn't care to waste any energy trying to figure it out. She was dressed in an elegant but tight, black sleeveless dress that accentuated her ample figure. She was a real beauty, in an *urban* kind of way, though. There was something slightly rough about her exterior, even though she looked very polished. Her face, perfectly symmetrical, was full of bold African features and Chinese angles; her dark and slightly slanted eyes gave her a bewitching appearance, almost as if she could cast a spell with a simple wink.

"I've been trying to get close to you all night," she said playfully.

"Why?"

"May I?" Before I could respond, she removed the cigarette from between my fingers and brought it to her deadly, crimson lips. She closed her eyes as she inhaled and made a face as if she was inhaling joy itself. "Ohhh, this is good," she said, shaking her head. "I used to really enjoy these before I quit. I haven't had a good drag in a long time."

When she opened her eyes, she slowly looked me up and down as if trying to scan me or see what was hidden beneath.

"Now, I see what Robert sees in you. You're spectacular."

Tell me something I don't know.

"I'm sorry, but do I know you? Have we met?"

"We're meeting now," she said coolly.

"Is there something you need from me, Ms.... I don't believe I caught your name."

"That's because I didn't throw it," she said with a wink. "From up here," she continued, "you must feel like you have the whole world at your feet. Being married to a rich and powerful man provides you with luxuries most people will never know. How does it feel?"

"It feels great."

"I guess you and Robert have a symbiotic relationship; you both get something you need from each other."

I frowned. "What are you talking about?"

"Robert gets the benefit of being married to a hot, young stud and you get access to unimaginable wealth. It sounds like a perfect match."

She was seriously starting to get underneath my skin and I really didn't have the patience to play these little games.

"I don't know who you are, but I love my husband very much and he loves me. Now, whoever you are, how about you go back to where you came from and let me enjoy the rest of the night?"

"Is that any way to treat a lady?"

I looked her up and down. "Am I looking at a lady?"

"Ouch," she said playfully, "that was harsh."

"I really don't mean to be rude, actually I do, but I'd like to be alone now, so you can scurry away."

"Don't you find it hard to be alone in a room full of people?"

I smiled out of sheer annoyance. "I've had just about enough of you. How about you give me back my cigarette?"

She politely handed it to me. "I see we've exhausted our conversation." She turned on her heels and moved toward the door. "I'll see you soon, Blues."

I doubt that.

I didn't know who she was, but she left a bad taste in my mouth.

CHAPTER 6

During the planning phase of Robert's murder, I continued to see Nigel; I saw no reason to stop. We continued to meet weekly, sometimes twice a week if I needed my batteries recharged. In between fucking Robert and Nigel, I was also fucking Marquis. I had to keep him satisfied so I could keep him on my side.

I couldn't wait to see Nigel, even as my mood soured. He was forty-five minutes late and I was already on my third cocktail. I didn't like to be kept waiting and the anticipation of his arrival built up into my system and mixed like a toxin with the vodka. Robert, being his usual crass self, had pissed me off that morning and I had been unable to shake off the bad vibe. Now, Nigel was late and I was agitated.

Being alone in the room allowed me too much time to think; too much time to remember.

The dreams kept me awake at night and I was beginning to hate quiet times by myself.

Sometimes, I heard things; little voices on the wind or I'd see an image of someone long ago dead and buried. I had done some very bad things in my day; usually, I forgot them as quickly as the deed had been done, but there were a few things over the years that had remained with me. I hoped Robert's murder wouldn't be one of them, like Jabari's had. My soul was bonded to Jabari's so I understood the lingering guilt; Robert would be different. I didn't care about Robert. Hell, I didn't even like him. He was an annoying little tick that was sucking the life out of me.

Planning a murder was not an easy thing. There were so many things to factor in and so many variables to consider. If one thing fell out of place, suspicion could land on me and I had no intention of going to jail. If Robert were to suddenly die, I'd be the prime suspect in any policeman's mind. I was much younger, much more attractive, and significantly poorer than Robert, and when the police found out that I'd inherit millions, they'd come after me. Most murders are committed by people the victim knew and if they were married, the spouse was always a prime suspect. I didn't want to risk letting a detail slip out as the police questioned me, as they were bound to do.

So, I had to be clever. I wasn't going to get caught; I was going to get rich.

Marquis was the perfect person to pull off the murder. He didn't know who Robert was and he certainly didn't realize that I'd inherit millions. Marquis thought he was my knight-in-shining-armor and was ready to rescue me from my tyrant of a husband. In his ghetto corner of the world, he had never heard of Robert Douglas or Robert Douglas Enterprises. And, because of his past dealings with the police, I didn't have to worry about him having loose lips. He lived and would die by the ghetto "no snitch" code and that would serve my cause admirably.

As I lay across the bed in the hotel suite, I heard a cracking sound coming from the bathroom.

Crack.

Crack.

Crack. Crack.

I swallowed hard and felt a lump in my throat. I was alone in the hotel room.

Slowly, I got up and eased my way into the room. I paused from fright. Then, I looked around and realized how silly I was being. I exhaled.

The room was empty.

As I turned to exit, I caught a quick glimpse of an image in the mirror—a familiar face that didn't belong to me. I jumped back and when I looked again, the image was gone.

I couldn't believe that I was still feeling this way, after all this time. All this talk of death must have conjured up feelings that I thought had faded. Now, I was dealing with nightmares and ghosts in the mirror. This shit had to end. When Robert died and I inherited his money, I was going to get some serious therapy to deal with my guilt.

I exited the bathroom cautiously and looked at the clock on the wall. The hour was getting late and Nigel still had not arrived nor had he sent me a text explaining why he was late. Our stolen moments together gave me the strength I needed to deal with Robert and I really needed an injection of energy. Anxiously, I paced across the hotel room, moving nervously from the bed, to the desk, to the chair, and finally to the chair on the balcony, wearing nothing but a white jock strap that contrasted nicely with my dark skin. I tried to shake bad memories from my head, memories of a dead boy that I once loved.

As I rested in the chair, I looked down at my sculpted legs and was happy that the years of running track were still paying dividends. My body was on point. If someone was watching me from another hotel room, then they surely got an eyeful. I wasn't ashamed of my body and didn't give a second thought to any lurking voyeur. In fact, I sometimes welcomed an audience.

As I sat on the balcony, one leg propped up on the table, blowing nicotine circles into the air, I tried to steady my nerves. My stomach felt like a great ball of serpents hissing and writhing around each other. Why was I so unsettled? Guilt was not an emotion I knew well—living life without a conscience prevented guilt from rearing its ugly head. So, what was happening now?

A gentle rat-a-tap-tap on the door brought me back to reality. Finally, Nigel had arrived to fuck these memories out of my head.

I walked calmly over to the door, as if I was in complete control, even though nothing could have been farther from the truth. I still felt unsettled, but it would soon pass. Slowly, I opened the door and as soon as I saw his face, all my troubles faded away. He stood there with a glorious smile carved onto his masculine face and looked me up and down, as if we hadn't seen each other in months.

"Are you going to let me in?" he asked, making such a simple question sound seductive.

I opened the door wider so that he could take in the full sight of my nearly naked body.

"That's what I'm talking about," he said in his smooth-as-silk voice.

I reached out, pulled him into the room by his tie, and slammed the door behind us. Without uttering so much as another word, I pulled him toward the bed, pushed him down onto his back, and immediately mounted him. Before he could protest or say a single syllable, I forced my tongue into his mouth and kissed him aggressively. He had never tasted as good as he did in that moment. He even tasted better than Jabari.

I sucked his tongue, bit his lips, and took control. His succulent red lips returned, in equal measure, the power of my passion. He wrapped his hands around my waist and held onto me tightly, as if holding on for dear life. I didn't want him to ever let me go.

"You're excited to see me, huh?"

"A little bit," I replied between heavy breaths. I no longer cared that he was over an hour late. I gave him a peck on the lips and looked at his honey-colored skin as he smiled, revealing his pearly white teeth. His full lips were made especially for kissing, and it was hard for me to resist.

He stood up with my legs wrapped around his waist and lowered me down on the bed on my back. He towered over me as if he was ready to claim me.

"I got tied up with Robert and I couldn't get away." He was offering an explanation, but at this point, one wasn't required.

"I don't want to talk about Robert."

I couldn't wait for him to be inside me. He stood over me and slowly and seductively began undressing himself. It took more strength than I realized I had to prevent me from getting up and ripping the clothing from his body. My breathing dug into my chest as I watched the various stages of his strip routine.

His tie fell to the floor.

Then, his dress shirt and T-shirt hit the carpet.

I looked hungrily at his thick, golden chest. I wanted to suck on his pink nipples and tug at the line of black hair that separated his pecs.

Then, he kicked off his shoes and pulled down his pants.

He stood before me, wearing nothing but his boxer briefs and his black dress socks. I could see his member pulsing in his underwear, threatening to break free from the thin cotton prison that kept it confined. He rubbed it several times before pulling his underwear down just enough for me to see the magnificent head of his perfect prick.

He took the tip of his right index finger and placed it in his mouth just enough to get it wet and then took the finger and rubbed it seductively across the head. My heart almost leapt out of my chest as I watched him toy with his manhood. I began to salivate and moved toward him. He raised his finger as if to say "stop" and I followed his command. I smiled. He wasn't finished playing with me. He wanted to work me up into frenzy.

Finally, he let his briefs fall to the floor around his ankles and he stepped out of them casually. Now he stood before me, completely naked with his dick in his hand, eyeing me. He spit into the palm of his hand and used his saliva as lubrication and began to stroke himself. He started off slowly; then as the pleasure rose, his speed increased.

His strong hand moved up and down his shaft as I watched with breathless anticipation, waiting for that moment when he would allow me to serve him as only I could. Watching him watch me as he masturbated stirred something deep inside, and it became hard to catch my breath. I had to have him and the glint in his eye told me that he was ready.

I jumped off the bed and was kneeling before him within seconds. A long moan rumbled from deep within him and filled the room with his pleasure.

"Damn, baby. Nobody does that better than you," he said as he pulled me up and kissed me so deeply, I swear his tongue touched my soul. "I love you so much, baby." There was something ferocious in the way that our lips met. No part of his mouth was left unexplored by my frenzied tongue. His hands pawed at my flesh, and I dug my fingers into the groove of his back. Passion rose from our heated bodies and filled the space.

"I want you inside me." I stood up and crawled into the bed and lay spread eagle. He reached over and grabbed the tube of lubrication I had placed on the nightstand and applied it to me with his thick fingers. He then unrolled a condom over his dick and eased his way into me. He started off gently and gave me enough time to adjust to the invasion. Slowly, he began to increase his speed, applying much more thrust and power behind the weight of his hips, and I felt each push.

When I looked up and into his eyes, I saw Jabari.

I closed my eyes and pretended that it was Jabari inside me. I could never escape his memories, not even in that moment. For a second, I believed it was Jabari until the sweat dripped from Nigel's face onto mine; that forced me to open my eyes. His breathing quickened and I slapped his ass—the way I used to do Jabari's ass—and forced him to push harder. I wanted him to push so hard that I could feel it in my throat. Then, I could feel his body quake, ready to release. He let out a grunt to announce his powerful orgasm, and I could feel the spewing flames from his lust.

He took a few quick deep breaths and rolled off me, still heaving from his top-notch performance. He leaned over and kissed me while I continued to masturbate and finally, I gave in to the mounting pleasure. I released all over my chest. He climbed on top of me and pressed his chest to mine, gluing us together in lust. Then, he rolled off me again and rolled onto his back. I rested my head on his chest.

As we lay intertwined in a messy pool of love, I remained nestled in his arms for a few moments until I had caught my breath. As we lay, my phone began to ring loudly, shattering our bliss. The obnoxious ring I chose specifically for Robert pierced the air and filled the room with panic and alarm.

"That old fucker always calls at the wrong time," I said.

"Just let it ring, baby."

"Trust me, I wasn't about to answer it." I reached over to the nightstand and hit the button on the phone to silence the death rattle. I lay back down and placed my head back on his chest and closed my eyes, momentarily losing myself in the warmth of his embrace. It felt like home.

"Blues, what's going on with Robert?"

"What do you mean?"

"How is his health?"

That's an odd question.

"You mean besides his heart condition, eczema, and being old as dirt?" I laughed.

"Hmm, yeah. Anything else?"

"Not that I know of, but hell, I wouldn't know. He could have Ebola for all I care." Nigel didn't smile at my joke. "Okay, Nigel, what's wrong?" I adjusted my position so that I could look in his eyes, which carried concern, as if he was pulled away in thought. He sat up in the bed.

"Are you and Robert okay?"

"We're as good as we usually are. Why?"

"Today, Robert called me into his office to talk about his will."

"Do I still get everything when he dies?" I asked eagerly.

Silence. Uh-Oh.

"Nigel..."

"I don't want you to get upset, but he wanted me to start working on drawing up a new version."

"A new version? What the fuck?"

"He wants to leave most of his estate to Howard University."

I leapt up in a rage. "You have got to be kidding me!"

"I don't understand it at all. I asked you about his health because it's common for dying people to start making sizeable donations and he has been very charitable lately."

"He wants to leave all his money to Howard University? He didn't even go to that damned school!" I was furious.

"Just calm down, Blues."

"How can I calm down when you just told me that Robert wants to give away most of his money. This is not a time for calm!" I took several deep breaths. "What about me? What does he want to leave me?" Nigel paused. "Nigel, what is he leaving me?" My voice was stern.

"He's leaving you about a half-million."

"Half a million? Are you fuckin' kidding me? That's chump change compared to what he's worth. What about the house?" Outside of Bob Johnson, Robert was probably the second richest black man in the D.C. area.

"He's leaving that to charity."

"He wants me to be poor and homeless? That old raggedy son-of-a-bitch!"

"A half-million dollars is hardly poor."

"It is, compared to what he's worth. I can't believe this shit."

Now, more than ever, I realized what I had to do. Robert had to die before Nigel completed the new will. "When does he want this change made?"

"Soon. He didn't give me a date, but soon. I could stall, but I don't know what good that will do."

"What about getting me a divorce settlement?"

"Well," he said in a low voice, "things don't look that promising."

"Don't make any changes right now. Let me work on Robert."

"You can't mention any of this to anyone; I could get disbarred."

I moved closer to him and planted a soft kiss on his lips. "I'd never do that. I just need a little time to get him to value me more, to see my worth. All this is worth a hell of a lot more than a half-million," I said as I pointed at myself. He grabbed me and pulled me into his arms.

I was worth far more than a half-million dollars. I could have any man I wanted, yet I chose to marry Robert, and he was now acting as if my sacrifice was practically worthless. Beauty is a commodity far more valuable than gold. He needed to understand what I had sacrificed to be with him. With each caress, he incurred a cost; each time he pressed his lips against mine or inserted his filthy tongue into my mouth, he was assessed a fee; each kind word or gentle embrace was taxed; each time he pressed his flesh into me, he was charged an exorbitant service charge. Surely, he didn't think I was free. If he thought he could buy me at a discounted rate, he was mistaken. The money he gave me each month as an allowance paid for nice clothes and jewelry, but that was simply a monthly maintenance fee. The seven-figure checks he was donating across town was money that I had already counted in my inheritance. I earned that money—each and every night—on my back, on my knees, with my legs in the air, and on all fours; I earned that money with my sweat and spit and lips and hips and now he wanted to cheat me out of what I had paid for with my body. Fuck that. He should have run the numbers and decided if he could afford me before he married me.

Sometimes, you have to pay the price.

CHAPTER 7

Once I got home from my tryst with Nigel, I walked up the staircase toward the bedroom, humming a love song underneath my breath. I wanted to relax for a couple of hours before Robert got home and I had a few minutes before Oprah came on. It was her final season so I wanted to see when she was going to buy a whole city and gift it to a lucky viewer—I knew she was going out big.

As I entered the room, I was startled to see Robert standing in the middle of our bedroom like a statue, staring directly at me; with that damn cat at his feet. His poker face didn't provide any hint of what he was feeling or why he was home at three-thirty in the afternoon.

"Robert," I said as I caught my breath. "You scared me. What's going on? What are you doing home so early?"

He picked up what I gathered was a glass of whiskey and took a long, slow sip.

"Where have you been?" he asked flatly as he set his glass down and picked up the cat and started stroking her.

I stepped deeper into the room and moved cautiously over to him, not sure whether this old bastard was ready to swing on me. The air was thick and his mood sour. I didn't know what was going on, but he had me spooked. He could be volatile and unpredictable and there were a few times, particularly after he drank a lot of tequila, when I was sure that he wanted to punch me. Now, it had never happened, but I never put it past him. So, I treaded carefully.

Could he possibly know about Nigel and me?

I eased my way over and kissed him on the forehead. As I tried to step away, he grabbed my hand, not forcefully, but with enough pressure to let me know that something was dreadfully wrong.

Oh shit.

"I asked you a question and I expect an answer. Where have you been?" He bent over and dropped the cat gently on the floor. She paused, meowed, and then strutted out of the room as if she didn't want to witness the ensuing bloodshed.

"Oh… I was out running errands," I said, trying to sound as if it was no big deal. Inside, an almost paralyzing fear that he had found out about my affair, or even my plot to kill him, overtook me. Had I left some evidence around? I swallowed hard. I could feel the strength of my heartbeat. "I wanted to get some new music, but didn't see anything I liked." I eased my hand from his grip, as if nothing was wrong, and walked on wobbly knees to the dresser. I took off my watch and set it on the dresser, trying to resume my normal routine.

"Really? I called you and you didn't pick up; you know I hate that. Today has been crazy for me and I really needed you, but you weren't around. I needed you to bring my file folder about the Purple Party. I had a meeting with Kevin, but apparently you had more important things to do."

"Baby, I went to Best Buy; it wasn't that important. And, what's with the third degree? I honestly didn't know you called. If I had, I would have picked up. I love talking to you."

Uggghhh.

"That's what you say," he said again, trying his best to make me feel guilty.

He stared at me with cold, blank eyes and took another sip. His left eye twitched, and I could see the nostrils of his thin nose flaring ever-so-slightly. His beady, black eyes sucked in all the light from the room.

He watched every move I made like a hawk. He was watching the way that I walked so that he could tell if I had been recently fucked. I tried not to panic and continued gliding casually across the room like he wasn't there.

Finally, I stopped and made eye contact with him.

"Robert, you're beginning to make me nervous." I could no longer bear the weight of his stare. If he was planning on punching or stabbing me, I could do without the build-up of drama. Just do it.

He walked over to me, maintaining an unbroken stare. I hoped he couldn't detect the fright lurking beneath the surface. When he was close enough, he reached out and grabbed me by the waist.

Finally, he smiled, slightly. "I didn't know where you were. Call it an old man's paranoia." He leaned in and gave me a deep, sensual kiss that lingered longer than I liked.

I hope you like the taste of Nigel's dick.

"I love you," he whispered. I felt the heat of his breath on my neck as he held me tightly. "I don't know what I'd do without you."

"Well, you don't have to wonder; I'm not going anywhere."

Robert hugged me tightly and inhaled deeply. Something still wasn't right with him.

I pushed back. "When are you going to tell me what's really wrong?" He released me from his embrace.

"I can't get anything past you, can I?" he said with a tiny, forced smile.

"No, you can't, so don't even try. Wassup?"

Robert looked at me as if a great weight rested on his shoulder. I wasn't sure if I had ever seen him so disturbed. It had to be something major for him to leave work early and that bit about me bringing him the folder was all a gimmick. He needed me for something else. Something had unnerved him; to his core.

"Robert, tell me what's wrong." He took my hand and led me out of the bedroom. We moved down the hallway and down the staircase. "Where are we going?"

"I have to show you something."

He tightened his grip on my hand and practically dragged me down the hallway into the solarium.

As we neared the room, he inhaled deeply again. I wasn't sure what he was about to show me, but I was sweating bullets. What if he knew? What if he had photographs and was taking me into the room to show me the evidence? I wanted to yank my hand from his grip and run in the opposite direction, but I didn't. I stayed the course.

When we got to the sunroom, I saw a pair of red bottom, high-heel shoes attached to a pair of smooth cocoa-colored legs. As we entered the room, a woman slowly stood up. As she turned to face us, I realized she was the same vixen who had accosted me when I was at the fundraiser the other night at RDE. *What the hell was she doing in my house?*

She smiled at me, almost triumphantly. She had said she'd see me later; she was right.

Robert walked over to her and put his arm around her waist.

"What the hell is going on here?" I exclaimed.

"Blues, it's good to see you again," she said in a tone far too casual for our relationship. We weren't friends and I didn't want her being so familiar with me, even if her arm was around my husband's waist.

"Oh, so you two have met?" Robert asked.

"Sort of. This…woman…approached me at the fundraiser you had at RDE the other day, but she didn't tell me who she was.

Now, I find her in our house, so it's about time someone told me what's going on." I looked her directly in the face. "Who are you and what are you doing here?"

Robert paused. He looked at her and smiled, like an old fool. I rolled my eyes.

"Blues, I'd like you to formally introduce you to Ashleigh Douglas; my daughter."

The words "my daughter" slapped me across the face and my mouth dropped to the floor. I knew Robert had a daughter, but he hadn't spoken to her in at least five years. I considered her dead. Last time he had spoken of her, it wasn't in pleasant tones.

"Your daughter? The crackhead?" I asked suddenly.

Robert winced, as if he felt pain from my very accurate description of her.

Once a crackhead, always a crackhead.

She smiled. "Blues, I had a little problem with crack when I was younger, but I've been clean for over two years." She spoke in a pleasant tone, as if being a reformed crackhead carried a lot of dignity.

"From what I was told, it was far more than a *little* problem. Robert," I said, turning to him, "what is she doing here? The last time she was here, didn't she steal fifty thousand in cash from you, out of your safe? Do I need to hide my pocketbook?"

"Blues—" Robert said.

"No, it's okay, Daddy. I did a lot of awful things when I was high. One of the things I learned in rehab was to own the harm that I've done to others and to make it right." Her voice sounded practiced, as if she had rehearsed an Easter speech for church.

"I bet." I moved into the room and took a defiant stance near one of the windows, my arms folded across my chest, my lips pursed together. "So, what are you doing here now? What do you want?"

"I wanted to see my father. I've missed him." She turned and hugged him tightly. To a less discerning eye, it would appear that she genuinely missed her father and that this faux hug was authentic, but she wasn't slick enough to fool me. I could see through her subterfuge; game always recognized game. She wasn't here for anything as noble as reuniting with her father. She was here for the same reason I was—money. Cold. Hard. Cash. "We have so much to catch up on, Daddy. I have so much to tell you."

As she hugged Robert, she looked at me, with a glint of satisfaction in her eye. Her wry smile hinted at a sinister motive. I was not about to be played. Robert may fall for her tricks because he was sometimes a sentimental old fool, but if she thought for one second that I was going to let her ooze her way back into Robert's life and take his money—money that would be mine—she was mistaken. I had put in far too much work to lose now. I win. Always.

I watched their embrace. Robert's face seemed to soften and his permanent scowl relaxed a bit. This whole scene played like a script out of some midday soap opera: the drug-addicted daughter of a millionaire businessman emerges from obscurity after a five-year absence to reclaim her inheritance.

"You two have a lot to talk about. I'll let you catch up." I turned and made a quick exit out of the room and ignored Robert, who was calling my name.

I was completely caught off-guard.

CHAPTER 8

I couldn't bear to be around Robert and his daughter anymore. Something about the entire situation turned my stomach. I grabbed my keys and got the hell out of the house. I didn't have any idea where I was going, but anywhere would be better than being in the house with them. I was already tired and this sudden surprise was too much for me to process. It made my head hurt.

Even though Robert had mentioned a one-night fling with an Asian girl that produced an offspring when he was in college at the *turn of the century*, I had somehow blocked it out of my mind. Never, not even in my wildest dreams, had I ever expected to meet this *love child*, particularly after the stories he had told me about her. On the rare occasion when he spoke her name, he didn't speak of her in flattering terms. He only told me what a nightmare she had been.

When she was fifteen, her mother had died and she had come to live with Robert. I couldn't imagine Robert taking care of anyone besides himself. I knew him very well and he wasn't exactly the nurturing type, so I could imagine the tension they had in their relationship.

As soon as she moved in, from what I was told, the trouble began. She was fighting, skipping school, and being a royal bitch to everyone. Robert talked about the many times he had to go up to school after she had gotten into a fight and the many times he had to call the police because she had run away. For no other reason than rebellion, she had fallen in with a bad crowd of girls from Anacostia—the bad part of town—and developed a ravenous addiction to crack. She stole from Robert more than once to feed her habit. He sent her to rehab several times, but she never took to it.

When she was twenty-five, he sent her to rehab again—for the sixth and final time—after she failed out of Georgetown University. After four days of a twenty-eight day program, she disappeared into the night. *Poof*, she was gone. That time when she ran away, he didn't bother to try to find her. Instead, he decided to wash his hands of her. Last he heard, she had hitched her way to Los Angeles.

That was five years ago.

Robert had once confessed to me that he loved his daughter, wished her the best, and sometimes wondered what had become of her. I heard a hint of disappointment and sadness in his voice when he spoke of her that time. I wasn't sure if the disappointment he felt was directed toward himself for not being a better father or toward her for being a terrible daughter. Maybe he blamed himself for her failures. I didn't bother to ask any follow-up questions because, honestly, I didn't care. She was out of his life and that's all that mattered to me. I didn't have time or the inclination to be a stepdad. He hadn't seen her in years so I assumed she had died from an overdose in a cardboard box somewhere on skid row.

Clearly, I was mistaken.

Now, here she was, in the flesh, in my house, after all this time. Something didn't feel right—at all.

As I darted down M Street, NW, in my shiny foreign car, the city was racing with the hurried energy of a city on the move. Cars whizzed by. Buses crawled along. People with their small lives and small concerns littered the sidewalks, like urban trash. As usual, throngs of hungry people lined up outside of Georgetown Cupcakes. The way people waited in line for a $5 cupcake, you'd think they were baking crack right in the mix. I had to admit, though, those cupcakes were on point.

I continued to dart in and out of traffic, even as the traffic snarled. I sped up, slowed down, and changed lanes all in an effort to get away. I needed to put some distance between me and Robert's unholy family reunion.

Then it dawned on me.

Why was I running away? I needed to be back at the house, trying to figure out what the hell she wanted with my husband—her father. No sooner than the thought formed in my head, I had already U-turned in the street and turned the car in the other direction—away from traffic—and was headed back toward the house.

Once inside, I slammed my keys down on the credenza, and marched into the solarium. She was seated on the couch, casually sipping a martini.

"Where is my husband?" I asked curtly.

"Blues, hey. He had to take a call upstairs." I turned to exit the room. "Blues, wait. I'm glad you came back. Let's talk. I'd really like us to be friends."

"Friends? Lady, I don't even know you."

"Come and sit with me. Let's talk. Can I make you a drink?"

With reticence, I stepped deeper into the room. This would give me an opportunity to size her up and figure out her game. She moved over to the bar and started mixing a cocktail. She didn't even wait for me to tell her my drink of choice. The familiarity with which she glided across the room unnerved me; it was as if she had already claimed the house as hers. Her feline smile told me that she was up to no good and she knew that I realized that she had ulterior motives.

I took a seat on the couch and she brought the drink over to me.

"What is this?"

"It's an Ashleigh special. Try it. I'm sure you'll like it." Once again, she smiled coyly.

I took a sip and she was right—the drink was refreshing and had a strong gin kick that I felt in the back of my throat. She moved across from me and lowered herself delicately down into the chair, as a proper lady would. She moved with grace and poise, as if she had had years of training in a finishing school, instead of a crack den.

"Daddy showed me your wedding pictures. You both looked so good. I'm sorry that I missed it."

"Where were you? On a crack binge?"

She gently set her drink down and looked at me straight on.

"Blues, let's not fight. I'd really like it if we got along together. I'd hate to be one of those clichéd families where the child is at odds with the stepparent. I don't want to feel like I'm in a bad Lifetime movie."

Stepparent. The sound of that made me want to throw my drink into her made-up face.

"Don't get it twisted. I'm not your parent."

"I know. You could be my little brother," she said sardonically. I heard the contempt for me in her voice.

"Let's cut to the chase. What are you doing here?"

"I told you. I missed my daddy. After I got myself clean, I wanted to see him, but I was afraid. It took me all this time to get the nerve to come home. I'm finally ready to be the daughter he always wanted."

"Eh-huh."

"There is no reason for us not to get along. We could be great friends."

"Listen here, Ashy—"

"It's Ashleigh."

"Whatever. Don't think you can come in here and start running things. You have been a constant source of tension for my husband and I'm not about to let you stress him out. So, I suggest you pick up your little pocketbook and crawl back to whatever crackhouse you undoubtedly clawed your way out of."

"Look at me, Blues. Do I look like I'm on crack?"

"That only means you clean up well. If you put lipstick on a pig, well, it's still a pig."

"Blues, what the hell did you just say?" Robert stood in the doorway, his brow scrunched with confusion.

Ashleigh stood up.

"It's okay, Daddy. I understand Blues's frustration. He's worried about you. He's worried that I'm going to hurt you. He's simply being a good husband."

"To be perfectly honest, Robert, I don't understand why she's here."

"She's here because she's my daughter."

"She's also a drug addict. I'm not sure I feel safe with her in this house."

"I'm sorry you feel that way, Blues. You have nothing to worry about from me. Daddy offered to let me stay here for awhile."

"He did what? Robert, may I speak with you for a second?" I didn't wait for him to respond. Instead, I turned quickly and made an exit out of the room. I walked several feet down the hallway, out of earshot. Robert was right behind me.

"Baby—" he began.

"You're letting her stay here? Can we have a conversation about it first?"

"What do you want me to do? She's my daughter."

"And I'm your husband. Are you forgetting all the shit she put you through? The money she stole from this house?"

"She's been clean for years now."

"How do you know that? Just because she said it?"

"I know because I know my daughter."

I tried to calm myself. I didn't want to push him too hard, out of fear he'd push back. I needed to win him over, not push him closer to her. "Robert, you haven't seen or heard from Ashleigh in years. You don't know her."

He stepped closer to me and hugged me around the waist. He exhaled.

"Baby, I really need you to support me with this. This may be my final chance to have a relationship with my only child. Can you support me and my decision?"

I rolled my eyes.

"No, because this doesn't make sense. I get that you want to have a relationship with your daughter, but why does she have to stay here? Can't she rent a room or something?"

"I won't have my daughter staying with some stranger."

"I'm sure she's stayed in much worse places."

"Blues, I really need you to get on board with this. Can you trust that I know what I'm doing?" His *it's-my-or-the-highway-tone* returned.

I paused for effect. "I guess. I'm just tired of you making decisions that affect us without talking to me, but if you want her here, who am I to object? I'm only your husband and it's your house."

"It's our house."

"It doesn't feel that way. You invited someone who is practically a total stranger into our house without so much as a text message to me."

Robert cupped my face with his hands. "You're right. I handled it badly. I apologize."

I was shocked and didn't know how to react. This was probably the first time Robert had ever apologized to me for anything. I liked the way the words sounded on his tongue, but I knew better than to get used to them.

"Fine, Robert. I'm going on the record to say I believe that if she moves into this house, it will end badly for all of us. Just remember I said it."

"It'll be fine. Pessimism is not your style. Now, can you make an attempt to get to know her? After all, she is your stepdaughter." He giggled.

Fuck you.

"Mr. Douglas, you have a call." We turned to our left and saw Margaret, our housekeeper, down the hall holding the phone in her hand. "Shall I take a message or would you like to take it?

"I'll take it." He released his embrace and I watched him walk down the hallway and disappear around the corner.

When I turned around, Ashleigh was standing there, smiling.

"It's been a long day. I'm going upstairs to take a nap. I'm a bit tired."

"You do that. Just remember, we can always put you out."

"And my daddy can always divorce you." She winked.

Bitch.

CHAPTER 9

Later that night, Robert and Ashleigh went out to dinner. Robert begged me to go with them, but I faked a headache so I could stay at home. I had had enough of her already and I needed time to think. How did her arrival affect my murder plot? With her skulking about the house, I would have to be particularly careful to not slip up and make a mistake. This unexpected variable put pause in my plot, but I would not be denied.

I casually moved around the house, looking at things, itemizing possessions in my head. Robert wasn't about to cheat me out of anything and I certainly wasn't going to lose a fortune to a drug addict. I was not going to lose anything—not one painting, candlestick, or flowerpot. She may have been his daughter, but I was his husband.

As I wandered through *my* house, I moved over to the fireplace in the den, and looked at the picture taken of me when I won the high school state championship in track. This was the only tangible thing that connected me to my past. I stared at the photograph; the smile on my face was electric. I remember being so happy that day. I put everything I had and everything I was into that race. I ran with a sense of urgency and of purpose that, even to this day, I have not been able to duplicate in any aspect of my life.

In the photo, I was dressed in my green track uniform with a bouquet of colorful flowers clutched closely to my chest. Underneath the picture the caption read:

Blues Carmichael, State Champion
100 Meter Dash

Even now, I smiled when I looked at that picture. It was one of the happiest moments of my life and I was thrilled that Jabari had celebrated with me that night because he also ran track; but, more than anything, I remembered wanting to get home as soon as possible so that I could share my good news with my parents, who hadn't bothered to attend the event. I had hoped that winning the track meet would engender some affection from my father, a proud look, a pat on the shoulder—I didn't dare hope for a hug—but he was too drunk to notice when I came home. My dear stepmother, on the other hand, dismissed my victory as a stroke of luck and minimized the hard work and effort I had put forth to be the best. She chuckled and said I looked like a "black blur" running around the track when the highlights aired on the local television station. One kind word would have sufficed; instead, I found only ridicule.

As I stared at the photograph, I said my name out loud, "Blues Carmichael," and it sounded oddly hollow, almost as if it didn't have any weight; the hollow sound mirrored my empty soul.

"Blues Carmichael," I said again. I thought about the lie that I had told so many times over the years to explain my unusual name. I told people that my mother had been a famous New Orleans blues singer and when she had gotten pregnant by one of her band members, she sang up until she made it into the delivery room. The real story, the one my father told anyone who would listen, is that while in her womb, I gave my mother the blues for the entire nine months. Still, in spite of all that happened and all I went through growing up, a part of me still clung to the silly notion that one day he would love me as his son. One day, before I died, I hoped to get one kind word from him.

Then, I'd make both of them suffer.

I couldn't wait to inherit Robert's money so that I could go home and show them how rich I had become; I'm sure my father would be too drunk to even notice my presence, but, when he sobered, he'd ask me to buy him something to drink. I wanted my dear stepmom to know that her unkind words about the blackness of my beautiful skin didn't break me. I survived. I wanted her to see that, in spite of her hateful heart and her efforts to tear me down, I continued to stand. I wanted my father to see that his pretty son used his pretty looks to overcome *his* distance and *his* drunkenness and *his* anger. And, when they begged for money— as I knew they would—I'd walk away. When I said goodbye that time, it would be forever.

I sat at the dining room table in complete silence with my stepmother and father and I watched him mechanically lift his fork to his mouth. This was one of those rare occasions that we sat down as a family—one of those rare occasions when he was sober enough to sit upright at the dinner table. Her smoked salmon and asparagus tips didn't have their usual flavor, but he didn't complain, which was unusual for him in regard to her cooking. In fact, he didn't speak at all. I think they were focused on me and just getting through this awkward moment.

During the first part of this meal, no one spoke. At all. When I tried, my father shot me a curt look that slammed the door shut on conversation. The distance that separated me from them was not measured in inches, but in miles. I wondered what it would take to bridge that distance or if the distance could ever be bridged. In spite of my pretense and feigned independence, the alienation of affection from my parents wounded me each and every day; each cold stare tore at me; every empty hug filled me with a bit of rage; each silent second sliced away a little part of my flesh, leaving nothing but hardened bones.

They despised me. It wasn't just my darkened skin or my pretty features that filled them with hate. It was because they knew. They had always known about me and it turned their stomachs.

I subtly gazed at my father's strong face and wondered what thoughts circled his head. When he wasn't drunk on gin, he looked like a respectable father, like the ones I saw in the park teaching their sons to throw a football or the ones who sat their sons down and gave them advice on becoming a man.

I didn't know the reason for this family dinner, but I waited for some conversation, but nothing came from my father. Not a word or a syllable. I didn't ask for anything a normal child didn't crave from their parents. I wanted to be loved by them. I wanted to be protected and made to feel like I mattered. They had never defended me or made me feel protected. Certainly not now and not the time when I was seven and little Brock Jackson tormented me with the slur "tar baby" in school and made me cry. Instead of making me love my skin, I heard her tell my father, "Well, he is black as tar—that ain't a secret." I died a little that day and realized I would get no protection from them.

We continued eating in silence.

I could deal with almost anything, except being ignored. Silence cut like a knife.

I sighed loudly, hoping to start a dialogue, but neither one even blinked. When I could stand it no more, I slammed my fork and knife onto the plate, causing a loud clanking sound.

"Is this how we are going to be for the rest of our lives? Sitting around, not talking to each other? You two acting like I don't exist?"

"We know you exist, Blues. You're sitting right in front of us." She casually cut a piece of fish and picked it up with her fork. My father took his massive hand and wrapped it around his wineglass and brought it to his lips. In a few moments, he'd be falling out of his chair drunk, or peeing on himself later in bed.

"For once, could we have a decent conversation? Could you act as if you cared about what's going on in my life?" I asked.

"We know what's going on in your life. Just eat your supper and don't bother your father."

"Bother him? Are you for real?"

She dropped her fork and looked at him. "What does that mean?"

"It means nothing I do ever bothers him. Does he even speak anymore?" I said as I glared at him.

"He speaks to me."

"What about me?" I said, looking directly at him.

"I speak to you. You just never listen." His voice sounded foreign. He then let out a deep exhale. "What do you want to talk about, son?" He spoke with impatience and frustration, as if we'd had this same conversation before and he was too busy to be bothered with it again. This lucid moment was the first time he'd looked directly at me in months.

"I want you to talk to me like I'm a human, like you care about what's going on in my life."

"I know what's going on with you, Blues, even when you think I don't."

"Then why won't you say something?"

"What the hell do you want me to say? You want me to show interest in your life? Alright then. Why don't you tell me about the nice young lady you're dating?" My father put his fork down, leaned back in his chair, folded his arms, and waited for a response. I eyed him and then my mother as if the question was in jest.

I looked around incredulously. "Are you serious? You want to go there?"

"You can't answer it, can you? Why can't you answer it, son?"

"Because I don't have a girlfriend. You know that."

"And why don't you have one? You're a handsome, smart young man. Where are all the girls?" My father's face tightened and he looked like he would burst.

"Are you fucking kidding me with this?"

"Blues, watch your language!" she cried out. I guess my language offended her genteel nature but the drunken, profanity-laced tirades my father usually unleashed were never admonished by her.

"When are you going to get past this?"

"I will never condone your behavior."

"My behavior? What behavior? What have you seen me do?"

"Don't quibble with me, boy. You know exactly what kind of behavior I am talking about."

"You have no idea what my behavior is. You walk around all day like you don't see me, like you don't hear me. I speak to you and you walk on by."

"What is it about you that you want me to see? Do you want me to see who you've been laying up with when you don't come home at night? Do you want me to see who you're talking to when you're giggling on the phone like a schoolgirl?"

"What the fuck is wrong with you?" I blurted out when his words had cut too deeply. "Why do you hate me so much? I am you. Look at me! I look just like you!" My voice sounded desperate as I made eye contact and waited for a response. I tried, with all my might, to hold myself together, but tears formed in my eyes and my lips quivered. I didn't want him to see me cry. "Why can't you love me? Am I really so bad?"

"Look at you now, crying like a woman. Man up! You're an embarrassment and I don't know what I did to deserve a son like you." His words stung.

"What you did? What the hell did I do to deserve a father like you? Isn't there a bottle of gin you should be sucking on right now?" He looked shocked. I stung him back. "What you see is what you get. This is who I am. You've taken me to therapy and to preachers; you've tried to beat it out of me, you've tried to starve it out of me, but I am who I am!" Rage, not hurt, now peppered my tone. "I am who God wanted me to be. Why can't you understand that?"

"Don't bring God into this," she interjected, as if my words were an affront to her thin religious convictions.

"I am your son and I'm asking you to love me in spite of what you feel about my life. Can you do that, Daddy?"

"I can't...not like you are."

They got up from the table and began moving down the hallway. I *stood there, almost paralyzed. In that defining moment, I realized I was fighting a losing battle and their love was lost to me—forever; I wasn't convinced that I ever had it.*

My rage grew. How could they treat me like this?

"Well fuck you! Fuck you both!"

My choice was clear. I could either live in misery or free myself. In that fateful moment, I decided.

I snatched a sharp knife from the table and fought the urge to run up behind him and bury the blade in his back. Instead of stabbing him, I did something else. I grimaced loudly as I ran the sharp blade horizontally across my wrists. Blood spilled out of my veins and fell to the floor in bright red splatters.

"Daddy!" I screamed out. When my parents turned around to see me, they gasped. She cried out with all the emotion a mother should have. She raced over to me and screamed at my father to dial 9-1-1.

"I am flesh of your flesh and blood of your blood." I fell to the floor and my mother's wails echoed throughout the house.

As I lay there, the magnitude of what I had done to myself caused me to cry out in pain, even as blood poured out of my open wounds.

I didn't want to die. I merely wanted to be loved.

I felt fear like I had never known. I didn't want to die. I wanted to live. This was their fault. My blood was on their hands.

In that moment, I decided to live, if for no other reason than to make them suffer for at least another twenty years.

Then, everything went black.

I still remembered how I felt that day. The bitter taste of their hate still lingered on my tongue. I remembered feeling profoundly unloved. No child should ever feel that from a parent. Even though she wasn't my real mother, she was the only mother I ever knew and she treated me like a stranger.

I moved upstairs into the bedroom, gliding my way into the

bathroom, and opened the medicine cabinet. Inside, a plethora of medications for Robert's various conditions stared at me. There were pills for cholesterol, tablets for high blood pressure, and creams for his eczema; he had medicated droplets for his eyes and special vitamins that supported circulation. If he ever lost RDE, he could make a fortune as a pharmacist.

I picked up the bottle of pills that were for his heart and twisted off the lid. I thought about pouring all of the pills out into the toilet and replacing them with fake pills, but I didn't; however, it would be wonderful to see him stagger to the bathroom in serious need of his medicine only to find an empty bottle. I could watch him clutch his chest and collapse to the floor in pain. It was a good thought, but it was too common a plot.

Just as I put the pills back in the cabinet, Robert appeared out of nowhere, like a spooky ghost.

I need to put a bell around this cow's neck.

I felt Robert's rough hands around my waist. "What are you doing?"

"Oh, nothing…just a little tidying up," I said. "How was dinner?"

"It was good. She's come a long way since I last saw her. I have a lot of hope for her this time."

"I'm sure." I moved by him and walked into our bedroom. He moved slowly behind me.

"This is really bothering you, isn't it?"

"What?" I knew exactly what he meant, but wanted to be difficult.

"Ashleigh being here."

"Well, since you brought it up, yes, it bothers the hell out of me. You don't find it strange that she appeared out of nowhere? After all this time?"

"She's my flesh and blood. It doesn't matter how long you've been out of touch with family. You can always go home."

"I don't have a good feeling about this. She's your daughter and I get it, but I can't understand how you could accept her so easily. She put you through hell. I just don't want to see you get hurt. I don't want her stressing you out. Your heart isn't as strong as it used to be."

"Don't worry about my heart, baby. I'm taking care of myself and she's not going to stress me out. We'll be fine. I really need this chance to make it right."

"If you say so." Robert moved behind me and I felt his hands underneath my T-shirt. They eased up my stomach toward my nipples and stopped. I knew where this was going and I didn't like it one bit. I felt his grubby hands rubbing my nipples, which were uber-sensitive.

Dear God, not again. I'm not even drunk!

He lifted up my shirt and licked my right nipple with his dry tongue.

Lord, give me strength.

CHAPTER 10

After two weeks, Ashleigh was still there and I made very little effort to get to know her. Each time she tried to talk to me, I blew her off, as if I didn't have the time or the patience. Robert asked me again to work on my attitude, but his tone made his plea sound more like a mandate and I wasn't in the mood to be commanded around.

While she was in the house, she adopted an attitude like she was mistress of the manor. A couple of times she had directed the housekeeper to do things contrary to the way I liked them and I had to get Ashleigh together about it. I made it clear that she was not to give any of the servants orders or directives—that was my job. This house would be run the same way it had been run prior to her arrival and if she didn't like it, she could kick rocks in open-toed sandals.

One of her more obnoxious tendencies was the way she doted over Robert. When she was around him, she tended to act like a little girl and it was a tad bit too sickening to watch; yet, Robert seemed to love it. He reveled in the attention she gave him. I had never seen this side of him and I hoped to not have to deal with it too much longer. She had to go.

She managed to talk Robert into hiring her as his assistant, on a temporary basis, at RDE. She was ingratiating herself with Robert's employees and it was part of a larger plan to worm her way into his life and take everything that was mine. I didn't know how she planned to do it, but I'd kill her before I let that happen.

After another one of my sleepless nights, I finally got some rest starting around three in the morning. Robert was usually up in the morning before the sun rose. Usually, I helped him get ready for work, if for no other reason than to get his ass out of the house, but this morning I slept in a bit and when I finally made it downstairs, I watched Robert pull out of the driveway and head to work. It was barely six in the morning, but he was an early riser.

Later in the morning, I went for my morning run to try to clear my head and by the time I returned, Ashleigh was in the kitchen ordering the cook around like she was the queen of the castle. I didn't have the energy to speak to her, so when I entered the room, I moved to the refrigerator and poured myself a glass of juice. She tried to say something to me but I dismissed her with a wave of my hand and kept it moving.

By the time I finished my shower and returned downstairs for breakfast, Margaret informed me that Ashleigh had taken a set of car keys and left. She told Margaret that she had some errands to run before she went to work. For someone who just blew into town, I couldn't understand what errands she had. She was probably making a crack run.

But, I needed to be proactive. I needed to find out information about her, so I took this opportunity to search her room. As I raced up the stairs, I wondered what I'd find in her room. I moved swiftly down the hallway, rounded the corner and approached her bedroom on the right. I knocked on the door to ensure that it was vacant.

Tap.

Tap.

Tap. Tap.

I couldn't detect any sound, so I slowly opened the door. I peered inside before I set foot into the room. The room smelled of lavender, probably some cheap perfume she splashed on before leaving. The queen-sized sleigh bed was neatly made and everything was set neatly in place. The curtains allowed in a few slivers of sunlight, which sliced through the room in sections. Besides the fragrance that hung in the air, the room hardly looked disturbed.

I stepped into the room and closed the door. My breathing was rushed and I quickly scanned the room to determine where to begin my search. I looked around the room for her luggage, but didn't find it. I moved over to the closet and slid open the door. I saw two Louis Vuitton suitcases and a small carrying bag.

How does a former crackhead afford Louis Vuitton?

I picked up each bag, half-expecting them to be heavy, but they were empty. If they were still half-packed, then I could assume she didn't plan on staying long, but clearly she had already settled in and emptied all her bags. I was grasping at straws for some hope of her departure. I closed the closet and moved over to the mahogany dresser. I pulled open the drawers, one at a time, to see if I could find anything, but all I found were her silk panties and slips.

I closed the drawers and turned to face the room, trying to determine a good hiding place. I dropped to my knees and looked underneath the bed, but there was nothing there.

I went back to the closet and picked up another bag. I placed it on the bed and unzipped the outside pocket. I pulled out several pieces of paper and threw them onto the bed. *Bingo!* Upon closer examination, I saw that the pieces of random paper were actually Internet articles about me and my wedding to Robert. She had pictures and the full details of the ceremony. I shuffled the papers around and found another article about me from the local newspaper about my high school track days.

"Hmmmm," I said out loud to myself. This bitch was checking up on me.

Then, I saw another article from the same paper. It was about a local athlete who had fallen to his death in an apparent suicide. I had been questioned by the police and my name came up in the article. In this day and age of instant Google searches, it wasn't unusual for someone to do an Internet search on someone, but I didn't like the feeling that she had the upper hand; she knew more about me than I knew about her.

There was nothing incriminating about the article and certainly nothing that linked me to Jabari's death. Many people had been questioned about his death and no one was charged. Still, I didn't like her snooping around in my past. I'm sure that Robert had run a complete background check on me prior to getting married. I had been arrested for possession of a small amount of a controlled substance—marijuana—but the charge was eventually dropped after I completed my community service.

I searched her room for a few more minutes and then gave up. Nothing I saw gave me much insight to her real motives, but I'd find out. I knew what she wanted—money—but I didn't know how she planned to get it. Robert would never leave the bulk of his fortune to a daughter who would smoke it up faster than Amy Winehouse. And, Ashleigh was a smart girl, so she had to know that, too. So, what was her endgame?

"Blues," I heard a voice say as I stood on the side of the bed with all of the articles spread out. "What are you doing in my room?" Ashleigh stood in the doorway. The look on her face was venomous. Her eyes were tightly drawn and her lips clenched.

"Technically, this is my room; my house, my room. Get it?"

"Oh, Blues," she said, releasing the tension from her face. She stepped closer to me and gently removed the papers from my fingers. "You don't trust me and I understand, but that still does not give you the right to invade my privacy." She stuffed all of the papers back into her suitcase and zipped it shut.

"Don't get all indignant. I'm the one that's pissed. What gives you the right to investigate me? Who do you think you are?"

"I'm nobody. I'm a daughter who's simply trying to get to know the man who married my father, that's all. Is that a crime?"

"Cut the bullshit, Ashleigh. I can see right through your games. The woman who approached me on the rooftop of RDE was not a concerned daughter. The woman who was talking to me that night had some tricks up her sleeve. You aren't fooling anyone with this little Ms. Innocent act."

She picked up her suitcase and walked it over to the closet, sliding open the door and sliding it closed before turning to face me. "When are you going to stop acting like I'm the enemy? I haven't done anything to you. I want a chance to have a real relationship with my father and to get to know you."

"I don't like people digging around in my past."

"Do you have something to hide? Something my father should know? Something about the mysterious suicide of Jabari West?" Her lips twisted up in the corner to reveal a taut, almost victorious smile.

Her words dug into me, but I didn't let her see me flinch.

"If there was something about his suicide that I knew, I would have told the police years ago, don't you think?"

"I'm not sure what to think. Exactly what was your relationship with him? The newspapers said you ran track together, but I think there was something more." She slithered across the room to be closer to me. "If you need to unburden yourself and talk about something, I'm here for you. I know firsthand what carrying a lot of guilt can do to a person's soul. Trust me on that."

"You don't know the first damned thing about me or Jabari. You are way out of line and way off base."

"Am I? I can see something in your lovely eyes. Is there something you want to tell me?"

"Yes, there is. Go to hell."

"Did I strike a nerve?"

"Ashleigh, you don't know me very well, so I'll give you the benefit of the doubt and I'll tell you politely...this one time. Don't fuck with me. If you've come here looking to start trouble, then you might want to think again. I'd hate for this to get ugly. If you want me to trust you and for us to get along, then I suggest you back off." I moved to the door.

"I wasn't starting anything with you. I'm only here to help. I found it odd—and so did the police—that you were the last person Jabari called before he died. According to your own statement, you and him weren't that close. So, why would he call you, of all people?"

Crack.

Crack.

Crack. Crack.

"If you read the whole report, you also read where I told them that Jabari called me by mistake. I'm not sure who he meant to call, but we had a short conversation and then I hung up the phone."

"Really? You make it all sound so innocent."

"We spoke for less than thirty seconds and then I— Why the hell am I explaining anything to you?" I said. This bitch was getting under my skin and making me lose my cool. I turned and walked toward the door.

"Blues, one last thing," she said coyly, "does my father know about your arrest for prostitution in New York?"

I stopped dead in my tracks. She was going to make me choke the life out of her.

I turned to face her and I smiled. "Your father knows everything he needs to know about me. I'm quite certain he ran a complete background check on me before we married. Robert isn't stupid."

"No, he's not stupid, but sometimes he can be blinded by the charms of a handsome, virile young man like you."

"Your father knows about that arrest. It was a simple misunderstanding and the charges were dropped."

"Oh, I see."

"You haven't seen anything, yet. You have lost your fuckin' mind, coming up in here talking to me like this. You may be his daughter, but you're still a crackhead and Robert will never trust you. *Never.* You can say what you want and try to spin stories about my past to fit your plans, whatever they are, but you'll never win. You see, Ashy, once a crackhead, always a crackhead. Everybody knows that." I walked out of her bedroom and closed the door. The sound of her voice and the sight of her counterfeit smile made me want to push her out of a twenty-story window. This bitch was really tripping. She didn't know it, but she had messed with the wrong man.

Her words had winded me and I paused outside her door to gather my breath. Who was this Ashleigh Douglas and did she know more about Jabari's death than she was letting on? If she knew something, she wasn't going to tip her hand right now. Instead, she'd wait for the perfect moment so that her disclosure would have the most impact.

If she thought I was going to take this lying down, then she was sadly mistaken. I wasn't going to let her play me, especially when I'd come so far. I had been through hell and back to get to the place where I was and I was not about to let it all slip through my fingers. I moved swiftly down the hallway and returned to my room, slamming the door behind me.

Crack.

Crack.

Crack. Crack.

I grabbed the remote control and clicked on the television. I needed something to drown out the noise in my head.

"Clever girl," I said to myself.

She had made her intentions clear. She had launched the first salvo. I had to strike before she did.

CHAPTER 11

"Marquis, I really need you to do this for me. I'm serious," I said to my little homo-thug as he sat on the off-colored brown sofa in a cramped, run-down rowhouse on Good Hope Road, SE. I didn't know why they called this road "good hope" because as far as I could see, there was no hope on Good Hope Road. Hope, along with any sign of decency, had boarded up and fled for safety a long time ago.

Marquis's place consisted of two rooms, a big open space that served as a living and dining area with a small, cramped bathroom in the back. The whole place reeked of cigarettes, beer, and faded dreams.

Marquis was a plaything—a diversion—that picked me up one day outside the mall some months ago. His whole thug-presence and machismo was so not what I was into or had ever been attracted to, but there was something deep and mysterious about his eyes that captivated me, so I listened as he spit game. He came at me hard, with all the bravado, cool pose, and hustle he had mastered on the streets. In spite of his extended effort, I didn't fall immediately for it. He amused me. I listened as he talked that talk in the parking lot with me leaned against my car; he didn't seem to care whether or not anyone around heard him come at me with his homo thug appeal. He was fearless.

He was every bit of five-feet-six-inches and 135 pounds, but when he stepped to me, his swagger reflected his image at twice its normal size. There was something raw and unchained in his spirit. I could smell danger on him like I could smell the marijuana. He excited me. He was thugged out from head-to-toe, with sagging blue jeans, a faded wifebeater, black utility boots, with a Black & Mild dangling from his thick and beautiful lips.

"Man, you cold-blooded, ain't you?" he asked with a hint of delight in his deep voice. His voice was deep and was tailor made for a much bigger man.

"I'm just tryna be like you."

He smiled. "Nah, son. Don't be like me. You betta than me, but you know I got you," he said. "Now, what I gotta do?" I explained to him the part of my plan that he needed to know. Ashleigh had crossed too many boundaries with me and I was not about to sit around and wait for her to strike. I had to take her out and Marquis was the perfect person to eliminate her. I kept Marquis on a strict need-to-know basis and the beauty of him was that he never asked any questions. If I told him what needed to be done, he'd do it, no questions asked. He didn't ask me what she did to me or why I wanted to do that to her; generally speaking, he never seemed to care what motivated me. He was definitely a follower. He would have made an excellent soldier, except for his aversion and rejection of all authority figures.

When he and I hooked up, we'd sometimes chill and smoke weed; other times we'd fuck like whores. I could tell he was no expert at sexing a man, in spite of his confidence, because his stroke game was like a jack rabbit, but I intended to teach him and he was willing to learn. He was more than curious and had already had several experiences with men. "Men give the best head," he said that day at the mall. He found out I had won trophies for my head game.

Over time, when he became comfortable with me, he shared with me the unfortunate circumstances of his upbringing; his mother essentially putting him out on the street every time she found a new boyfriend. Finally, at sixteen, when she put him out, he didn't return. He'd been on the street doing what he had to do to survive for a few years, which translated to mostly slingin' rock. Now, at twenty-three, he had managed to carve out a slice of the Southeast D.C. drug trade for himself. He wasn't a baller by any means— he wasn't that ambitious—but he made enough to survive; surviving seemed to be the extent of his ambition.

"If I do this for you, what I get in return?" he said with a grin as he rubbed his penis through the black sweatpants that he wore.

"Baby, you can get anything you want."

"That's wassup. You know what I like." He dropped the joystick to his Xbox game and pimped his way over to me, grinning from ear-to-ear. He was a simple little thing, but his swag was on point. I liked him more than I cared to admit.

He pushed me down on his sofa, climbed on top of me, and kissed me forcefully. I wanted to resist, but his lips had a power of their own that I couldn't resist. He tasted of liquor, chicken wings, and peril, but he had never tasted so sweet.

This little man was my savior.

I had charged him with the task of killing Robert. Marquis, eager to please and possess me, was all too willing to oblige; especially when I lied and told him how Robert abused me mentally and physically. When I told him how Robert punched me in the face one day, I saw anger sweep across Marquis's face; it took refuge residence in his heart. His whole demeanor changed; hate filled his eyes. Right in front of me, he transformed into a wild thing, ready to strike and kill. If Robert had been anywhere near him at the moment when the lie left spilled from my mouth, Marquis would have blown his head off, without a second thought.

To be rid of Robert, I only had to tell him when and where;

but, I had to be careful with Marquis. I had to do all of the planning. I didn't have faith in his ability to devise and execute the plan. He was a trigger man, nothing more, nothing less.

Danger is alluring and that was part of Marquis's appeal. He kept things exciting. Every day I spent with him was a new adventure, but behind my heart, a small measure of fear lingered when I dealt with him. It wasn't something I'd ever show or tell him. He'd never hurt me, but Marquis was no stranger to murder. He had first killed when he was eighteen, in a drive-by, after a rival gang shot and killed his cousin; that man was his first kill, but not his last. Marquis told me how pulling the trigger made him feel powerful, as if he was God. It freaked me out a little bit. He felt little remorse after the deed was done; in fact, he and his boys had gone to play a game of basketball on a beat-up court on Benning Road, NE.

We connected because we were kindred spirits. Killers. I never shared with him or anyone what I had done to Jabari; that secret would follow me to my grave, but I listened when he sometimes confessed his sins. I listened, but I could offer no absolution.

Marquis shared with me so much of himself, things he had never told anyone, because there was never anyone to tell. He was alone in the world for the most part. He wasn't a depraved killer, wandering the streets murdering without thought and conscience. He was a thoughtful killer, who killed with purpose, only when it was necessary.

Robert's death was both purposeful and necessary.

Even though I had strong feelings for Nigel and thought we might be together one day, I entertained fantasies about running off with Marquis. I wanted to show him parts of the world that he had never imagined. I wanted to be there to see his eyes light up when he saw the Eiffel Tower for the first time or when he saw the pyramids of Giza. It would be cool to see his eyes light up at the splendor of the Grand Canyon or the Statue of Liberty. I wanted to use Robert's money to uplift him, rescue him from his poverty and make him mine.

But, it was only a fantasy; a small one, at that.

Marquis and I both knew we were too different for each other. He'd never fit into my world, nor did he desire to. He was content on smoking weed, selling rock when he needed to, and playing video games.

I pushed him gently off me.

"What, a brotha can't get no love today?"

"You know I love you, Marquis. I just have to be somewhere in a few minutes."

"Fuck that shit. You in Souffeast now, muthafucka. You don't leave until I say you leave," he said playfully, his thick D.C. accent in full effect. He stuck his tongue down my throat hard and forcefully.

I didn't resist.

✪ ✪ ✪

I pulled into the driveway of our house around six in the evening and was surprised to see Nigel's car. Robert was never home this early—let alone with Nigel—so I couldn't imagine what was going on; however, I was happy Nigel was there. If I was lucky, maybe I could get Nigel alone and steal a kiss. With the taste of Marquis on my lips, I thought it would be an interesting mix.

Before I stuck my key into the lock, I took a deep breath and shook off thoughts of Nigel so that my eyes didn't betray our secret relationship. I also took a moment and steadied myself for Robert's inevitable berating. He'd make his displeasure known at my silent treatment; I had ignored his calls all day. Even though we had guests, he'd find a way to express his emotion, even in the smallest way. His anger, simmering right beneath the surface, would manifest itself in passive-aggressive ways throughout the evening until we were alone. He could be such a juvenile. After our guests had moved on, he'd scold me like a child—his thin lips quivering with anger—as he wagged his emaciated finger in my direction like an old Catholic school nun. Eventually, his child-like tantrum would shift into lust and we'd have angry sex, maybe break a table or an expensive vase in the process. Either way, he'd get over it.

When I stepped into the house, I was immediately greeted by the rich and aromatic smell of exotic spices. The appetizing scent hung in the hair and beckoned me toward the kitchen. As I neared the area, I saw a couple of people dressed in white uniforms scurrying about the room, tending to simmering pots and peeking into the oven.

"Excuse me, what's going on here?" I asked the tall thin man wearing the chef's hat.

"Blues, I'm glad you're home; there is a lot to do before the guests arrive." I was startled by Ashleigh, who greeted me affectionately. I don't know where she came from. It was like she materialized in a puff of black smoke. "We need to make sure everything is set before the guests arrive."

"What the hell is going on?"

"You didn't get the messages? Daddy is hosting a dinner for the executives from some charity…Corey's Room, Kyle's Room—"

"Keevan's Room?"

"Yes, that's the one."

"Really? When did he decide this?"

"This afternoon; very short notice."

I shook my head. "I hate when he does that."

"Blues," she said, "you have to learn to be more flexible with Daddy. He's an important man and sometimes these things can't be helped."

I know she wasn't trying to give me advice about Robert.

"Whatever, Ashleigh. I know more about Robert and his business dealings than you could ever hope to know. "

"Well, if you knew so much you should have known that he needed you today and you should have been available tonight. Daddy starting yelling at me, asking me why you weren't answering your phone, as if I knew. I could've made a guess, but luckily for you, I didn't."

"I don't have the patience to deal with you right now."

"Why? Have your extracurricular activities tired you out?"

I exhaled heavily. "What time does this dinner start?"

"At seven."

I looked down at my watch. It was 6:20. "How many people are coming?"

"Eight, including Nigel."

"I saw his car outside. Where is he?"

"He and Daddy are out by the pool." She moved about the kitchen like she was the queen bee. I followed her over to the stove as she raised a lid on one of the pots. I looked at the colorful dish.

"This isn't Catering by Estelle," I said flatly after taking one look at the dish and because I couldn't think of anything else to say.

"Excuse me?"

"Robert only uses Catering by Estelle; he won't be happy."

"He'll be fine. Estelle was completely booked tonight and couldn't accommodate us on such short notice."

I inhaled. "Fine. What do you need me to do?" Just as I spoke, the doorbell rang.

"You can get the door," she said as she turned and walked toward the chef, leaving her comment to sizzle into my ears. Luckily for her, living with Robert had taught me to temper my tongue. I let her flippant comment pass and, as she had instructed, I answered the door.

I was not happy to learn that Robert was hosting this dinner party. Usually, when folks came over, it was because they needed something from him, something like money—my money. I didn't usually take too much interest in Robert's affairs because, quite frankly, I didn't much care. He sat on the boards of several not-for-profit organizations that I never cared to learn about, except this Keevan's Room mess. Robert talked about it more than I cared to listen.

Keevan's Room was just that—a mess. This organization, from what I understood, provided shelter and support for gay men who were victims of domestic violence. From what I gathered, the founder, some dude named Kevin, named the organization after his dead brother who I guessed must've had his ass kicked on a regular basis by his lover or some shit like that. I didn't ask Robert for the details, nor did I ask how he came to be on the board of such an organization. I could only imagine the kind of weak-ass men that would need that kind of protection.

Robert did mention that Keevan's Room operated three shelters: one in Washington, D.C., one in Houston, and the newest location in Los Angeles. The Purple Party, going into its second year, was a huge fundraiser for the group. I didn't care for charity, but I loved a great party.

I made it to the door on the third ring of the bell. When I answered it, I was surprised to see two very striking men standing before me. My disinterest in Keevan's Room quickly changed to '*how you doin'*?' The shorter of the two men wore a blue and white striped shirt and dark slacks. I could see that he worked out, but his body wasn't nearly as good as mine; even still, I wanted to lay hands on him. His skin tone was an earthly color brown and his dark and inviting eyes sparkled in the evening light. I noticed a couple of errant gray hairs protruding from his neatly trimmed mustache and goatee, but it only added to his appeal. He looked yummy. I was beginning to understand Robert's interest in Keevan's Room.

"Hello, I'm Kevin Davis and this is Daryl Harris. We have a dinner meeting with Robert; I think we're a bit early," he said as he glanced down at his Cartier watch.

I could spot an expensive watch from another room. *Hmmmm, good-looking and rich—my favorite combination. Maybe he'll be my next ex-husband.* Kevin's booming voice projected much more confidence than I expected. I felt a spark in my pants. He had better watch out.

"Of course, come in. I'm Blues Carmichael-Douglas, Robert's husband." I stepped aside and let the dynamic duo enter the room, taking full stock of the specimens as they eased by. There was nothing sexier than a black man who was completely confident in his black skin.

"Blues. That's an interesting name," the taller one said as he moved into the room. I had already forgotten his name, but I remembered that it started with a D. He exuded a quiet sexuality that intrigued me and made me pay attention. His strut, his height, his lips, and his smile suggested there was more to this man than met the eye. He was dressed a little more casually than Kevin, but he looked great in his khaki pants and short-sleeved shirt.

"I'm an interesting person," I said with a wink. Kevin seemed a bit put off by my comment. *Hmmmm, could they be lovers?* I didn't really care.

If I couldn't make a happy home, I certainly could break one.

"Follow me, please." I led them into the den; I didn't know where else to place them. "May I offer you something to drink while you wait for Robert?"

"Nothing for me," they both said in unison and then giggled at the simultaneous outburst.

Ugghhh, silly fags.

"I don't mean to be presumptuous, but are you two a couple?" I asked, even though I already knew the answer. They lapsed into an awkward silence and shot mysterious glances at each other, as if they were at a loss for words.

"Umm, what are we, Kevin?" Daryl asked with an impish smile.

"Let's just say we have a history together," he said, exchanging glances between the two of us. He looked at Daryl with an uncomfortable smile. I smiled, too.

"I didn't mean to offend you. If you were a couple, I was going to mention how cute you look together; that's all."

"Well, thank you. Kevin and I are very special to each other," Daryl interjected. I could tell from the look in his eyes and the silly expression on his face that he really cared for Kevin, but there was something standoffish about Kevin that kept him at bay. I wondered what that history between them really was about.

I quickly bored of the conversion. "I'll see what's keeping Robert." I could feel two sets of eyes locking onto me as I exited the room. *They're looking at my ass.* As I stepped out of the room, I paused right beyond the door, out of sight, because I knew they were going to talk about me. Jealous fags always did.

"I don't like him," I heard Kevin say plainly. He said it as a matter-of-fact, as if his dislike of me was permanent.

Well, fuck you, too.

"Don't be too hard on him; he's just young."

"Yes, very young; too young for Robert."

"Kevin, stay out of grown folks' business."

"I'm just saying. There is only one thing that boy could offer Robert and I know it ain't conversation."

"And that's okay. As long as Robert is happy."

"Whatever. And you, if you eye Little Boy Blue one more time, you gonna need shelter from Keevan's Room," Kevin said, in an *I'm-laughing-but-you-know-I'm-not-playing-with-your-ass* tone.

"I don't want that boy, but you gotta admit, he's got a big booty," Daryl said with a chuckle. I peeked around the corner just in time to see Kevin give him a playful jab to the ribs in protest.

"That may be true, but I don't like his vibe. Something is off about him. That boy can't be any older than twenty-five and his eyes are empty. I thought Robert had better taste."

Better taste? Bitch, it doesn't get any better than this.

"Now, who's being shady?" They snickered.

Uggghhh.

"I ain't worried about that little boy. I am, however, worried about this party. Everything has got to go off without a hitch; this is our biggest event of the year."

I made a mental note to fuck Daryl at some point in the near future for coming to my defense. Now, it was time to find my husband.

As I made my way out to the pool, I saw Robert and Nigel seated on stools at the outside bar, drinks in hand, and sharing a private laugh. I exhaled as I neared.

"Ahhh, there he is," Robert said with a genuine affection. He hopped off the stool and pulled me into his body when I was close enough. He planted a firm kiss on my lips. "How are you, baby?"

"I'm fine. I'm sorry about this afternoon. I went to see a movie and then snuck into another theater after it was over." They both looked at me like I had lost my mind. "It's something I used to do when I was a child." I chuckled.

"Whatever makes you happy." Robert smiled.

"Good to see you again, Blues."

"Likewise." These phony pleasantries were painfully transparent. Robert held me tightly by the waist. For some reason, he wanted me close to him; maybe he was going to stab me for ignoring him this afternoon. Even though he was smiling, he really wanted to cuss me out. I certainly wasn't expecting this level of affection from him; in fact, I expected the opposite, considering my afternoon disappearing act.

"Nigel and I were talking about the Purple Party; it'll be bigger, better and wilder than any previous party. It'll become legendary."

"Oh, I forgot to tell you. Two of your guests have arrived. Kevin and Daryl, I think. I put them in the den and told them I'd get you."

"Great. I asked them to come a few minutes early so that I could discuss something with them."

Nigel said he had to make a phone call and would join Robert in a few minutes. Robert and I entered the den, breaking up their frivolous conversation. Robert still held onto me and I wasn't sure if he missed me or he wanted to mark his territory. *He might as well pee on me.*

Kevin stood up and smiled like a grinning idiot as he greeted Robert, who returned an impassioned smile. They hugged like they were old friends, a bit too long for my taste, but I shrugged it off. He then introduced Robert to his partner in crime, Daryl. Robert and I both had cocktails in our hands and something told me that I'd need it.

"Blues, did you offer our guests something to drink?"

Fuck, I don't work here.

"We're fine now," Daryl answered. I loved the way his lips moved.

I bet he could suck a mean dick.

"You sure? It's no trouble," I added. I prayed hard that Kevin would opt for a drink this time; I was dying to pee in his cup. I always liked to leave a taste of me on the lips of the people I didn't like. "I could get it for you," I offered with a smile. To my dismay, they both declined. I smiled innocently.

I tried to escape from the room before the conversation got too deep, but each time I wiggled away, Robert would pull me back into him or engage me in conversation. I sat next to Robert like the adoring spouse, when all I really wanted was a kiss from Nigel.

"The entertainment for the event will be spectacular," Kevin continued. "The guests will be treated to a wonderful performance by the main attraction, the one and only Danea Charles, who just so happens to be a great personal friend of mine...of ours," he said as he placed his hand on Daryl's knee and smiled.

"Ticket sales have significantly increased over the last month since we announced Danea, but we need a couple more big-dollar donors and sponsors to really meet our fundraising goal," Daryl added.

Fuck. Here it is. I knew it was coming—the begging; they wanted money. I could see it in Kevin's shiftless eyes. *Haven't we given enough to this ridiculous cause?* If some man was getting his ass kicked by his lover, that was between them and I didn't want Robert spending another cent of *my* money on that bullshit.

"We have every faith that you'll get your donations," I said, smiling. "It's a great cause, and folks are willing to give." *Just not us.*

The party was to take place at the Georgetown Palladium in one week and, in spite of my lack of interest in the cause and my growing dislike of Kevin, I was looking forward to the event. It would be a virtual Who's Who of D.C. A-listers and I couldn't wait to hobnob with the elite of the city. The ensemble I had selected, a designer original, was nothing short of dazzling. Regardless of who was there, I'd be the finest thing in the room. Purple was my color. Hell, every color was my color.

After about half an hour, Ashleigh sent one of *her people* up to inform us that the other guests were starting to arrive. I finally figured out that Robert was entertaining the board of directors of Keevan's Room and a couple of high-rollers. As much as I hated to admit it, Ashleigh had done an excellent job of preparing this event. She had already ushered folks out onto the patio for cocktails before the dinner. Robert complimented her endlessly on her effort. When he was with her, I saw a tender side that he rarely showed. He seemed genuinely happy to have his daughter back in his life; too bad it would be short-lived.

When we finally sat down at the table for the four-course meal, the conversation was bold and lively; the drinks really loosened up these stiff-ass people. Every once in a while, I would cut my eyes at Nigel to see if he was enjoying himself, but he paid me no attention. I had to admire his poker face.

I was disappointed that the night ended without a quick private moment with Nigel, but I understood.

Soon enough, our kisses wouldn't have to be in private.

CHAPTER 12

After my morning workout, Robert sent me on an errand to bring a file to him at RDE and to meet him for lunch. He was always leaving something at home for me to fetch. I was so tired of being at his beck and call. I used to think he'd leave stuff behind because he was old and couldn't remember shit, but now I knew better. He did it to keep tabs on my comings and goings. If I had to stop what I was doing in the middle of the day to bring him a file, he thought I couldn't be fucking around on him.

I stepped off the elevator on the fifteenth floor—the executive floor—and all the busy worker bees were going about their day. My presence went virtually unnoticed. Their secretaries' phones rang; delivery boys dropped off packages; people darted off to the various meeting rooms and offices; a hundred frantic voices seemed to be talking at once. It was all pretty annoying. Now, I was no stranger to work—I had slaved for years in restaurants, retail stores, call centers, and offices before Robert came to my rescue. As much as I disliked him, I disliked this kind of work even more. I wasn't strong enough to endure having to be at the same place at the same time just to see the same people five days a week. When Robert was dead and Ashleigh was out of the way, I'd never have to fear that kind of life.

By the time I made it to Robert's office, Ashleigh was at her desk, slumped over her computer. When she saw me approach, she looked up briefly and then quickly back down, not making eye contact. The small fan on her desk gently blew the ends of her midnight black hair. Her form-fitting green and black dress hugged her curvaceous frame and accentuated the parts she wanted to put on display. Her full breasts sat upright and the plunging neckline gave everyone more than a glimpse of her lady parts.

"Ashleigh," I said dryly.

"He's in there with Nigel." She motioned toward Robert's office. "Just go in." When she looked at me, there was a horrible hate in her tight eyes and I could feel her glare tearing through me. She could pretend to be a sweetheart all she wanted, but I had the prescience to understand that this sweet, darling child was gunning for me.

I swept past her and opened the door to his office. He was on the phone and Nigel sat in front of his desk. I hadn't expected Nigel to be tied up with Robert in a meeting. There goes my afternoon foreplay with Nigel. Damn.

Robert exhaled loudly before he spoke into the speakerphone. "Charles, there is a lot of money at stake here and I am not letting this deal go to hell 'cause some old woman won't move."

"She's pretty determined to stay in her house. Her husband died there and she said she will, too. I don't think there is an amount of money you can pay her to make her move." I was surprised that Charles was still on the payroll. I had put in a half-hearted word with Robert to save Charles's job and I guess it had worked. Who knew?

Robert saw me enter the office and waved for me to come forward with his file. "Charles, I don't care if the Virgin Mary died there. You get her to move. You are already on shaky ground with me. This is your last chance. You find a way to convince her to move before this whole thing falls apart. This is your responsibility;

this is your project." Robert disconnected the call as Charles was in mid-sentence.

"Hey, baby," I said nervously. I treaded cautiously because he was in a dangerous mood. "Hey, Nigel."

"Give me the file, Blues. Can't you see we're in the middle of something?" Robert looked down at his desk and I turned my head toward Nigel and rolled my eyes as a reaction to Robert's attitude. I stepped closer, handed off the file, and turned to exit. I wanted to get the hell out of the line of fire.

"I'm sorry, Blues. I'm a bit tense. There's a lot going on right now," he said in a more relaxed tone. He realized that he was being a complete ass to me—again. When he was dead, I would certainly not miss his acid tongue.

Robert focused his attention on the information in the folder. After a few seconds of silence, he looked up at me. "Blues, we really have to get back to work." He dismissed me in his usual rough manner. I turned and made a beeline toward the door. I couldn't get out of his office fast enough if I was Carl Lewis. Right before I got to his office door he called out to me again.

"Blues, wait. Ashleigh has to run an errand for me. Go with her and make sure it gets done right."

"Huh? I have plans. I was going to—" I cut myself off in mid-sentence when he looked at me like I had cursed out his mother. "Okay, baby. What do we need to do?"

"She'll tell you." With those three little words, he ended the conversation. "And close the door on your way out." I walked around to look at Ashleigh, who was ruffling through a stack of papers.

"I guess *we* have an errand to run."

✪ ✪ ✪

Once we got into my car, she placed her can of Dict Coke in the drink holder, popped open her handbag, and pulled out some makeup. She pulled down the visor to reveal the mirror and began to reapply. She dusted her face, applied mascara to her eyelashes, and added color to her already-crimson lips. I should've slammed on the brakes when she applied the mascara and hoped the pencil popped her eyeball.

After she instructed me to get onto the freeway, we didn't speak for awhile.

After several minutes of watching and being annoyed by her beauty regime and waiting for her to say something, I finally broke the silence.

"Where are we going?" I asked casually, not sure what to say.

"To Fairfax; over near Tysons Corner Center."

"Fine. I'm not sure why I'm here, but I guess Robert didn't think you were smart enough to do this yourself."

She glared at me. I could see her hatred for me reflected in her eyes. Her face revealed nothing but contempt for me; she was pure fire and ice. Sometimes she was as cool as a cucumber, other times she burned as hot as a star. As she eyed me, her expression was stone cold, but the fire in her eyes burned with intensity. "You know, Blues, I really am about tired of you. I have gone out of my way to be nice to you since I got back and all you've done is be an ass to me."

"If you call accusing me of being a gold-digger and a prostitute being nice, then I'd hate to see when you're being a bitch."

She turned her head and looked out of the window. "I can't wait until you're gone," she uttered under her breath.

"Gone? I'm not going anywhere."

She turned toward me with a smirk on her face. "Really? Is that what you think?"

"That's what I know."

"Then you don't know too much. Blues, let me tell you something. My father has always had a weakness for pretty boys like you. He plays with them for awhile and when he's done, he throws them away like yesterday's trash. Please don't think you're any different. You can't be that simple. It's only a matter of time before you're sent away."

"Your father didn't marry any of the others. He married me."

She chuckled. "Marriages can be undone."

"Robert loves me. I ain't worried."

"Maybe you don't have to worry about him divorcing you, but what about murder?"

My heart skipped a beat. I quickly turned my head her direction, careful not to swerve into traffic. Did she know about my plot? Had she heard me talking to Marquis? "Murder? What the hell are you talking about?"

"I'm talking about your ex-boyfriend, Jabari; the high-school football star who had the world at his fingertips, but decided to jump off a building and kill himself. You were the last person he spoke to. It sounds like the police need to open another investigation. There is no statute of limitations on murder."

"Are you still on this? I didn't kill Jabari; no one ever thought I did. I have nothing to hide. They can investigate me until the cows come home and they won't find anything. If they didn't find anything then, then they won't find anything now. I don't know what you think you know, but you know nothing."

"Hmmmmm." She looked at me through squinted eyes. "Well, I'm just saying it doesn't sound right to me."

"If you really think I'm capable of murder, shouldn't you be worried about pissing me off?" I looked at her sternly. She'd never admit it, but I saw a bit of fear flash across her eyes. "Besides,

I don't care if it doesn't sound right to you. The truth is the truth. Who cares what a crack bitch has to say about anything?"

She snapped her compact closed and slammed the visor up.

"Please don't take me for a fool. I know why you married my father; what you want from him."

"Really? Why don't you lay your wisdom on me?"

"If my father was broke as hell, there's no way you'd be with him."

"I wouldn't be with anyone who is broke as hell."

"Look, I love my father, but I know what kind of man he is. He's part of the reason for my drug problem. I had to have an escape."

"See, that's some bullshit. Don't try to blame your crack problem on your father."

"You've only known him a couple of years. I've known him most of my life. You have no idea what it was like growing up around him. Nothing I ever did was good enough. I could never say or do the right thing. I grew up apologizing for just about everything all that time." Little did she know, I knew exactly how she felt, but I'd never admit it to her.

"Ahhh, you poor baby."

"Fuck you, Blues. Just fuck you."

"If you hate him so much, why are you back?"

"I never said I hated him. He's my father. I love him."

"Why are you back, Ashleigh?"

"I'm back to claim what's mine."

"I knew it! You didn't come back to work on your father-daughter relationship. You came back for money."

"Isn't that why you married him?"

"I married your father because I..." I tried to say the words, but they got caught in my throat.

She laughed. "You can't even say the words, can you? How fucked-up is that?"

"I married Robert because…because I love him. It has very little to do with his money." I didn't sound very convincing and she looked at me incredulously.

"Say whatever you want, but I know the truth. I've looked into your background and you've been a hustler all your life. You didn't come from shit, you don't have shit, and you ain't gettin' shit out of this marriage. Believe that."

"Bitch, you need to watch what you do and what you say. You don't know me like that."

"Bitch? Is that all you got? Whatever, Blues. I'll tell you one thing. If you think I'm going to sit here and let you cheat me out of my inheritance, you have another thing coming. I've put up with a lot of shit from my father to let some simple-minded pretty boy suck and fuck his way into my money."

"As soon as you showed up, I realized it was about money."

"It's always about money. Fuck what you heard."

"If your father decided to not give you any money, it has nothing to do with me. It's because you're a drug addict and you would smoke up everything that wasn't nailed to the floor."

She reached down into her purse and pulled out a small manila envelope and tossed it in my lap while I was driving.

"What the fuck is this?" I asked, trying to not take my eyes off the road for too long.

She smiled. "It's a surprise. Why don't you open it?"

"Because I'm driving."

"From what I've seen, you're very talented. I'm sure you can multi-task."

I kept my left hand on the steering wheel and reached down and grabbed the package from my lap. I looked ahead and saw the traffic light change from green, to yellow to red. I pressed the brake pedal and brought the vehicle to a slow halt. I turned my head to meet her gaze. The gleam in her eyes unsettled me. *What did she know?*

"I had planned on showing this to you in a more dramatic fashion, something more formal, but you've pissed me off."

I ripped open the package and pulled out photographs of me and Nigel having sex in our hotel room.

"You bitch. How…how…did you get these? What the fuck?" My chest swelled and burned with an anger I had not known in years. I balled my fist, ready to strike her down where she sat, but pounding her to death on a busy street wouldn't help me avoid jail.

"You didn't think I'd show up after all this time without doing my homework on you, did you? I was in town a few weeks doing surveillance on you before I made my appearance. As soon as I saw you, I knew it would only be a matter of time before I found some shit on you. I know your type. You're shady. And greedy. And there's no way a man like you would be with my father without getting something on the side. So, all I had to do was follow you for a few days to figure out your routine. You and Nigel fuck in the same hotel room every week. Not very smart. In fact, I'm surprised my father hasn't found out yet. He's not big on trust. He must think you are too stupid to cheat on him in such an obvious way."

It took all the strength I could muster to contain my rage.

"If you take me down, you'd take Nigel down, too. Are you prepared to do that?"

She looked at me with those cold, black eyes. "I don't care about Nigel. I'll do what I have to do to win. After all, I am my father's daughter."

The traffic signal turned green and I pressed hard on the accelerator and bolted down the road, weaving in between traffic. The sun was shining and the day was very bright, but all I could see was red. I didn't know what I was going to do. She had caught me completely off guard.

"So, here's how this is going to go down," she began again calmly, "you're going to go to the house, tell my father you're leaving him and pack your raggedy little duffel bag. When you break his heart, I'll be there to comfort him, like the good daughter I am. I'm already back at RDE. Soon, I'll be completely back in his good graces."

"Ashleigh, listen. Okay. I admit that you have me by the balls and there ain't shit I can do about it. Can you just give me a little time? I don't have any money or any place to go."

"Are you kidding me? You've been living with my father all this time and you don't have any money stashed away? That's a damn shame."

"It is a shame, but it is what it is. You wouldn't have me living on the street, would you?"

"With that face and that body of yours, I'm sure you'll land on your feet, or your back. Either way, you'll be fine."

She continued sipping on her Diet Coke as we pulled into the parking lot of the building.

"Please, Ashleigh. Give me a few days. That's all that I'm asking for."

She took another sip and glared at me.

"I'll think about it. I'll let you know when I drop this off inside. Be right back. I know you're upset, but it would be a mistake to leave me."

"I'm not going anywhere."

She opened the car door and practically danced down the sidewalk into the building. Quickly, I reached into my gym bag in

the backseat and shuffled the items around. I had recently pur-
chased a few vials of GHB from my dealer and I had not yet
placed them in the house. I was pretty sure that I had left them
in my gym bag. Frantically, I tore through the items in my bag.

Shoes.

Jock strap.

Deodorant.

Towel.

Condoms.

Lubricant.

Suddenly, I remembered I had placed the vials in a jewelry box
and placed them in my glove compartment. Quickly, I reached
over and shuffled through the stacks of miscellaneous papers and
found the magic I was looking for. I yanked opened the top of
the box and with haste, I opened the tubes and emptied two vials
into her soda can. I closed the box and threw the tubes into my
gym bag and zipped it up just in time. I looked up and saw her
exiting the building, moving at an obnoxiously slow pace to irri-
tate me. The smile on her face was electric.

I took a few deep breaths and tried to calm myself. I hated this
bitch, but more to the point, I hated the fact that she was privy
to my secrets.

She hopped in the car and smiled at me. "I'm back. You miss
me?"

"Just put on your seat belt."

"Awww, I didn't know you cared." She reached over her shoulder
and pulled the strap across her body and locked it in place. As I
pulled off, I saw her pick up her soda and drink.

She sealed her fate.

CHAPTER 13

"Marquis, grab her feet!" I said in a desperate whisper that wafted into the night air as we lifted Ashleigh's limp body out of the backseat of my car.

"Shit, I'm tryin'. This bitch is heavy!" Marquis struggled to lift her dead weight off the ground. I was beginning to panic; it was taking much longer than I expected to remove her body. Even though I didn't worry about anyone in that neighborhood snitching, I had concerns that a patrol car might roll through and see my car parked in the alley that ran perpendicular to the main street.

"I got her," he said as he lifted her feet off the ground. He strained to carry her and I could see veins popping in his neck from the effort of carrying her. She wasn't a large woman, but dead weight is dead weight. When we reached the side of the house, Marquis dropped her feet and I propped her against the wall so that he could open the gate. I held her firmly against the wall so that she wouldn't collapse. The side entrance to the rowhouse was tucked away in a darkened alcove protected by a dilapidated wooden fence that looked like the ragged teeth of some urban monster.

He moved quickly to the gate and reached his hand into a tiny slot. I heard the hook of the flimsy metal lock clink against another piece of metal. I looked around to make sure no one was watching. The clinking sound was low, but in my head, it sounded like the blare of a trumpet.

The darkened alley was illuminated by a single flickering street light about thirty yards in front of me. A bit of light spilled into the alleyway from the main street as car headlights cut the night into pieces. My breathing was rapid and my palms sweaty. At any moment I expected to see a car from the Metropolitan Police department drive by. After all, this was a high-crime area. We'd have a hell of a time trying to explain what we were doing in the alley outside of a crackhouse with an almost comatose woman.

"Hurry up before someone sees us!" I hissed.

"I'm trying. Something is wrong with this fuckin' gate!"

"Shhh. Be quiet," I said. As if my words spoke it into existence, I suddenly heard faint voices that grew in volume with each passing second. My heart raced. I couldn't discern which direction the voices were coming from, but I instinctively looked toward the main street and waited with bated breath for some sign of pedestrian movement. As the group neared, I could clearly distinguish male and female voices engaged in robust conversation and laughter. Their voices swelled in my ears and I prayed that this alley was not their chosen route. For all I knew they could be thieves, drug dealers, or gangbangers. Whoever they were, I certainly wasn't prepared to meet them that night. Their voices got louder and louder as they neared. It sounded like at least five people and I could hear some impassioned and mindless chatter about some rapper they'd never meet and his music video.

Then, they appeared out of the shadows—a group of menacingly-dressed, rambunctious teenagers of varying heights and widths who seemed to care little for the volume of their conversation, which consumed all the noise around them. They spoke all at once in thunderous voices that laid waste to any sound that didn't match their level. They oozed along the sidewalk, almost as one entity, and claimed for themselves whatever lay in their path. Their formation was tight, like a battalion, and it was hard to determine where one person ended and the other began. They acted as urban royalty and the sidewalk and everything in their path belonged to them.

Marquis and I remained deathly silent until the mob passed. When they are out of sight and earshot, I released a heavy sigh. I couldn't remember a time when my heart had beat as fast.

Now, the ragged wooden gate was the only thing that stood between us and the safety of the crackhouse; the irony of that thought wasn't lost on me, but standing outside this house in this neighborhood put us in jeopardy of being discovered and safety, at least from being seen, would be found in the shelter the house provided.

Marquis continued to struggle with the lock on the gate.

"Fuck! I can't get it!"

"I thought you pretty much ran this house?"

He cut his eyes at me. "I do, but somethin' is blockin' the latch."

"Shit, let me try. Here, hold her up." Quickly, we switched positions. The sight of Marquis's little ass trying to hold up Ashleigh against the wall was comical to me, but I held in my laughter; now was not the time for levity. Even though he was a thug, he was still sensitive about his small stature and I could not risk offending him at such a crucial time.

I stuck my hand between the splintered wood and felt for the lock. I tried not to worry that I would mess up my manicure as I fidgeted with the hook, but I had just gotten my nails done yesterday. I continued to feel around, but there was something that was blocking the lock. I pulled my hand out and peered inside the gate. From what I could see, the place was a real dump. Trash—paper, liquor bottles, old food containers—littered the landscape, making it hard to see the ground. Cigarette butts and broken crack vials added to the décor.

Sudden movement in the corner of the fenced yard caused me to jump back.

"Shit. There's someone back there!"

"What you talkin' about? Here, hold her ass up."

Marquis peered through the hole in the fence.

"Sheila! Sheila! Get yo' stupid ass over here and open up this fuckin' gate!" The sternness in his voice was intoxicating, even on a night like this in a situation as crazy as this. "Hurry up!"

She moaned.

"Who the fuck is that?" I asked.

"Just some crackhead."

Seconds later, I heard the woman unlatch the door. Marquis quickly kicked open the door and I heard a commotion on the other side of the gate as the woman fell to the ground. She moaned and huffed, but I heard her scamper to her feet as Marquis quickly moved over to me and helped me move Ashleigh into the yard of the compound.

"Close the fuckin' door, Sheila," he said again, with equal bravado. "I can't stand a fuckin' crackhead." With each one of Ashleigh's arms draped around our necks, we labored to get her inside the house.

"Sheila, open the door. Damn. I gotta tell her er'ry fuckin' thang." The woman scurried by us and raced up the three concrete steps and pushed open the door to the house. As soon as the door opened, the stench of crack and old liquor assaulted me, throwing me off balance for a split second. For some odd reason, I wasn't expecting the stench to be so pronounced.

We entered the darkened house through what I can only assume was the kitchen; however, this kitchen was covered with so much black grime that it was hardly recognizable. The stove, once white, clearly hadn't been used in years and balled pieces of tin foil and crack vials covered the top. Chicken bones and other pieces of decaying food particles decorated the table that sat in the middle of the room. I looked over to my left and saw something scurry in the opposite direction. Something told me that I didn't want to know what it was.

"Let's put her in here," Marquis said. He led the way into a room with a tattered tan couch and we pushed her onto the sofa.

"Damn," he said as his chest heaved up and down. "You owe me big time for this."

I looked around the room and part of me—a very small part—actually felt sorry for her. This place was like a house of horror. I had never seen anyplace so filthy. Garbage lay on top of garbage, as if it had reproduced. There was so much dirt and dust on the floor that it was difficult to ascertain its real color. The house, dank and dark, clearly was a menace to the neighborhood as evidenced by the "do not enter" tape and the "Condemned by Order of the City" sign that someone had removed from the outside of the house and brought inside.

I continued to look around and just ahead of me I saw a shadow move.

"Marquis, there's someone else here," I said calmly.

He chuckled. "Of course there is. This is where they come to smoke. I'm sure there's at least ten people here now." He looked at me. "You sure you wanna do this?"

I looked down at her. In her quiet state, she looked peaceful and innocent. She didn't look like the hellcat who was trying to bring me down. I decided not to kill her because the death of both Robert and his daughter would look too suspicious. Instead of killing her, I opted to return her to her former state. Once she relapsed on crack, she'd be in no position to cause a stir about Robert's estate. No one would doubt why he hadn't left her anything.

"Yeah, I'm sure."

"You know there's no guarantee that she'll smoke anything. She could wake up and leave."

"Nah, I don't believe that. Once a crackhead, always a crackhead. The smell of this place is enough to make her remember what it felt like to be high. She'll be salivating like a dog. You make sure she has some crack nearby when she wakes up. And, I don't want her harmed. Don't let none of these crackheads rape her or anything."

"Bruh, I ain't gon' be here all night, so I can't guarantee nothin'."

I inhaled. "Well, do what you can. I need to get out of here before someone steals my car."

"Blues, I wanna see you tomorrow so we can settle this debt." He licked his lips and eyed me from head to toe.

"Not a problem." I hurriedly moved out the living room and raced through the kitchen. Once I exited, I saw Sheila in the corner getting high. I didn't know her, but wondered what she had looked like in her other life. Right now, she looked like the stereotypical crackhead. She was rail thin, wearing dirty blue jeans and a torn T-shirt that I'm sure was once white. Her hair was knotted and clumped together like clay. She looked up at me.

"What the fuck you lookin' at? You want some of this pussy?" she said as she gyrated her hips in a provocative manner.

I didn't bother to respond to her. Instead, I walked on by.

Soon, that would be Ashleigh in the corner.

I smiled.

CHAPTER 14

When I got into my car and sped off into the night, a hundred thoughts raced through my head. Had I done the right thing? Had I been hasty in dealing with Ashleigh? Would this plan work? How long would it take for her to relapse? What would happen if she didn't get high?

I didn't have answers to any of those questions, but the deed had been done. Now, I had to pray for the best outcome for me.

I bolted down the city street, swerving to avoid cars turning left and parked cars on the right. I needed to put some distance between Ashleigh and me and what I had done, because, in spite of the necessity of my plan, a nagging sense of guilt crept into my spirit. And, I became annoyed at myself for feeling this way. I despised this weakness in me. As ruthless as my actions were in leaving her behind, her actions to destroy my marriage and my life justified it. She would have no sympathy for me, so why should I have any for her? Regardless of how I felt, I wasn't changing my mind, nor was I going back to fetch her from that house. She was there and that's where she would stay.

I pressed my foot on the accelerator, my feelings quickly changing from guilt to anger. I thought about the gleam in her eyes when she threw those photographs in my lap. I remembered the triumph that echoed in her voice as she told me to get out of *my* house and to leave *my* husband. *Fuck her*. The slight guilt I felt moments ago faded underneath my rage. This woman was ready to cast me out into the street with no more than a "raggedy" duffel bag. She didn't care that I had no money and nowhere to go. She didn't give a fuck what happened to me, and I wouldn't care what happened to her.

This wasn't exactly how I had planned to deal with her. Ashleigh had tied my hands today with her bombshell and forced me into acting affirmatively in my defense. Through her hateful actions, she had thrown me off kilter and forced me into acting desperately; I did not like acting desperately. Desperation led to mistakes. I was more of a planner. After I killed Jabari, I learned how to not react out of emotion. I had learned that a carefully laid, methodical plan was always best, but today I wasn't afforded that luxury.

It was either her or me.

Whatever wretched fate happened to her in that crack den was her fault and she had only herself to blame. Before today, I knew I had to get rid of her. I just wasn't sure how, but I wanted to do it on my own terms. Before today, I was still devising my plan, but the more I thought about dropping her off in a drug house, the more I realized that things might work out after all.

Anger now colored everything I saw. I viewed the city through a hazy shade of red. She needed to suffer. I didn't want her to die like Robert. I wanted a very different fate for the woman who planned my demise. I wanted her to die a little bit every day. Wandering the street as a strung-out crackhead, eating out of garbage cans, and selling her body for drugs—if it was necessary— was what she deserved. No one fucked with me and got away with it. Not back then with Jabari. Not now with Ashleigh.

When I faced a red light on Alabama Avenue, I took the opportunity to take a few deep breaths to assuage my frayed nerves. I looked around at the decaying buildings, carryout restaurants and liquor stores that lined the street. I was so far removed from hard living that it was difficult to imagine that people still lived like this; yet, I remembered that once upon a time, I, too, had lived this way. I could never forget that. *Never*. Each day I carried a heavy fear in my heart of returning to poverty and being forced to live in a rundown tenement; that fear was my motivation for every major decision I had made recently; that fear forced me to dump Ashleigh in a dangerous crackhouse. No one would return me to the streets. Not Ashleigh. Not Robert. No one.

As I looked around, I felt the familiarity of it. This area was an urban replica of the decaying Brooklyn neighborhood I lived in when I first landed in New York. I remembered how scared I'd sometimes be just walking down the street. Vulgar graffiti, aggressive prostitutes, deranged drug addicts, and shell-shocked homeless people were commonplace. Thugs, thug-wannabes, bad-ass children and welfare mamas screamed at the top of their lungs at all hours of the day and night. Rarely was there a quiet moment in the entire neighborhood. Half of the houses in the neighborhood had been condemned years ago, like the houses and buildings I now saw.

That was then. This is now. My mansion on the other side of town was a world away from that kind of life and I intended to keep it that way.

When the light turned green, I felt my anger and anxiety lift. Still, I prayed that my rushed plan would work. It couldn't be that hard to induce a relapse in a known crackhead; I don't care who it was. When she awakened, everything about that place should remind of her what it felt like to be high. I imagined her palms sweating and her body twitching as the familiar scent tickled her nostrils and her taste buds. If I knew the girls she used to get high with when she rebelled against Robert as a teenager and young adult, I would have found them and made sure they were around her when she woke up. I was certain they were still getting high; after all, they were from this part of town and they grew up, from what I'm told, in abject poverty.

By the time I made it home, the house was empty. Robert had not yet made it home from another one of his late-night meetings. I had time to search Ashleigh's room and claim the spoils of war. I found her digital camera that had the photographs of me and Nigel sexing. She hadn't had a chance to put it in a safe place. I only hoped that she hadn't made dozens of copies. From the hasty way in which she'd dropped her bombshell on me, something told me that she hadn't yet taken the necessary precautions, which is why the camera was sitting in plain sight on top of her chest of drawers. This was exactly why I hated to act without thinking—it led to mistakes. She had, like I had so long ago, let anger dictate her actions. Acting out of anger will always keep you off-balance.

To seal the deal, I placed a few empty crack vials in one of her drawers. I figured that if she relapsed and was gone for days, Robert would probably have the maid search her room and when the vials were found, Robert would know that his sweet daughter had once again fallen. It would break his heart. If I was lucky, it might even cause a heart attack.

By ten o'clock, I was lounging at the pool on my second Jack and Coke; the cool breeze tickled my skin and helped to relax me, but my thoughts and feelings vacillated between nervousness and a sense of triumph. Had she awakened? Had she started smoking? Had I won my battle with her? If she didn't relapse, I was doomed. I reached over to the table and sent Marquis a quick text message, checking on her. I placed the phone back on the table and before I could pick up my drink, my phone vibrated. I looked at the text from Marquis that read, "HIGH AS A KITE."

I smiled and deleted the message. A quick victory.

I lay across the chair on the patio, trying to enjoy the picturesque view when I suddenly felt as if my breath had been stolen. I inhaled deeply, trying to force myself to relax, but some force gripped me and held me tightly. I had had sudden panic attacks before, especially after Jabari's death, but I hadn't felt a sense of panic like this in years. As I lay there, held in place by some nefarious force, I tried to calm myself, to no avail.

Then, I saw a shadowy figure emerge from the house and come slowly into view. I squinted my eyes, hoping to get a better look before this stranger was upon me. He looked familiar, even from his distance. I could tell from the great stride of his gait that it wasn't Robert; there was too much youth in his step.

Then, he came fully into view.

I watched, in horror, as Jabari sauntered over toward me wearing blue swimming shorts, his beach towel casually thrown across his shoulder. He looked as if he had a planned swim date with me. His face looked the same as the last time I had seen it. His face did not reveal his emotions or hint at his intentions, but nonetheless, I was terrified.

I watched him closely as he moved closer to me.

Was this some cruel trick? Did my eyes deceive me? My breathing, labored and thick, dug deeply into my chest. I wanted to flee, but I couldn't move. I was simply powerless.

And terrified.

When he reached me, he leaned over and slowly kissed me in a way that was so familiar. He did not hesitate or waver with his display of affection. The softness of his puffy lips did little to ease my fright. His lips, although soft, were cold as ice and I could see his breath in the air, even though it was a warm summer night.

Was this apparition here to do harm? Was it my time to pay for my sins? After killing Jabari, condemning Ashleigh to addiction and plotting to kill Robert, had my day of reckoning finally come?

He pulled away and stared down at me. He seemed to be examining my face, every line and contour, and his eyes, those beautiful eyes, showed no malice or ill will. A fondness in his eyes eased my fear and my panic began to melt. He was a beautiful man, even more beautiful than I had remembered. I wanted to reach out and touch him to see if he was real. I longed to feel the touch of his flesh; after all these years, he remained my one and only true love. I remembered how he used to touch me and make me feel complete. His gentleness always set my soul at-ease.

Did I still look the same to him? Had time been kind to me? Did he see the fresh-faced boy he once loved or did he see the hideous creature, full of venom and vice, that I had become?

As he continued to examine me, my guilt swelled. I stared into the face of my long-lost love and was overwhelmed by thoughts of what I did to him. In a fit of rage, I had killed the man I loved and had never found a moment's peace, in spite of my efforts to forget and to pretend that everything was alright. That night—his death—would forever haunt me. Some things can never be forgotten.

I could still see the look in his eyes as he fell over.

In my ears, his anguished screams echoed like they did that night. Sometimes, I heard those screams in the still of the night.

Crack.

Crack.

Crack. Crack.

The sound of his body crashing to the jagged earth below stayed with me.

Yet, I never really grieved for him.

I never grieved for myself, either.

I often wondered what his last thoughts were. Did he realize what happened, what I had done to him?

I had carried the weight of my crime in my spirit for so long that his death became a part of me. His death polluted my soul.

I stole from this world its most precious gift and would one day be held accountable for that. I accepted that fact long ago.

Maybe that day was today.

Whatever I had done to him, I also had done to myself. I died that day, too, and was reborn a tortured soul.

Jabari set his towel down on the chair next to me, without so much as a word. His silence was heavy; it occupied so much space that it started to suffocate me. I waited for him to point the accusatory finger at me and scream bloody murder. I waited for him to recognize in my face a reflection of the shame I carried. In part, I wanted that condemnation; it might free me, but he didn't give me what I needed.

Jabari dove into the pool and the splash of cool water leapt high into the air; the droplets hung in the air for a few seconds, suspended in time. When they finally fell, a few drops landed on my feet and they burned with hellfire. I tried to scream, but could not. The pain I felt was only a sample of what was to come—I was sure of that.

I wanted to move, to run, and to hide while he was submerged, but I could not command my own limbs to respond. It was only a matter of time before he exacted vengeance. I was forced to endure this tortured moment of watching him circle endlessly in a pool of blue. His presence had rendered me utterly motionless, except for the tears that ran down my face.

Moments later, he leapt from the shallow end of the pool with sudden fury. He jetted from the pool as if he had been expelled. He, like the water moments ago, hung in the air, hovering above the pool for a few seconds before falling back into the water. He rose from the shallow end of pool and stepped onto the concrete, dripping wet. His face, now twisted and terrible, told me my time had come. A cool breeze blew across us as his body became wrapped in flames—he brought the hellfire with him to claim my soul.

I tried to close my eyes, but I couldn't. I was forced to watch him move toward me, step by step. Each step he took left a smoldering footprint on the concrete. I took a deep breath and with all the force I could command, I screamed. My scream must have startled him because he stopped, for a second.

Then, I realized I could move.

I jumped up and ran in the opposite direction around the pool. When I got to the other side, somehow he was already there, blocking my path. In spite of the fire around him, I could clearly see his face, which had once again transformed back into his usual face. I looked into his eyes and saw me pushing him off the building. I saw me driving away into the night as I left Ashleigh to rot. I realized what I had done; I didn't need a reminder. I wanted to get away from him.

I moved to the right.

He moved to the right.

I moved to the left.

He moved to the left.

I took a step backward.

He took a step forward.

He moved with perfect agility.

Then, he let something escape from his mouth that I could only describe as a yell. It was a sound like no other and carried force. I actually stumbled back, as if I had been struck by a mighty fist. Anger twisted Jabari's face into a contorted ball of fury; his eyes became tight, like thin, sharp splinters and his lips were drawn tightly together. He was about to strike.

Out of sheer defense, I threw myself into his body but he did not move; not even an inch. I was no match for him. I stumbled back hard, as if I had run full speed into a brick wall. I completely lost my balance and hit my head on the side of the pool, before falling in. Immediately, blood gushed from my wound and colored the pool water. I was fading away, losing myself to utter darkness.

❂ ❂ ❂

"Blues, Blues, wake up." The sound of Robert's voice brought me out of my nightmare. When he touched me, my body jolted and I screamed. "Are you okay? You must've had a bad dream." Slowly, I opened my eyes. He stood over me, shaking me gently, with a concerned look on his face. "Come on into the house."

Even though I was awake, I was still shaken by my nightmare, which was the most vivid one I had had about Jabari in years; maybe God was trying to tell me something. If He was, I wasn't ready to listen. Robert was still going to die.

I shook off my dream and let Robert lead me into the house. His arm was wrapped around my waist in a supportive way.

"What were you dreaming about?"

"I...I don't remember."

"I'm getting concerned about your dreams. I think you need to see someone."

"I'm fine. Really." He looked at me incredulously and I changed the subject. "How was your day?"

He took a deep breath. "It was a long one. I fired Charles."

"Really? Why?"

"He is grossly incompetent. I need someone on my team who can get the job done. That was not Charles." His voice sounded agitated and since I had enough going on, I didn't press it. "Where is Ashleigh?"

"I don't know. She's not in her room?"

"No, the house is empty."

"She wanted to do some shopping so after we took care of your errand, I dropped her off at the mall. I thought for sure she'd be back by now."

"No worries. My daughter was always a super shopper. I'm sure she'll be home soon. Come on. Let's go inside."

Nothing had changed in my mind. Robert would still need to die. I was not about to change my plans because of some random images about a dead lover. Soon, I'd have another dead lover and, as far as I was concerned, the two of them could sit around in the afterlife and lament over their loss of life at my hands.

CHAPTER 15

The next few days leading up to The Purple Party were filled with a mixture of anxiety, excitement, and apprehension. Robert's moods shifted with the wind and his attitude became more and more obnoxious as the days passed by. The disappearance of his dearly beloved daughter weighed heavily on him and I encouraged him to call the police, but he balked at the suggestion. He wanted to spare himself the public embarrassment and he said he wasn't worried because this was how she operated. She'd come home after a long absence—clean and sober—and then relapse into another drug binge. Robert, with tears in his eyes, told me this was the last time. He had completely given up on her. I wanted to ease his pain by telling him that he needn't worry too much about her because his time on this earth was winding down, but I refrained. Instead, it was inside that I smiled.

I gave Marquis the go-ahead to kill Robert. It would happen on the Monday morning following The Purple Party. On workdays, Robert left the house often before sunrise. He prided himself on being the first in the office in the morning and the last to leave at night. That, he articulated on many occasions, was the key to success. Since I knew Robert's routine like the back of my hand, I gave Marquis exquisite details on Robert's route to work and his usual stops. Robert's downfall—excluding marrying me— would be his almost fanatically regimented morning routine. He'd get up in the morning at the same time, eat at the same exact time, be out of the house at the exact same time, and take the same exact route to work. His whole morning was a choreographed effort that he rarely, if ever, deviated from. And, because his routine was so precise, I could tell Marquis exactly where Robert would be and at what time.

On an ordinary Monday morning, a simple bullet to the head would put that dog down. I salivated at the thought. Marquis would kill him and then rob him, to make it look like a mugging.

Robert met with Kevin and Daryl a few more times, late into the evenings, to make sure that everything was going well for the party. I couldn't remember a time when I'd seen Robert so wrapped up with a charity. I don't know if it was the mission of Keevan's Room or if he had an attraction to Kevin or Daryl, or them both, or if he needed a distraction from Ashleigh's disappearance. Either way suited me fine. As long as he remained busy, he could avoid thinking about changing his will, which was my main focus. He had to die before any significant change could be made.

I was beginning to pull Nigel into my plot without his knowledge. The last time we met in the hotel and sexed, I lied about how Robert appeared feeble and asked Nigel had he noticed any changes at work. After thinking for a few moments, he told me that Robert didn't seem as "on it" as he usually was and how he had forgotten a couple of meetings in the last few days. I told Nigel that I was trying to get Robert to a doctor, but he refused to go. Then, I told Nigel that if something were to happen to Robert that I'd be at a loss as to what to do with RDE. I told him that if I was left RDE, I'd probably sell it because I had no interest in the business. Once I mentioned selling RDE, I saw the light flicker in his eyes. Ambition was Nigel's greatest weakness and I had just made him the offer of a lifetime. If Robert died—and he could put together the financing—I would sell him the business. Nigel had hopes and dreams of being the main act, instead of being the sidekick. My hope was that Nigel would slow the process of changing his will as long as he could. Maybe he'd even try to talk Robert into not changing the will.

The Saturday morning of The Purple Party started off with gray skies and rain clouds. I stood out on the balcony of our bedroom and surveyed the landscape as the rain came down hard. I had not seen this kind of rain in months, but I appreciated it. It would wipe clean the sins of a lost city, giving us another opportunity to sin again. I spent several minutes watching individual raindrops as they fell to the ground and became a part of something larger. I was fascinated by the rain's ability to be absorbed by the earth and how it was the key to life. While the rain fell and made life possible, I plotted to take away life.

Soon, very soon, I'd be free.

Now, I did have my plan B. I didn't have very much money, but I was able to sell some jewelry and stash a few thousand dollars over the last few weeks that I would use as my getaway money. If shit hit the fan and things didn't go as well as I had hoped, I'd make my way to Mexico, preferably Puerto Vallarta. There I planned to land on a rich man and start over; maybe, I'd find some rich European who would whisk me away to some fabulous French estate or to Monte Carlo.

I stepped inside from the balcony and heard a hacking sound coming from the bathroom. As I entered the bathroom, I saw Robert sitting on the closed toilet seat, gazing down at the floor. When he heard me enter, he looked up at me. His eyes looked cloudy and his skin pale—well, paler than usual.

"Robert, are you okay?" I asked with fake concern as I rushed to his side.

"I'm fine. Just help me to the bed." He clutched his hand to his chest and took shallow breaths. "Get one of my pills for me."

He reached his hand out to me and I helped lift him from where he sat. Slowly he stood up on wobbly legs and made his way to the bed with my assistance.

"I'm going to call Dr. Glenn," I said, knowing full well that he would protest and forbid me.

"No, don't do that. I'll be fine. I need one of my pills and to rest for a minute."

"Are you sure? You don't look well."

"I'm fine. Just a little tired. Get me my pills, will you?"

I rushed into the bathroom, opened the medicine cabinet, and grabbed the bottle of medicine for his heart. For a fleeting second, I thought about not bringing him the pills, but realized that was too risky of a strategy. What if he wasn't having a heart attack? What if it was just gas and he recovered quickly? Then, I'd be fucked.

I poured two pills into my hand and grabbed the glass of whiskey he had left on sink. I poured the whiskey down the sink, rinsed the glass out, ran some cool water into it, and raced back into the room as if I was really concerned.

"Here, baby."

He popped the pills into his mouth and downed the water. "I'm just going to rest a bit."

"You sure you don't want me to call the doctor?"

"I'm sure."

"Well, I'm not at all sure about you going to this party tonight." Again, I knew he'd protest, but it just felt like the right thing to say.

"The only way I won't go is if I'm dead. I just need to rest. I'll be fine."

I paused for dramatic effect.

Death is closer than you think, old man.

"Okay," I said slowly, "but, I'm going to check on you in a bit. Get some rest." I leaned over and kissed his clammy forehead. If I were lucky, maybe he'd die in his sleep and save us all the trouble.

As I made my way out of the room, I turned to look at my husband. As he crawled into the bed, he seemed smaller than the larger-than-life persona he projected. His Herculean image, based on bravado and confidence, was much bigger than the actual man. In his weakened state, he seemed almost... human. Gone was the puffed-out chest and the machismo; illness had laid low the arrogance and the hubris he wielded like a weapon. In his weakened state, he was mere mortal, of flesh and blood. He wasn't the giant that produced awe and fear from those around him. He was simply a man. A mortal man.

I exited the room and quickly focused my attention to the big party. I was so excited and my ensemble was stunning: a pair of form-fitting purple pants with a white silk shirt, with a patch cut out across my chest to reveal my nipples. I'd top it off with a purple hat, cocked to the side. I looked like an old school pimp from a Foxy Brown movie. And, I had a purple umbrella that I'd lucked upon in a vintage store in Eastern Market. Even if Robert died in his sleep, I was still going to the party.

I couldn't wait for this party. When I walked into the room, all eyes would be on me. Where else would they be?

A few hours passed and I realized that I had forgotten to check in on Robert. *Maybe he had died gently in his sleep.* I walked up the staircase and was startled to see Robert moving in my direction, with a bounce in his step. He looked vigorous, lively—alive—much to my dismay. This man had had more heart attacks than Dick Cheney, and was *still* standing. It's true: evil never dies. Now, he was coming toward me with much more speed than a man at his advanced age and weakened state should have. Before I realized it, he was upon me. Before I could stop him, he grabbed me by the waist and planted a wet, sloppy kiss on me. I pushed him away.

"Robert, what are you doing? You should be in bed."

"Baby, I feel fine; almost like a new man," he said as he thumped his chest.

What the fuck?

There had to be some secret chamber hidden behind a wall in our bedroom where he held kidnapped children and stole their life force—that was the only way he could have recovered so swiftly.

"You look...good," I said with confusion.

"I feel even better. I told you that I just needed to rest a bit. Make me a drink, will you?" He patted me on my ass and proceeded to move downstairs, leaving me standing on the landing dazed and confused. I turned my head and watched him take the stairs two at a time! Whatever he was on, I needed to be on as well.

This man simply refused to die.

CHAPTER 16

The moment finally arrived and excitement could be felt in the air. Luckily, the rain had stopped mid-morning and the sun came out. Everything was electric and intoxicating. The fanfare, pomp and circumstance made the night seem almost enchanted. I was so excited, I could barely contain myself. My excitement alone charged the air. My smile was wide and complete, as if no trouble would ever come to me.

Tonight, while all the guests danced and partied, I'd celebrate Robert's death.

We pulled slowly up to the curb at the Palladium in Robert's navy blue convertible Bentley, taking time to make sure that the crowd envied our splendor. I wanted to take the limo, but Robert insisted on driving. He smiled as if he was king of the hill and I was his willing concubine, but when people looked at us, they were really looking at me. Robert was dressed in a simple purple suit, but he did look dapper, like a pimped-out elder statesman.

The valet attendants immediately rushed the car and opened the doors for us both. I watched Robert slither out from behind the steering wheel and hand them the valet key and some money that he stuffed into their hands, but I couldn't tell exactly how much. His old ass probably gave them each $100 to park the car. Usually, I cringed at the thought of him spending my money, but since his hours on earth were winding down, I didn't care if he splurged one last time.

As we stepped forward, I took a moment to really take in the

over-the-top decorations. The sidewalk leading up to the building was covered with bright purple carpet that looked soft like
cotton candy. The outside of the building had streams of purple
cloth blowing in the wind like streamers. Robert locked arms
with me and we walked the carpet like kings at a ball. Purple rope
separated us from the mass of photographers who had gathered
to snap pictures of the guests as they arrived. Even though we
weren't famous, we stopped and posed like the happy couple. *If
only they knew these would be some of Robert's last photos.*

As cameras flashed, we continued our journey into the building
and stepped into the grand foyer. People had gathered in the
area, drinks in hand, smiles plastered across their faces, all wearing various hues of purple. By the skimpy outfits people had on,
the motif of the party was *provocative purple*. I thought my shirt
was edgy, but it paled in comparison to what I saw. I watched a
huge, tanned muscle boy move through the crowd wearing a
purple sarong and a purple bowtie—nothing else. He looked like
a big purple Hercules, but I didn't mind the view.

We moved toward the entrance of the Grand Hall and the
room was packed to the nines. Around the perimeter of the room
were huge floor-to-ceiling, Roman-like columns that gave the
room a regal appearance. Centered in the back of the room was
a huge staircase that must have been ten feet wide that connected
with smaller staircases that protruded off to both the left and right.

Thumping sounds from the speakers pumped power into the
enthusiastic crowd. An almost tangible kinetic energy permeated
the air and ignited the entire area with a feeling of freedom.
Subtle purple lighting accentuated the enormous space, coating
the already electrified atmosphere in a psychedelic haze. A huge
picture of Danea Charles, in a purple frame—of course—hung
above the staircase. The whole scene was a bedazzled spectacle,
but I loved it!

We continued walking through the room, passing out winks, nods and smiles. Robert stopped a few times, shaking hands and making small talk with a group of small men who looked even older than him, if that was possible. I surveyed the room and flowers of every kind—including roses—seemed to be growing from the building itself, all purple, of course. It was a spectacular effect and I made a mental note to figure out how they accomplished that. *Maybe I could use the same effect at Robert's funeral.*

I continued to be mesmerized by the crowd. Flesh spilled over thin purple straps and from tiny shirts and skirts. Glitter and sparkles reflected light off bulging biceps and thick chests. The crowd was in a trance, intoxicated by the freedom of the spellbinding music and I was titillated by sight and sound. Acrobats in tight, purple leotards twirled and twisted from the high ceiling, à la Cirque de Soleil. I was amazed at the sight of dancers hanging from the ceiling while performing majestic feats of wonder that defied gravity.

Interspersed throughout the magnificent crowd were a few familiar faces. Kevin had told Robert that Danea had worked hard to get some of her celebrity friends to attend the event. I saw Janet move by with an entourage in the back. To my left were a couple of cast members from *Will & Grace* and *Queer as Folk*—I was impressed. I think that I saw a member of Destiny's Child in the corner, but she disappeared into the crowd. Rumor had it that Madonna might make one of her *unannounced* appearances. If that happened, the crowd would probably explode!

As I stood there surveying the crowd, I hadn't noticed Nigel approaching us from behind until I heard his deep voice greeting Robert. I felt his bravado in the small of my back and I took a deep breath, slowly turning around, trying to keep my composure. I smiled. He smiled, subtly. Robert put his arm around my waist. Did Robert sense my attraction to Nigel? Before long, it wouldn't matter anyway. Nigel and I would vacation in some fabulous place, all on Robert's dime.

"This whole place is…amazing," Nigel said, trying to mask his excitement at seeing me.

"Of course it is. Did you expect anything less?" Robert said, beaming with pride. "Everything came together magically."

"Hello, Blues," Nigel said as he turned his attention to me. "Are you having a good time?" He reached his hand out to me for a shake. When I grabbed it, I'm sure everything I felt for him flashed across my face. The warmth of his hand and his strong grip made my dick twitch. I had to get away from him before our secrets were put on display.

"Mr. Wright, good to see you again." I *loved* calling him by his last name. It just felt…right.

"Yes, I'm having a good time. Look around this room; it's hard not to. They did an excellent job with the decorations."

"This is fabulous. I knew Kevin would pull it off," Robert chimed.

"I need a drink." The sound of Kevin's name grated on my nerves like you wouldn't believe. It was his event, but I had no intention of sitting around all night listening to people praise his pompous ass.

"Blues didn't think I was going to make it," Robert continued, "but I told him that 'nothing but death could keep me from here.'" Robert laughed, thinking he was being funny by referencing that played-out movie line; he ended up laughing himself into another one of his hacking coughs.

Ugh, just die, will ya?

"Are you okay, Robert?" Nigel asked. He grabbed Robert's arm and helped steady him. "Why don't we go to the VIP room and sit down for a minute? Kevin is probably up there. He was looking for you a minute ago."

"Yeah, let's go up there."

"I'll meet you up there. I'm going to grab a drink," I said as I looked for the bar.

"We have plenty of drinks in VIP," Robert stated. "Come on."

I forced a smile. Robert adjusted his jacket and stood erect, trying to puff out his miniature chest. He took a deep breath before proceeding.

"Let's go." His tone carried the cadence of a general giving his troops marching orders and since he was the man with the money, both Nigel and I marched behind to Robert's tempo while trying not to eye each other. I was going to fuck Nigel before the night was through. I didn't know how it would happen or when, but I was determined to find a nice, quiet spot somewhere so that we could do what came naturally to us. And, by the expression on his face when he looked at me, I'm sure he was thinking the same thing.

As we made our way through the dense crowd, I lingered a few steps behind since I was still in awe of the sights. I took notice of the men, the music, the flashing purple lights, the colors, the costumes, the purple drinks, the glitter, the glam, and the gorgeous gals. It was a sight to behold. To my left, several feet away, I saw the most beautiful waiter carrying a tray of purple champagne. If he wasn't the hired help, I'd fuck him, too. I turned my head to the side and pretended not to see him seeing me. I turned my nose up at him and bobbed my head back and forth as if caught up in the rhythm of the music and moved closer to Robert.

At the top of the stairs to our left, I saw a glass room covered with purple silk curtains—the VIP. Robert nodded at the huge doorman who flung open the door to let us in and we stepped inside as if he owned the joint. The room was a big purple exhibition: purple velvet couches and chairs, purple lighting—hell, even the waiters looked purple. At this time, there were only a few people inside, Kevin being among them, along with a small group sitting in the back corner of the room.

Pictures of Danea were plastered across the VIP room as one of her songs played in the background. I appreciated that Danea sang about real-life shit, like love, pain, and relationships; she told stories in her songs, unlike most of the ignorant shit they played on the radio these days about big booty hoes swinging from a pole, barked out by illiterate rappers with gold teeth who grinned like jigaboos. Danea kept it real. Maybe I could commission her to sing a song about a murdered husband.

When Kevin saw us, he smiled. He was dressed in black pants with a purple, fitted shirt. I was right about his body; he did work out. His arms were well-defined, but not overly muscular. I had to admit that he looked good, but I still didn't want to be in his presence, so I lingered in the background, not wanting to be a part of the obligatory and mindless exchange of pleasantries. I could hear them—Kevin, Nigel, and Robert—doing exactly that.

Gimme a break.

"Blues, come here." Robert motioned for me and he pulled me into him, placing his hand around my waist when I was near enough. "Please tell Kevin to stop worrying because he's done a terrific job. Kevin, you should have seen Blues's face downstairs—he was mesmerized. Go ahead, tell him, Blues."

"You've done an excellent job. The crowd is on fire." As much as I disliked Kevin, I had to give credit where credit was due. The party was hot.

"I can't take full credit. Daryl was a huge part of organizing this and bringing it all together."

"Speaking of Daryl, where is he?" Robert asked as he looked around the room.

"He went downstairs to check on something. He'll be back shortly."

"Kevin, will I get to meet Danea?" I asked enthusiastically.

"Hmmm, I'll see what I can do," he said quickly and turned his attention back to Robert. He totally dismissed me like I was some common guest. I looked over at Nigel, who could tell that I was bothered by Kevin's remarks. He shrugged his shoulders awkwardly while Robert's attention was on Kevin. Robert would be dead soon and I'd cancel any check he had given Kevin that hadn't cleared the bank.

I moved over to the bar to get some champagne.

"Are you having a good time?" Nigel asked when he joined me.

I nodded my head in the affirmative, but he really wasn't asking how I was. He was really asking, *Can I fuck you tonight?* I'm glad we shared the same thought. We had developed our language and code so that we could avoid detection.

"Are you?"

"Most definitely. The party has just begun," he said with a wink. "I'm sure it'll heat up later, if you know what I mean." I followed behind him and pulled up right next to Robert, grabbing his cold hand in the process. Even in the middle of hot-ass D.C. in the middle of summer his body remained perpetually cold; it was baffling. He *was* old, but not dead—yet.

"Baby," I whispered in his ear. "I'm going to check things out downstairs while you all talk. Is that okay?"

"That's fine. I'll find you in a bit," Robert replied and turned back to his conversation without missing a beat.

I made my exit out of the room, anxious to get away from Kevin and excited to see what was going on downstairs. I couldn't wait to see who had made it to the party. I moved through the crowd and made my way to the bar in the back so I could have a clear view of the entire room. There were quite a few celebrities in attendance, a few A-listers and several D-listers. I'm sure most of them didn't give a rat's ass about the purpose of the party; they wanted their red carpet moment—in this case, their purple carpet moment. Even still, the excitement of the room was palpable and everyone appeared to be having a great time.

After about half an hour of people watching, I made a pit stop into the restroom. As soon as the door closed, I felt someone grab me from behind and push me into the wall, face first. Before I could properly respond, I felt his lips on the back of my neck.

"Don't move!" he demanded. Damn. My dick stiffened against the wall as Nigel continued to assault me. I felt the heat from his breath on the back of my neck. I looked him up and down and licked my lips. He licked his. He looked ravenous and I was ready to be his meal. I wanted to take him into a stall and fuck the shit out of him.

"Where's Robert?"

"He's still upstairs with Kevin. I had to sneak away so that I could get a few minutes alone with you. I miss you."

"You like living dangerously, don't you? What if Robert walks in?"

"Unlike most people, I'm not afraid of Robert. And, I'm willing to take a chance for a kiss from you." Nigel always knew what to say to turn me on. I loved that fearless quality in him and he realized it. I was playing with fire by continuing to deal with him. If I wasn't careful, I'd fall in love with him, if I was capable of it. As he pressed me against the wall, I longed for the soft touch of his lips upon mine. Just as I moved within inches of his face, we heard voices on the other side of the door. Someone was about to enter the room, but they were finishing a conversation in the doorway. Whew. Luckily, it gave Nigel enough time to move into a stall and remain out of sight.

Then, Kevin burst into the bathroom like a fucking hurricane. *I should call that bitch Katrina 'cause he just royally fucked up my shit.* I moved over to the sink as if I was washing my hands.

"Blues," Kevin said as he eyed me slowly. "Robert was just looking for you."

"Really? What did he want?"

"I didn't ask."

"Thanks for relaying the message." I moved away from the mirror and toward the door. I didn't like the look on his face or the tone in his voice. I stopped before I exited and turned to face him.

"You don't like me, do you?" My bluntness took him by surprise.

"Excuse me?" Clearly, I had caught him off-guard.

"You heard what I said." I stepped closer to him. "I'm not sure what I've done to you, but every time I come around, you seem to get an attitude. Have I done something to offend you?"

Kevin turned to face me. "Blues, I don't even think about you. I'm sure that's all in your head, little boy."

"Little boy? I got your little boy." I stepped even closer.

Kevin looked at me like I didn't even register with him. "What is this you're doing? Why are we even talking?"

"I'm sick and tired of you turning your nose up at me. Remember, you're coming to my husband to pull off this little party of yours."

"You're right. I went to your husband; not you. You and I don't have to have a conversation about anything, so why don't you go out there and do what you do best; stand by Robert and be pretty."

"See, I knew it. You're jealous of me."

He looked at me and burst into an annoying laugh that angered me so much I wanted to punch him in his smug face. I didn't know how to respond, but I could feel my chest getting tight and my temperature rising.

"Are you serious? What do you have that I could possibly be jealous of?"

"For one, I'm a lot younger than you are. Your gray is showing, old man. Secondly, you couldn't get a man as fine as me if you paid him."

"Wow, you really put me in my place." His sarcasm-drenched words only fueled my anger toward him. He wasn't taking me seriously and that pissed me off. "Blues, I could throw a rock out of a window in any direction and hit a man a lot finer than you. If your looks are all that you have to offer, then clearly, you don't have much. When I look for a man, I look for a man who can handle his business and not some little boy waiting for someone to take care of him. If you think I'm jealous of you, then you're more delusional than I thought. Delusional; that's a big word. If you don't know what it means, look it up. Now, if you'll excuse me, I have to get back to the party."

Kevin eyed me up and down and then flitted by me and right out the door. I didn't know what to say, but I wanted to beat the holy shit out of him. After Robert, he might be the next one to die.

When the coast was clear, Nigel emerged from the stall. I was fuming.

"Did you hear the way that bitch was talking to me? I ought to go out there and kick his ass!"

"Don't worry about him. He's nothing to us. Now, back to where we were." Nigel kissed me suddenly and pulled me into the stall, slamming the door behind him.

CHAPTER 17

When Nigel and I finished our dalliance, I went back into the party and decided to return to the VIP room to find Robert before he sent his henchmen to track me down and drag me kicking and screaming back into the room. His patience was often short.

When I reached the top of the stairs near the VIP, I looked down to take in a full view of the crowd. The crowd bristled with energy and swayed with the beat of the music. It actually made me smile to see people having a good time and forgetting about the troubles of the world, if only for one moment.

As a gazed into the crowd, I noticed an odd figure moving through the crowd. The figure's face was hidden from my view by a purple hood, but he moved with ease and grace through the mass of people. Inexplicably, my eyes were fixated on his movements. He wasn't dancing or attempting to get into a groove; he moved with what seemed to be a singular purpose: to get through the crowd to the staircase that led to the balcony where I stood. I noticed something odd about the figure. Something about the way he walked—no, glided—through the room filled my heart with dread. As crowded as the room was, he moved in an uninterrupted straight line and no one seemed to notice his presence.

No one, except me.

My eyes remained transfixed on the figure. He moved in a beeline toward the staircase. When I realized he was indeed moving in my direction, I gasped. Just below the balcony where I stood, he stopped. Slowly, he removed his hood. I still couldn't see his face because he was almost directly below me.

When he looked up at me, I was staring into the face of Jabari.

I gasped out loud and quickly shook my head. How was this possible? Had someone slipped a hallucinogen into my drink? A horrific feeling seized me and I felt myself getting lightheaded. I grabbed the railing of the balcony to steady myself.

The glare of Jabari's eyes pierced my lungs. I couldn't breathe and my skin felt hot. Surely, my eyes deceived me. Jabari was long dead, yet he stood below me, eyeing me with contempt. Had he really died? Had I really thrown him off the building?

I looked around at the few people near me and they didn't seem to notice anything odd. I closed my eyes and prayed that he'd be gone once I opened them, but I wasn't that lucky.

When I opened my eyes, he was standing on the staircase, as if he had been teleported from the spot below me to where he now stood. He was coming closer to me and I was sure he wasn't coming to release me from my sins; in fact, I was certain that he demanded retribution. Quickly, I gathered myself and raced toward the VIP room. If I could make it there before he did, maybe I could save myself. I pushed and shoved my way past the few people, snatched open the door, and ran directly into Daryl's chest.

"Blues, are you okay?" he asked.

"Huh?"

"Are you okay?"

I took a moment to collect my thoughts. I looked at him and suddenly felt very stupid. Here I was cowering from shadows like a frightened child when I should have been standing tall like a gladiator. This nagging guilt was getting on my nerves. Now, I was seeing things when I was awake. Maybe it was all the alcohol I had consumed. I needed to pull it together.

"Uh, yeah. I'm okay. Just felt lightheaded."

His eyes remained curiously fixated on me. "Maybe you should take a moment and go and sit in VIP. Robert is in there. He was asking for you a minute ago."

"Uh, okay," I said.

"Tell Kevin to meet me out front. I'm getting the car from the valet. We're already running late."

"Uh, sure."

I walked into the room and moved slowly to the back where Kevin and Robert were sitting. I turned around a couple of times to make sure I wasn't being followed my some ghost.

When they saw me coming, there was a noticeable shift in their mood and conversation. Kevin leaned over and whispered something to Robert and stood up.

"Daryl and I have to pick up Danea from her hotel," Kevin announced to Robert so that I could hear. "We'll be back in about half an hour. If you need me, call me." Kevin's tone carried a bit of solace, as if he was trying to comfort Robert. He walked past me, shooting me a curt look and a sarcastic smile while shaking his rather large head.

I stepped closer to Robert, who stood up, his face twisted as I moved in closer.

"Where have you been?" he hissed.

I felt really uncomfortable.

"I was downstairs. At the party. Why?"

"Where's Nigel?"

I swallowed hard. "I guess he's downstairs somewhere. How would I know?"

Robert's eyes tightened. I could see the tension in his face by the protruding vein in the middle of his forehead, a sure sign that he was angry. He moved closer to me and pulled me into him forcefully. He kissed me hard, pressing his cold lips against mine. His kiss wasn't intended to be sensual. It was an empty gesture to remind me that he still had power over me.

Gently, I pulled away from him. "Robert, are you feeling okay? You seem…stressed, or something."

He curled his top lip. "I am…something."

"I don't want you getting all worked up. You wanna tell me what's up?"

"How about you tell me?" His question was much more of a dictate than a question. I could feel the weight of his words pressing against my chest. I took a step backward. I wanted to be out of arm's reach.

"Robert, what's going on?"

He sucked in a deep breath and exhaled a puff of hot air. "You know, when I married you, everyone thought I had lost my mind. They could not understand the attraction we had." He smiled as he reminisced. "We burned so brightly that we outshined everybody and everything. Never, not once, did I think you'd hurt me." His smile quickly evaporated.

"Robert, what are you talking about?"

"You know damn well what the fuck I'm talking about!" He threw his glass against the wall and it exploded with a loud bang. The few other people in the room looked around suddenly at us. "All of you, get the fuck out of here!" They, mostly RDE employees, left the room quickly, leaving me alone with Robert.

"How could you do this to me? I trusted you, even when I shouldn't have."

I wanted to step closer to him, but fear held me in place. I wasn't sure exactly what was going on, but from the pronounced scowl on his face and the anger in his voice, I gathered that one of my many affairs had come to his attention. I was not about to confess anything. At this point, I didn't know who he was refer-ring to. Surely, Ashleigh could not have been behind this. Last I heard, she was damn near close to overdosing.

I took a cautious step closer to Robert. He was right in that he still had power over me—he still controlled the purse, but I had power, too. Seductively, I moved toward him and reached out for him. I thought if he could just touch me again, feel the warmth of my body, feel the movement of my hips or the smoothness of my skin, that it would settle his spirit, but the hurt in his voice was so deep that even my power was rendered ineffective. He moved away from me as one would if they stood too close to an open flame.

"What have I done?" I asked gently. "Please tell me."

He did not utter a word. Instead, he stood without motion and glared at me. I could feel his stare cutting into me, clawing at me. It was difficult to maintain my cool disposition. I wanted to flee, to run for safety, but I had to know what he knew.

"You're gonna make me say it? You want to know how you've embarrassed me in front of the whole fucking city by acting like a two-bit whore?"

His words punched me in the chest.

"Two-bit whore? Robert, I assure you—"

"You shut the fuck up! Don't you say another fuckin' word or I swear I will cut out your heart!" He turned his back to me and then turned back in my direction so quickly that I jumped back. "Why, Blues, why? I gave you everything!" The alcohol in Robert's system mixed with his rage and created a toxic mixture. He was ready to explode. I needed to coax my sin out of his mouth so that I would know exactly what I was accused of. Had he found out about Nigel and me? Marquis and me? The waiter from the restaurant and me?

"Robert, baby. Would you please tell me what I've done?"

"Don't you mean *who* you've done? I feel so fuckin' stupid for ever trusting your ass."

"What are you talking about? What did I do?"

"Fuck you! I'll tell you what you're going to do. You're going to get the fuck away from me before I stab you in the heart, like you've stabbed me. You were the only one that I trusted and you had to go and fuck somebody else!"

"I don't know what you're talking about."

He quickly sobered up and looked me directly in the eyes. He turned around and grabbed an envelope off the purple sofa. As soon as I saw the envelope, I knew the deal. It looked exactly like the one Ashleigh had tossed into my lap in the car. How in the hell had she gotten this to him? I thought back to our conversation in the car. She did say that she wanted to show me the photographs in a more dramatic way. I guess the bitch had this already set up and when I turned her into a crackhead, she of course, wouldn't be worried about this. *Fuck!*

Robert rushed over to me and stuffed the envelope into my hands. The heat from his breath singed the hair on my face.

"Open it!" he commanded.

"Robert—"

"Open it!"

With reticence, I slowly opened the unsealed envelope and pulled out a photograph of Nigel and me.

That fucking bitch. I hope she gets raped by a dozen crackheads.

"Robert—"

As soon as I opened my mouth, he reared back and punched me so hard that I fell onto the sofa. He jumped down on me and started choking me with all the force he could muster.

"You son-of-a-bitch!" he yelled repeatedly. I placed my hands on his forearms and tried to pry his hands from my neck, but it was like a vise grip around my neck. "I should kill you now!" The vein in his forehead pulsated so hard, I thought it was going to explode.

Finally, he released his grip and rolled off me. He was breathing hard and he clutched his chest.

"Don't even think about coming home tonight, or any other night," he said between deep breaths.

I lay on the couch, trying to catch my breath. "Where am I supposed to go?"

"You can go to hell."

"Robert, please; we can work this out," I said as I rubbed my neck. "I am so sorry. Let me explain." Just as the words left my mouth, a few loud popping sounds rang out like fire bells in the night. Then, we heard the screams.

Pop.

Pop.

Pop. Pop.

"What the fuck is that?" Robert, still clutching his chest, pushed past me in a flash and moved toward the door to the VIP room. Slowly, he opened the door and took a peek outside. I leapt up from the couch and ran to his side.

"Robert, let me explain," I said as I ignored the sounds.

"Will you shut the fuck up," he whispered in a forced voice. "Go and hide."

"What?"

"I said, hide. Somebody is shooting!"

Pop.

Pop.

Pop. Pop.

It took a few seconds for his words to really register. When they did, foolhardily, I moved around him and looked out of the door. I saw a hooded figure in a purple velvet robe standing on the balcony, firing randomly into the crowd below. Even over the blare of the music, I could hear the sound of bullets tearing apart flesh. Terrified screams echoed throughout the great hall and ricocheted off the columns.

I watched as the gunman turned the gun on a woman who raced for the staircase that led to the bottom level. Without so much as a pause, he turned in her direction and fired a single shot that tore through her midsection and sent her spiraling down the long staircase. Her screams chilled me to the core.

"Oh my God! What are we going to do?" I asked Robert in a panic. Terror covered my entire body like a blanket. In order to get out of the VIP room, we'd have to run down the hallway to the staircase, in perfect view of the gunman.

There were no exits from the VIP room. We were trapped. Sitting ducks.

Pop.

Pop.

Pop. Pop.

Robert closed the door. He looked around the room and I could see the wheels in his head spinning. He and I were the only ones in the room and it was completely sealed off. There was a bar in the back and some furniture, but beyond that there were no knives or guns in the room. We could hide behind the bar in the hopes that if the gunman did enter the VIP, he'd open the door, not see anyone, and move on. On the other hand, if he entered the room and saw us cowering behind the bar, we'd surely be dead.

My mind raced. I didn't know what to do. I didn't want to die. Not now. Not like this. I wondered if Jabari had had that same thought as he plummeted to his death.

"Here, help me." Robert raced as fast as he could to the back by the sofa. His stride was unsteady and his legs looked wobbly, but he pressed forward. "We need to barricade the door so that he can't get in. Here, grab an end."

I raced over to the opposite end of the couch and lifted. Robert tried to lift, but the couch fell down to the ground with a thud and he looked as if he was about to pass out as he grabbed his chest again.

Fine time for you to have a heart attack.

"My medicine. Get it out of my jacket." He pointed to his jacket that was strung across a chair at the bar. I raced over and tore into his pocket and pulled out his pills. With unsteady fingers, I removed the caps and poured the pills into my hand. I ran back over to him and watched him swallow the pills.

"I need a minute," he said.

"We don't have a minute, Robert!"

"Just…just hide." He looked at me. "Go!"

Quickly, I raced over to the bar and balled up into a corner. I wished that I could fit into one of the compartments and disappear.

Just as soon as I tucked in my legs tightly, I heard the door to the VIP open and I heard Robert's voice. From my vantage point, I could see him struggling to stand.

"You? What the fuck?" Robert said with some effort.

The door to the VIP closed.

"Aren't I lucky? You're the one I was looking for."

Instantly, I recognized the voice as that of Charles, the executive at RDE that Robert had recently fired. I realized the odd figure that I had seen moving through the crowd moments before wasn't my guilty conscience manifesting itself in my reality. I had seen Charles and a prelude to murder.

"So, is this how it ends? You just gonna gun me down like some kind of dog in the street?"

"Yes." Charles's voice was plain, but firm.

Robert's breathing was heavy. I could hear it digging into his chest as he took a few steps forward.

"I should have known you'd take the coward's way out. Do you wanna know why I fired you? I fired you because you're weak. You've always been weak. You couldn't handle the pressure of being on top. You couldn't make the big decisions."

I heard the gun cock. I held my breath. My heartbeat pummeled my chest. Robert's machismo would get him killed.

"Is this how you really wanna go out? What about your wife and your children? What are they going to think of you, Charles?"

"Since I have no job now, thanks to you, I'm worth more to them dead than alive."

"You can get another job."

"Are you fucking crazy? Nobody is hiring!"

"Do you want to come back to RDE?"

"No, I want you dead, you son-of-a-bitch."

A gunshot rang out in the small space. The single shot sounded like cannon fire and the boom of the gun startled me. I tried to stifle my scream, but a squeak escaped from my mouth; that squeak was enough to betray my location.

"Whoever is hiding behind the bar should come out now. I won't ask again." His voice was hard and stern. For a few elongated seconds, I didn't know what to do. I wanted to pretend as if I hadn't heard the words, as if he hadn't heard my scream, but that was fantasy.

Slowly, I stood up.

I expected to see Robert lying on the ground with a bullet in his skull, but he was still standing, his eyes bulging in his head.

"Blues. How nice to see you again. Go stand by your husband."

"Charles—" I said.

"I didn't say speak. I said move over to your husband."

I did as I was told. Robert pulled me close to him, as if he was trying to shield my body from the bullet that would fire from Charles's gun at any second.

When I looked into Charles's eyes, I didn't see the eyes of a madman. I saw the soul of a wounded man; a man who had lost his way in a cruel world. His eyes, wide and bright, reflected a sad sort of madness that, oddly enough, reminded me of myself. I, too, was a wounded man who had lost my way, but under different circumstances.

I wanted to say something to Charles to let him know that he was not alone. He needed to know that we were kindred spirits and that his pain was my pain, too. We were united and inextricably bound by our wounds. But, words escaped me.

"If I'm going to lose everything, then I'll be damned if I let you sit up and enjoy your riches."

"Charles, you don't have to do this. Let me help you," I said.

"Help me? You can't even help yourself. This bastard treats you like a fucking slave and talks about you like a dog. What possible help could you offer me?"

I looked at Robert, who avoided my gaze. "You're right about Robert. I know how he is. He's an asshole, but he's not worth your wife and kids losing you. What legacy will you leave your children?"

My words seemed to stun him. He stared at us, but I could see my words drilling their way into his brain.

"Stop this before it gets any worse. It doesn't have to end like this," I said.

"This is the only way it's going to end. I've already killed people." He pointed the gun directly at Robert. Robert stood fearlessly and looked into the eyes of his assassin and did not flinch. Robert grabbed my hand and he squeezed, waiting for the bullet to be expelled from the gun. I squeezed his hand, too. I was truly afraid for him. And for myself.

I looked into Robert's face and I could not detect an ounce of fear. He stared at Charles as if they were in the boardroom of RDE and he had just berated Charles for doing a poor job. Robert did not quiver or beg for mercy. He stood like a soldier, resolute and strong.

I admired him for that.

As they eyed each other, I noticed the door behind Charles beginning to crack open. Slowly, I saw a head peek into the room. It was Nigel.

Oh shit.

Charles continued to stare at Robert.

"What are you waiting for? You can't pull the trigger? You're too weak to do it, aren't you?"

"Don't test me, old man. I've already shot up a room full of people. I'm not playing with your ass today."

"Robert, stop it," I found myself saying, my voice colored with panic, almost as if I cared whether or not he lived or died.

Clandestinely, Nigel tried to ease into the room, but the door made a sound, which caught Charles's attention. In an instant, he turned his head.

Robert lunged at him.

A shot rang out.

Robert screamed and fell backward.

I lunged at Charles. He stumbled backward.

Nigel charged into the room.

I didn't know if Nigel was coming to my defense or if he was coming to save Robert; either way, he charged into the room like a hero, risking his life in a hail of gunfire.

Charles didn't have time to turn the gun and fire with any accuracy at Nigel. I knocked him off balance and, like a cheetah, Nigel pounced on him and pummeled him with rapid-fire blows. The gun sailed across the room as they struggled.

Charles never had much of a chance. Nigel beat him to a bloody pulp and made sure that he was unable to move.

I moved over to Robert. I needed to check on my husband.

The bullet had struck him in the chest, near his heart. I felt unexpected pain.

I looked at him and he looked at me. With great effort, he reached up and touched my face with his hand. I leaned down and planted a farewell kiss on his lips.

He was dead and tears poured from my eyes.

I stood up and moved over to Nigel. I looked down at Charles and kicked him in the face and then hugged Nigel. With our arms around each other and with Charles's gun in his hand, Nigel and I moved toward the door. We heard sirens so the police were on the way. When we reached the door, Nigel stepped in front of me so that we could walk through it one at a time.

I looked back at Charles. He had a small pistol in his hand and was taking aim at us, mainly me, since I was in the back. There was no time to warn Nigel, not without risking injury to myself. It was as if the next few seconds happened in slow motion. I saw flashes of my life playing before my eyes.

My father.

My stepmother.

Running track.

Jabari.

New York City.

Nigel and me making love.

Marquis's lips.

Ashleigh smoking crack.

Overall, I didn't like what I saw. My life had been horrible. I had been horrible and in that instance, I wanted to repent, but instead of praying, I made a decision. I grabbed Nigel with both of my hands by the back of his shirt and pulled him behind me, essentially using him as a human shield.

Three shots rang out and tore through Nigel's body. His body violently rocked as his flesh was ripped by the metal. He screamed out and hit the floor hard.

I screamed and ran out of the room, unscathed by any bullet. As I ran, I turned and saw Nigel in the doorway, bleeding. His right arm reached out to me as if to say "help me," but I didn't stop. I couldn't stop. I wouldn't stop. I could not risk my life, even to save his. In the flicker of time that I turned to see him, even more prominent than his outstretched arms, were his eyes. They glowed in a way I had never seen before. It was as if his eyes were illuminated by his soul; they were bright and eerie. In his eyes, I could see shock at my betrayal. I had sacrificed his life to save my own.

If Nigel had known anything about me, then he would have expected nothing less from me.

The light in his eyes dimmed. In my heart, I realized that his life had been extinguished.

As I barreled down the staircase, I was met by armed policemen who stormed the building. They grabbed me and pulled me to safety. I screamed and pointed to the VIP room to indicate where the killer was located.

As they moved me to safety, I heard a single gunshot and knew that Charles had taken his own life, after creating such chaos.

CHAPTER 18

The few days after the carnage of The Purple Party were filled with chaos, questions, and sympathy. The city mourned. Seven people, including Robert, Nigel, and Charles, had died from a madman's bullet. Many more had been wounded.

Ironically, it was a madman that Robert had created.

In part, I wished that I could have thanked Charles for doing my dirty work. His vengeance had set me free and made me a very rich man since Robert's will had not been changed.

I hadn't been really affected by Nigel's death; not as much as I thought I should have been. I thought about the times we had spent together and I was grateful that he had been there when I needed him the most. I would never forget his *sacrifice*. I'd miss him, but I'd miss his sex more.

By design, Robert's funeral service was small and dignified and attended only by a few. As expected, Ashleigh was a no-show. My plan to turn her into a crackhead had worked better than I had expected. Marquis kept her doped-up and, according to him, she was a "crack fiend"—she simply couldn't get enough. When he told her that her father had died, it barely registered with her. He said she cried for about fifteen seconds and when the pain became too much for her to bear, she begged for more crack.

For his service, he'd be handsomely rewarded with some good dick, ass, and some cash. Once things were settled, he and I would take a fabulous European vacation. I could show him the world, like I had dreamed; but only for a short while.

During the service, I played the role of the distraught widower to perfection. I shook my head at the right moments. I trembled with sorrow when the right words were spoken. I appeared weak and consumed by grief just when the small crowd needed to feel my pain. I let unrestricted tears stream down my face. The funeral may have been Robert's, but it was all about me.

As we lowered Robert's casket into the ground, I looked up beyond the crowd and in the back, standing near a lonely tombstone, was Jabari. His face was like stone and revealed no emotion. I wasn't entirely surprised to see him. He'd been with me on this journey from the beginning. I surmised he'd be with me all of my days on this earth.

Crack.

Crack.

Crack. Crack

I was surprised, however, when my crocodile tears actually became real. As I watched them lower Robert into the cold earth, I cried.

I cried for so many reasons.

I cried for Jabari, the way I should have years ago.

I cried for Nigel, my secret lover whom I sacrificed to save myself.

I cried for Ashleigh and for Marquis, who had never known love or family.

I cried for Robert, too. His death was kismet; if not by my hands, then by Charles's.

More importantly, I cried for myself; for the hurt inflicted upon me over and over again by an uncaring world. I cried for all of the pain I had caused so many people over the years. I cried for the little boy that needed protecting so many years ago. I cried for the naïve teen who had landed in NYC to learn about hard living and harder loving.

I cried.

And, I cried.

And, I cried.

I cried, but I didn't change. I was still a monster. Some monsters are born; others, like me, are made. Monsters never change their skin, only their clothing.

Once a monster, always a monster.

CRAZY IN LOVE

CHAPTER 1

Brandon Heart felt the familiar throbbing in his pants as his powerful erection grew, threatening to break past the thin blue material of his school uniform. His erection bulged with the unrepentant lust of a typical red-blooded American teenager who was full of heat and blinded by desire. A small, licentious smile formed in the corners of his lustful mouth as he watched, with an obsessive focus, his English teacher—Mr. Cross Jones— scribble an obscure quote from some dead author on the chalkboard. Brandon paid little attention to the words; he was far more interested in admiring the way Mr. Jones's ass looked—firm and high—in his khaki slacks as he faced the blackboard. Brandon focused his attention on the lower extremities of his own bulging anatomy, fantasizing about the day his erection would be introduced to *that* ass. It would be highly inappropriate—possibly illegal—but he didn't care; he had long ago fixated his mind on conquering Mr. Jones, and Brandon, even at such a tender age, had already learned the virtue of never taking "no" for an answer. He wasn't even sure that Mr. Jones swung *that* way, but Brandon always felt that his teacher's pants were just a bit too tight, his clothes a bit too coordinated, his face a bit too perfect to be entirely straight. Still, he wasn't completely sure that he was into guys, but he had no doubt that he could get Mr. Jones into *him*. Once he focused his mind to the task at hand, it would only be a matter of time before Mr. Jones succumbed to his charms. After all, Brandon had conquered far straighter men than Cross Jones.

At an impressive six-feet-two-inches in height, Brandon's young body was bursting with promise and power, muscles bulging underneath taut, flawless, coco-colored skin that yearned to be touched and caressed. He was like an ebony dream, composed of rich milk chocolate, sweet honey and fantasy and he was fully aware of his exquisite beauty; it was the kind of loveliness that people wanted to possess, as if beauty was something tangible that could be captured and contained. His beauty, along with his unique athletic prowess in football and track, put him at the top of the high school food chain. All at once, Brandon was envied, worshipped, despised, pitied, sexualized, demonized, idolized, objectified, and even loved; such a diverse tapestry of competing emotions kept his life interesting. After money, beauty was the most powerful force in the world—lovers had killed for it; nations had warred over it and over the years, Brandon had harnessed his power. His enchanting puppy dog eyes and kissable lips had been used to sway circumstances in his favor, like flirting with Mrs. Henderson, his chemistry teacher, so much so that she had changed his final grade from a "B" to an "A." Beauty is sometimes subtle, like the delicate petals of a flower or like the flickering splendor of a distant star in a darkened sky; however, Brandon's rarified beauty was far from subtle—it was a force—announcing itself with the subtlety of a hurricane. It demanded to be worshipped and admired. He wielded it like a weapon, sometimes a flame-thrower that, on occasion, created such beautiful disasters.

Even at such a tender young age, he was fully aware of and had complete command over his sexuality. It was evident in the way his body glided down crowded hallways; he was all legs and stride; all angles and curves. His sexuality was seen in the grace-ful way in which his lips moved when he spoke a thousand lies; it could not be denied in the way his strong hips rocked, with so much possibility, as he raced down the football field or around the track; his presence was felt when he stood fully erect in the hallway, towering over his peers. His sexiness spilled over even in the slightest movement of his body and people noticed and fantasized. He was regal, like an African prince, who could command the forces of nature simply by the thunder of his voice.

Brandon had long ago recognized a dangerous longing in the eyes of adolescent girls who swooned at the sight of him; they smiled coyly and tried to steady themselves as their knees weakened and their panties moistened; it was a longing so deep and so passionate that it was hard not to see—lust sometimes burned brighter than daylight. And, he saw envy in the eyes of his male peers who wanted to be him or at least be near him, hoping that some of what he had would rub off on them; but, even at such a tender young age, Brandon was astute enough to recognize, even in its smallest measure, what was concealed behind the eyes of his male counterparts; it was buried within their youthful bravado and it was more than petty jealousy and secret admiration; it was almost imperceptible but, nevertheless, it made them flock to him. Brandon recognized it and tacitly encouraged it. It was a desire so illicit that it could only be acknowledged inside the safety of their masturbatory dreams.

Yes, Brandon knew that some of his male classmates also desired him.

This twisted gift, the gift of beauty that was bestowed upon him by fate, gave him dominion in this world.

Brandon looked nervously down at his watch and wondered when his gift would arrive. He had carefully planned for the timing and left explicit delivery instructions, but now he began to worry a bit. He wanted to see the look of surprise on Cross's face when the gift arrived, but from the looks of things, it may not work out.

Class would end in about fifteen minutes, but Brandon was determined to be present when his gift arrived. Brandon shifted hard in his seat and inadvertently sent his textbook crashing to the floor. It landed with a harsh thud that echoed throughout the room, startling the half-comatose students.

"Is there a problem, Mr. Heart?" his teacher asked.

"No. Sorry."

"Don't be sorry. Just be quiet," he said with some irritation. "Pick up your book and read the next passage out loud."

Brandon looked around incredulously. "For real?"

"No, for play." Mr. Jones sounded annoyed and did not smile as Brandon picked up his book. "I assume you know what page we're on because I know you were paying close attention." His sarcasm was heavy. Brandon smiled uneasily and shifted through the pages in his book, hoping something would jump out at him. He had no earthly idea what page they were on; for the last thirty minutes, his mind had drifted off. "Brandon, I'll see you after class."

"But—"

Before Mr. Jones could respond, there was a light tapping on the classroom door and his attention was directed toward the unexpected visitor. The door slowly crept open and in walked Mrs. Greenberg, the school secretary, carrying the most spectacular bouquet of Calla Lilies that Brandon had ever seen. Brandon delighted at her uncanny timing—his gift arrived just in time.

"These are for you, Mr. Jones," she said playfully as the classroom burst into a chorus of cat-calls and whistles.

He smiled oddly, took the flowers from Mrs. Greenberg and placed them on the left corner of his desk. He opened the card quickly, read it, and slid it into his pocket. A reddish hue colored his face as a smile formed in the corners of his mouth; it was a smile that he fought off and dismissed.

"Quiet down," he said to his class in a voice meant to sound authoritative, but ended up without much force. He couldn't hide the fact that he was excited by the gift. The sudden arrival of flowers for him had clearly thrown him for a loop. This was the second secret gift he had received in as many weeks.

"Someone has a secret admirer," Mrs. Greenberg said with great affection and interest. She lingered there for seconds, hoping Mr. Jones would toss her a morsel so that she could run back to the teachers' lounge with the latest school gossip on the hottest teacher at school.

"Thank you, Mrs. Greenberg, for bringing these down to me. Have a great afternoon," he said as he returned his attention back to his classroom.

She continued to linger until he shot her a thorny look. She smiled politely and exited through the door. Brandon could tell that she was disappointed that she had left with no more information that she had arrived with. Now, she'd have nothing to gossip about. Brandon knew better than to sign his name to the card; those nosey crows in the school office would probably read the card before they delivered the flowers.

The sudden sound of the ringing bell signaled the end of class and an end to the awkward moment. Brandon slowly gathered his belongings, barely taking his eyes off the object of his infatuation, as the rest of the class, full of the roar of rowdy seniors, sprang to life at the end of the school day and the beginning of the weekend.

"I was disappointed with the class participation today. I strongly urge you to read the rest of *Moby Dick* for Monday's class," Mr. Jones called out to the students as they shuffled by, checking text messages and voice mail, paying little attention. "I *strongly* urge you to read it," he said, wagging his fingers at the disinterested group. "If you expect to pass my class and graduate in May, then

I suggest you pull it together these next couple of months." Mr. Jones stood at the front of the room, his arms folded and watched as his students vacated his classroom.

Brandon tarried in the back row, slowly putting away his belongings. Mr. Jones moved over to his desk, took a seat, and started shuffling paper, paying little attention to the flowers. After all of the students vacated the room, Brandon stepped gingerly up to the front of the room, over to Mr. Jones's desk where he sat, leaving in his wake the strong scent of testosterone and lust.

"You wanted to see me?"

"Yes, Brandon, I did," he said as he looked up. He took a deep breath and leaned back in his chair as he peered at Brandon above the rim of his designer glasses. "What's going on with you?"

"Huh? What do you mean?"

"For the last few days, you have seemed…distracted. Is there something going on, something I should know about?"

It's hard to pay attention to what you're saying when all I can see is your ass, Brandon thought but didn't share.

"Nah, it's just that I don't get Moby…*Dick*…at all. Do you think you could help me out?" Brandon smiled and stared into Mr. Jones's brown eyes.

Mr. Jones pursed his lips and looked curiously at his student. "How much of it have you read?"

"Enough to know I need some help. This shit, I mean stuff, doesn't make any sense."

"You need to take your time with it and focus. Really think about what the author is trying to say."

"See, that's the problem. I don't get all this symbolism. I mean, if he wanted to say something, why not just say it instead of having people guess at what he's talking about? That's some bull—"

"Watch your language, Brandon. Are you trying to get detention?"

If it means I could spend some more time with you, then the answer is yes, he thought.

"My bad. I just feel comfortable around you; I mean, you're only a few years older than me."

"For the record, I'm about eight years older than you, but that's beside the point. I am your teacher; not one of your peers."

"Dang, I'm sorry Cross—"

"What did I tell you about calling me by my first name? It's Mr. Jones. I'm not going to tell you again." Brandon smiled—he liked a man with a little fire in his belly—even though the frustrated look etched across Mr. Jones's face didn't change.

"Okay, I'm sorry. It won't happen again."

"Now, as far as *Moby Dick* is concerned, you have to take your time and learn to use your critical thinking skills. That's what all of this is about, training you to think differently so that you can learn how to be an effective problem-solver in life."

"Well, I still don't get it. Are you gonna give *it* to me or what?" Brandon inched forward.

"Excuse me?"

"Help, extra help. Are you gonna give it to me? I mean, you're supposed to be available for us slow students, aren't you?"

"Brandon, you aren't slow, lazy maybe, but not slow." They both laughed out loud.

"That was cold, Cross. I mean, Mr. Jones. Why you tryna play me? You know I need you," he said with a wink.

"If you need help, I'm here every morning at seven o'clock," he said while having no discernible reaction to Brandon's flirtation.

"The early bird gets the worm, huh?" Brandon smiled again.

This time, Mr. Jones smiled back, albeit slightly.

"All jokes aside, if you need help, come to my tutorial." Mr. Jones took a deep breath and inhaled deeply. His eyes focused on

Brandon's face. "Brandon, are you sure nothing is going on with you? You seem…different."

"Nah, I'm fine. Really. Just a few things going on at home. No biggie," Brandon managed to stammer out. "But, wassup with these flowers, Mr. Jones?" he said as he changed the subject suddenly. Mr. Jones blushed ever-so-slightly as Brandon leaned his face into the bouquet and took a whiff, never once taking his eyes off Mr. Jones. "Ahhh, look at you smiling. Somebody got a crush on you!"

"It's nothing like that. Just one of the parents saying *thank you*."

Brandon couldn't believe Cross had lied to his face.

"I doubt that. These ain't no everyday 'thank you' flowers. It looks like somebody put some thought into this. I bet these are your favorite kind of flowers, too, aren't they?"

"Actually, they are. How did you know?"

"Because it's easy to send roses; everybody loves roses. If someone sends you a different flower, that means they have to know you like it; it means they thought about it." Cross paused and appeared to ponder the simple truth of his words and then stood up from where he sat. "Who sent them to you?"

"I don't know. The card was unsigned."

"Ahhh, a secret admirer; that's wassup."

"Enough about these flowers. Let's get back to you."

The sound of Mr. Jones's authoritative voice slowly dug into Brandon's heart, causing it to flutter wildly—almost uncontrollably—but he didn't let it show. Brandon's breathing deepened and burrowed into his chest as he eyed his instructor through the smoky haze of adolescence, which made everything look shiny, new and within the realm of possibility. He took a step closer—a bit too close—invading the personal space of his teacher. He put his hand on Mr. Jones's shoulder in a friendly gesture of goodwill.

"Don't worry about me. I'll be okay. I promise," he said with a coy little wink.

"I just don't want you losing focus so close to graduation. A failing grade will wreck your GPA."

"What? Am I close to failing?"

"No, no, calm down. I just want to be proactive, but you did get a C on your last quiz, which is unlike you. To be successful in life you've got to focus and know what you want."

"I know exactly want I want," Brandon said in a voice that did not hide his adolescent attraction.

Cross paused. "I want you to do better on the quiz."

"Okay, I'll do better. I don't want to disappoint you, Cross."

"Cross?"

"I mean, Mr. Jones. My bad."

Mr. Jones exhaled and eyed Brandon closely.

"Brandon," he began as he removed his designer glasses from his face. "How are your parents? Have you been able to talk to them about whatever you're going through?"

Brandon grimaced. "My parents, hmmmm, let's see. Julia and William Heart don't really *get me*, you know? Besides, they ain't never around. My dad sold his business last year and they been around the world, twice, without me." Brandon hoped his faux sob story would win him favor with Cross.

"Oh. I'm sorry to hear that."

"Don't be sorry. I'm fine. In fact, I'm better than fine. I do better when they leave me alone."

Brandon moved away from Mr. Jones and wandered leisurely over toward the window. He gazed out into the daylight, hoping the piercing sunlight would pierce through his pain.

"Did you know that I have a brother? I mean, *had* a brother? He died almost four years ago." His tone was dry and even though

Cross was in the room, Brandon's question seemed to be directed to the empty space that separated him from Cross.

"No, I didn't know that."

"Tomorrow would have been his birthday." Brandon spoke plainly, without any emotion, as he stated the facts.

"Oh really? That must be tough for your family. Does your family do anything to remember him?"

He chuckled. "Yeah, my parents find some excuse to go out of town every year around this time. Hell, they'll probably be gone by the time I get home."

"I don't understand. What about you?"

"What about me?"

"Why don't you go out of town with them? It's at times like these when families have to stick together."

As he faced the window in an Academy Award-winning moment, a single tear slid from his eye and moved slowly down his cheek. He wanted to wipe it away, but didn't; instead, he let it linger on his face and glisten in bright light of day.

"Mr. Jones, that's a long story."

He became acutely aware that Mr. Jones was watching him and, in dramatic fashion, he wiped the tear from his face. He then felt a strong hand on his shoulder, offering warmth and support.

"Listen, Brandon. I lost my mother when I was about your age, so I know what you're going through."

"No one knows what I'm going through. Do you know what it's like to go home to an empty house every day and have to deal with this shit by myself?"

"I can't say that I do."

"Do you know what's it's like to know that your parents hate you?"

"Brandon, I'm sure that's not true."

"Whatever. They can barely look at me sometimes."

"Why do you think that is?"

"You wouldn't understand."

Cross walked back over to his desk, scribbled something down on a small white notepad, and returned to Brandon.

"I don't usually do this, but here is my home number. If you need someone to talk to this weekend, don't hesitate to call. You shouldn't have to go through this by yourself."

Before he turned to face his teacher, a tiny, but wicked grin formed in the corners of Brandon's mouth. A few crocodile tears could go a long way.

"Thank you, Mr. Jones. This means a lot to me. I'll only call if I really need to speak to someone." Brandon turned and hugged his teacher. He wrapped his arms around him and placed his head on his shoulder but suddenly pulled away out of fear of overdoing his performance.

"Oh, wow. I'm so sorry. I didn't mean to—"

"It's okay, Brandon. It's okay."

"Shit, I'm so embarrassed. You won't tell anyone I cried, will you?"

"It's okay to cry."

"Not for me. I have a reputation," he said with a silly smile that eased the mood.

"Don't worry. Your secret is safe with me."

And yours is safe with me, Brandon thought.

Brandon delighted at the thought of flirting dangerously close to the edge of desire with his teacher; desire could quickly become so much more. From the day Cross Jones had taken over the class from Ms. Keys who had gotten married mid-year and moved to Denver with her new husband, Brandon had felt a peculiar closeness to him. From the moment he had walked into the room, broad-shouldered and head held high, Brandon was intrigued. The way Cross moved, so confidently and sleekly, enticed Brandon. Cross carried himself with pride and walked with a formal gait. Brandon loved everything about him, from the way his broad shoulders looked in his tailored shirts to the way he stood, proud and erect, as if he placed himself above trivial things. And, Cross was something of a celebrity in the literary world and Brandon liked the thought of basking in Cross's fame.

Early on, Brandon recognized something familiar within Cross that connected with his spirit; it was something that caused his gaze to linger a little longer and his voice to deepen ever-so-slightly when he spoke to his teacher. It wasn't something that Brandon could articulate or even think about consciously; it was something that resonated deep within his core, something so innate and salient that words were not required; it was a feeling that simply *was* and whatever it *was* piqued Brandon's interest on a visceral level. He was compelled to know more about this man, as if it was his destiny. Something lonely in his spirit connected with something hollow in Cross's presence. Brandon believed their relationship to be kismet, ordained, and blessed by the universe itself.

As soon as Brandon stepped into the bustling hallway, he slung his backpack across his right shoulder and headed down the hall. Thoughts of Cross Jones still danced in his head and poisoned his thoughts; never had he been so affected or distracted by a man. It was he that usually served as the distraction. This unexpected reversal of fortune somehow intrigued him. There was something mysterious, something intoxicating—something dangerous—about this unholy attraction that he had for his teacher. Deep down inside, he knew that he was playing with fire, but the rewards outweighed the risk of burning.

"Hey, Brandon." He heard a sweet female's voice calling out to him as he rounded the corner toward his locker. He looked back and saw Sheila Kilpatrick, his ex-girlfriend, coming around the corner wearing her cheerleading uniform. She was all breasts and ass, the way most men liked. Brandon rolled his eyes and plastered a fake smile across his face.

"Hey, Sheila. Wassup?"

"Well, my parents are out of town and I thought maybe you could…stop by tonight."

"For what?" He didn't attempt to mask the annoyance in his voice.

She inserted the head of a red lollipop into her mouth slowly, all the while maintaining her eye contact with him.

"Girl, you trippin'. If I know you, and I do, then you've been sucking more than lollipops with that pretty little mouth of yours."

"Why you always got to be an ass?" She exhaled loudly and folded her arms.

"Bye, Sheila." Brandon turned on his heels and walked away, laughing. He had no time or patience for her vacuous attempts at seduction.

"You ain't all that!" she screamed as he heard her stomp down the hallway.

He smiled. He knew he was way more than *all that*.

CHAPTER 2

Cross entered his three-bedroom palatial townhouse just in time to hear the phone ringing. He yanked his key out of the lock, slammed the door shut, darted over to the table by the sofa, and snatched the phone off the hook.

"Hello?" he said, slightly winded by his sudden burst of energy.

"Where is your manuscript, Mr. Man? See, you gon' make me come to Atlanta to bust the windows out of that pretty little car you drive," the familiar voice said in a recognizable rhythm that caught Cross off-guard.

The sound of Lorenzo's voice blared through the phone with no warning. Cross suddenly wished he had looked at the caller ID as he rubbed his face with his hands and plopped down on the sofa.

"Hey, Lorenzo. How are you?"

"Don't try to sweet talk me. I got a call from your publisher asking when she's going to get your new book. I've been covering for you for two months now."

"I know and I appreciate it, but—"

"But nothing. You need to get it done and stop bullshitting around. I'm your agent, so I got your back, but I can't keep covering for you. If you don't get that manuscript to me in thirty days, Kathy is going to send her henchmen out to hunt you and me down. You know her ass is fanatical about your work."

"Thirty days? You got me another extension? See, that's why I keep you around."

"You keep me around because I'm the best agent in the free world and don't you ever forget it."

"You are da man!"

"Now that that is all settled, how are things in *High School Musical*?" he injected, but didn't wait for a response. "I don't know what you get out of screaming at a bunch of hard-headed, bad-ass kids all day. Clearly you don't need the money. I saw your last royalty check, remember?"

"It's not about the money. I enjoy teaching; inspiring young minds."

"Why you'd want to relive high school when you could be lounging by the beach with some hot, naked Latin papi serving you some fruity concoction is beyond me, but to each his own. Shit, we couldn't wait to get out of high school; I still can't believe you'd voluntarily go back."

"Cut me some slack, aight? The kids are cool; they just need some guidance. I want to inspire a new generation of writers. Who knows, I could have a new Baldwin or Morrison in one of my classes and Lord knows we need it. Have you looked at the shit people are writing nowadays?"

"Here we go again. Yes, Cross, I've seen the plethora of *urban* books being published that you claim are dumbin' down our communities. Stop being such a snob. At least black people are reading."

"I guess."

"Look man, I gotta go. I have an appointment in twenty min-utes, but you better get me that book!"

"I will. I promise."

"One last thing: make sure you don't get in trouble with one of those big, corn-fed high school boys. They didn't grow 'em like that when we were in school."

"You don't know the half of it," Cross said as he plopped down onto the couch. "I have this one kid who is…gorgeous. I mean, if you saw this boy on the street you'd swear he was at least twenty-five. That little Negro is the shit, and his young ass knows it. He reminds me of Lucas, a little bit." Cross found himself laughing out loud at the thought of his over-grown high-schoolers and how most of them were so much more physically developed than the ones back in his day.

"Lucas? This is the first time you've said his name since the break-up."

"I know. I'm moving on."

"If this boy reminds you of Lucas, you need to be very careful with that *boy* and make sure you have boundaries set. Don't let him work you. As much of a prude as you've become lately, I knew you back when we were fucking like porn stars."

"Ahhh, those were the days," he said with laughter. "Don't worry. I've got this under control. I'm much too cool to ever be worked. And, I'm not into jailbait. And, remember, I don't have fond memories of Lucas."

"Cool. I'm going to check in with you in a couple of weeks and finish that damned book!"

Cross returned the phone to its cradle and sighed. The sound of Lorenzo's voice brought back happy memories of the days when the two of them *lived* life. Part of him longed for those days again, but it conflicted with the part of him that desired exile.

He grabbed the bag that he had dropped in front during his mad dash to the phone. He dropped his Blockbuster movies onto the coffee table and then moved over to the stereo. He hit "play" and listened as the sounds of Ledisi singing "In the Morning" filled the vacant space in his house and in his soul. As she purred out the song, he poured himself a glass of red wine and stepped out onto the deck of his home. The fresh Georgia air filled his lungs as the soothing warmth of the early spring evening covered his body like a blanket. He looked out into the wooded area behind his house and felt peace.

It had been almost two years since he had absconded from the grit of New York City in search of a more tranquil existence. He settled Marietta, Georgia, right outside of Atlanta, hoping to get back to his roots. The daily toll of living in New York—in spite of the ease his money provided—had become toxic, even more damaging than the smog and pollution from the innumerable taxicabs; the city grew stale, in spite of its fury and glimmer and its spectacular towers had grown dull and lifeless, no longer offering enchanted possibilities for an eager heart. Even before his heart had been irreparably shattered by the one who still held its pieces, New York had lost its luster and Cross had lost his patience.

He settled into a chair on the deck and tried to relax. Living alone was sometimes rough for him. The quiet of his home attached itself to him in the still of the night; it latched onto his skin like a leech and it embedded itself into the furniture and onto the walls, leaving a smell that sometimes offended his nostrils; the stench of being alone, of being lonely, of being abandoned, of being disconnected—even from one's own self—stank up the entire house. His profound heartache, though two years buried in the past, still tainted his world. And, because of this, he had grown cautious in his step—despite his youth—afraid that stepping too boldly would lead to pain as it did in his past relationship. He carefully ordered his steps, never venturing too far from the sidewalk and avoiding anything that required emotional risk.

Gone was the carefree lad who, years ago, had left his home in LaGrange, Georgia, for Columbia University; gone were the wild New York nights, bouncing from one club to another, in a desperate search of whatever the young sought. He searched and partied and searched, finally realizing that the joy he sought was never in finding *it*, but in the journey itself; a journey fraught with trials, tribulations, and excitement. Those life lessons had fueled his literary fire and turned him into a star at a young age.

The prodigal child, now in his mid-twenties and a successful writer-turned-teacher, called Marietta home, a city that derived its life from the metropolis of Atlanta.

So, he worked.

And taught.

And prayed.

And wrote, though these days his listless existence began to manifest itself into a seemingly impenetrable form of writer's block. Being emotionally disconnected from the world would never produce a great novel, but still he wouldn't let go of the pain. He wasn't even sure he knew how to.

CHAPTER 3

Early Saturday morning, Brandon lay in wait. His long, big, black car with the black tinted windows was parked down the street from Cross's townhouse; it had become a part of Brandon's weekend routine to follow Cross and document his journey. A few weeks ago, he had followed him home one day after school so he would know where he lived.

Now, Brandon was quickly becoming an expert in all things Cross. Every Saturday morning Cross would leave the house by eight-thirty to make his nine o'clock workout class. After the gym, Cross usually stopped by Whole Foods on Roswell Road to pick up something for lunch. He usually bought some kind of fish and some kind of organic side dish. He'd buy a bouquet of fresh flowers from the flower shop across the street; he had a thing for Calla Lillies.

In order for his seduction to work, Brandon needed to have as much information about Cross as possible. So, he had spent several Saturday mornings surreptitiously following him, always lingering a few cars behind or hiding on a different aisle of the supermarket. Brandon wanted to know what made Cross the man that he was; he wanted to know the kinds of foods he ate, the places he went, the movies he liked to watch, and the kind of things he did when he was home alone. He often wondered if he sat around reading all day or was he the type to turn up the volume on his stereo and dance around the room naked?

Brandon had gone back and read each one of Cross's published novels, in hopes of gaining some secret insight, which was one of the reasons he had fallen behind in school. In his head, he could see Cross hunched over his computer, hammering the keyboard into the wee hours of the night, churning out the next great novel. Brandon longed to be there to bring him comfort when his fingers tired of typing.

As he sat waiting for Cross to exit his home, he laughed to a repeat of Miss Sophia's Girl Talk on V-103 emanating from the speakers and he paid attention to the women in the neighborhood who busied themselves with their wifely chores. He watched the real housewives of Atlanta pass by, one by one, as they pounded the pavement during their early morning jogs.

As he adjusted the volume on his radio, he noticed Cross's car pulling out of the driveway at 8:28 a.m. Usually, he would follow him, but this morning he had something else on his mind—he wanted access into Cross's house. He had at least two hours before Cross would return and he hoped that he could find a way into the house before he was spotted by a neighbor. He waited about fifteen minutes before he made his move, giving Cross enough time to get a good distance away. As Brandon stepped out of his vehicle wearing jeans and a nondescript T-shirt, he looked around for any neighbors or prying eyes.

Brandon walked up on the porch and rang the doorbell as if he was there on official business. He rang it again and waited. He wasn't sure if Cross had company so he waited to be sure. No detectable sound or movement could be heard from the other side of the door.

When Brandon was sufficiently satisfied that no one was home, he walked back to his car and drove around the corner to park. To fool the eyes of any nosey neighbor, he wanted to make it look as though he had left. When he parked the car, he got out of the vehicle and walked down the road, trying to figure out how to get to the backside of Cross's house without being detected. He eased his way down a narrow alleyway, cut through some bushes, and finally hopped a low fence, on the side of Cross's house. When he landed, he looked around at the neighboring houses to see if he noticed anyone watching him. He had done some crazy things in his days, but breaking and entering was new to him; yet he remained undeterred in his quest.

He took a deep breath, trying to calm himself, and then moved to the window on the side of the house. He tried to ease it open, but it didn't budge. He then moved to the backside of the house and tried to slide open the patio door, but it was locked also. Like a determined burglar, he moved to the other side of the house and noticed a window that wasn't completely closed. He smiled at his good fortune. Slowly, he opened the window, climbed inside, and lowered the window behind him.

Brandon stood absolutely still for a few minutes, almost afraid that his breathing would disturb the quiet and alert the world to his presence in his teacher's home. He steadied himself and gathered his wits as he finally felt courageous enough to look around the room. He had landed in Cross's office and when he felt comfortable, he moved freely about the space. He looked around at the various book awards and accolades that his *husband-to-be* had received over the years. Upon doing his due diligence, Brandon discovered that Cross's four published books had sold a total of more than 2.5 million copies and had been optioned for movies. Not only was Cross attractive, but he was also rich and successful.

Brandon then started perusing through papers on Cross's desk and books on his shelf. He wanted to get to know more about this man. He needed to know what made him tick.

After a few moments in the office, Brandon ventured into the rest of the beautifully decorated house. He walked down the hall-way, carefully taking in as many details as possible before moving into the den and looking around. He looked at the abstract art on the walls and the deep brown leather couch. He was tempted to sit on it, but this room offered little insight into *the man;* Brandon wanted to see the bedroom—the place where he hoped the magic would one day happen.

Slowly, he walked up the staircase to the second level of the home. He moved down the long hallway with the stealth of a feline, peeping into each room until he reached the master suite. Slowly, he pushed open the door and stepped inside. It suddenly felt like he was home. He fell in love with the deep red painted on the walls. Brandon loved red because it was so strong a color that it conjured a range of emotions from love to rage. He was excited by the fact that Cross was bold enough to paint his bed-room walls such a brave color; it showed he didn't mind taking chances; Cross Jones the schoolteacher was far too conservative to make such a bold statement in his bedroom. Brandon hoped the blood-colored walls meant that Cross would be a strong and passionate lover.

He moved over to the chest of drawers and started thumbing through Cross's unmentionables. He grabbed a pair of blue under-wear and pulled them into his face, hoping to get a whiff of Cross's intoxicating scent. When he realized the underwear smelled of Downy, he quickly put them back into the drawer.

He turned his attention elsewhere. He eyed the huge, perfectly made, black king-sized bed that was centered against the wall. Four huge pillars on each corner of the bed gave the room a Roman-esque feel, as if Cross was Caesar. Brandon, almost unable to contain himself, ran over and jumped onto the bed and rolled around on top of the bed. He pulled the covers back, grabbed his pillows and pulled them into his face. He inhaled deeply, taking Cross's scent fully into his body. It was almost as if his scent was a drug and Brandon couldn't get enough; it drove him wild. He then sat up in the bed and looked around the room. A huge flat-screen television hung on the wall directly in front of the bed.

"I wonder what you like to watch," he said as he picked up the remote control from the nightstand and turned the television on. He noticed a remote control for the DVD player and picked it up. Once he figured out how to operate the device, he hit "play" and before he knew it, his eyes grew wide with excitement as they were bombarded with images of naked flesh on top of flesh—porn! Brandon loved it.

"Ahh, you're into the group thing," he said as he watched the group of naked interracial men on the television with *growing* interest. He watched as five or six men went at it like there was no tomorrow and Brandon's eager hand had found itself around his own willing flesh. He spat in his hand for lubrication and started jerking himself into a frenzied state. The excitement the men on screen shared with each other spilled over into Brandon's own reality. He was excited watching them but more excited by the thought of Cross walking in and catching him in the act of self-gratification. He closed his eyes, even as the men on screen continued, and imagined that Cross was in the bed with him, on top of him, under him, in him, and that they were making love like newlyweds. He reached over and grabbed one of the pillows and put it over his face so that he could smell Cross again. Within seconds of doing that, he reached his *peak* and his young excitement exploded out of him like a geyser expelling its hot gases. He lay in the strange bed, breathing hard, even while his release oozed down his sides and was soaked up by the sheets.

When he was able to compose himself, he got up from the bed

and walked into the master bath. He opened the cabinet and grabbed a small towel from the shelf—it was as if he knew exactly where to look. He ran some warm water over it and cleaned himself up. He looked for and found a place to dispose of the towel—a hamper in the corner by the walk-in shower. He opened the basket, dropped in his towel. Then he had another thought. He looked in and pulled out a pair of Cross's underwear—a pair of black bikini briefs. He brought the underwear to his nose and inhaled deeply. *Yes!* Cross's masculine sweatfunk scent permeated every inch of the fabric and when Brandon inhaled, his dick stiffened again. Quickly and frantically, he jerked off again and when he reached orgasm, he used the pair of underwear to catch his seed. His teenaged lust had been satisfied yet again. He stuffed the pair of underwear into his front pocket as a keepsake.

Twenty minutes after his last orgasm, Brandon snuck out of the house the same way he had entered. He was careful to put everything back exactly the way he had found it and made sure that he made the bed. He had successfully entered Cross's home and had had his way with his belongings. He felt powerful, like he could do anything he wanted to do and get away with it. Now, all he had to do was *have* Cross. Being in his home, amongst his personal effects and inhaling his most intimate scent solidified Brandon's desire. Cross's pheromones lingered in Brandon's nostrils like no other scent had ever.

He was even more determined to have Cross.

✪ ✪ ✪

Later that night, after a couple hours of messing around at the mall and spending his parents' money on sneakers, CDs and a pair of $250 jeans that made his ass look like a work of art,

Brandon entered the empty home he shared with his mother and his father. Even though he resided there, he felt like an interloper skulking about the fringes, hoping for an invitation to really come inside.

When he walked into the grand foyer, he called out for his parents and listened as his voice echoed throughout the rooms. His voice bounced off the walls and returned to him without a response to his call. He took a deep breath and inhaled the emptiness that had already become a part of his character.

Out of habit, he made a quick sweep through the downstairs to see if anyone was around. He knew they wouldn't be, but just to be sure, he called out for them again and again his call went unanswered. He was alone, as usual. He knew he'd be. It was that perilous time of the year when his parents' pain spilled over its shallow embankment. It was that time of the year when they fled the city in a blaze like Bonnie and Clyde. Even if they had stayed, Brandon would have felt their absence from him, even in their presence. Over the years, their relationship settled into uneasy and awkward peace, much like enemies staring across the line of demarcation, carefully avoiding that one moment when their cold war would erupt into fury.

They would always blame him for the death of his older brother four years ago. Their favorite son and his perfect brother had died in a car accident after picking Brandon up from school one evening. The car had flipped three times and his brother, who was not wearing a seat belt, was catapulted from the car and flung across the highway like a rag doll, breaking almost every bone in his body. Brandon barely survived with help from his seat belt, but as his body recovered, his relationship with his mother and father flat-lined. In his heart, he knew that if they were presented with the option of choosing which child would live and which one would die that he'd be rotting in the ground in a cheap casket. His brother had been the perfect child, the kind of child that parents dreamed of; the kind of child that made a father's eye sparkle with pride; the kind of child that mothers vociferously defended. He was wildly intelligent, super-athletic and hugely popular, with a personality that lit up the room like a spotlight. His parents fawned over him as if he were the Prince of Wales; and Brandon looked up to him, too; in fact, he wanted to be him. In spite of the fact that he hated football, he played because his brother played; regardless of the fact that he didn't have a natural liking for school, he studied hard so that his grades would be comparable to his brother's. Despite the fact that he didn't feel a strong attraction to girls, he dated the prettiest of them so that they could be just as pretty of a couple as his brother and his beautiful girlfriend.

But none of this mattered.

His parents saw through the façade. His parents *knew* what Brandon was. There was a long list of offenses over the years that they could easily reference in order to prove their point beyond any reasonable doubt.

When he was nine years old, his father caught him "wrestling" with his best friend, William. He banished the child from the house and forbade Brandon from seeing him again. And, when he was alone with his child, Mr. Heart tried to beat the feeling out of Brandon.

When he was eleven, his parents received a call from his teacher saying that he had been caught in the bathroom kissing a boy. His mother locked him in his room all weekend, without food.

When he was fourteen, the maid found an old copy of *Black Inches* magazine underneath his mattress and turned the contraband over to his parents. His father made him take a shower and lay across the bed wet (so that it would sting more) while he beat him with a leather strap, all the while pleading with God to remove the demon from his son.

Brandon knew the only demon was the one his parents were creating.

And he didn't feel sinful, only misunderstood.

And, he felt no love from or for those that gave him life.

Later on that same year, on a dark autumn night, his mother had found a note from Brandon's first "boyfriend" wedged between the wall and his computer stand. The note described, in detail, their first sexual encounter. She sent Patrick to school to retrieve Brandon so that they could deal with his growing sexual deviance. She was determined that his perversions would not sully the family name. That was the night Patrick died.

When Patrick died, their love for their remaining child died, too. Brandon tried in earnest to be the son that they needed. He put forth a full measure of devotion to right the *wrongs* of his life so that he could grow closer to his parents. He excelled at sports, which had a wondrous effect on his body, and received excellent grades, dated and *fucked* his way through some of the school's most prized debutantes; their cotillion-bred morals fell by their ankles as easily as their pretty pink panties. He did all of this to win his parents' approval, but none of it worked, because they *knew*. They had always known.

Had his brother lived, he'd be celebrating his twenty-second birthday on Sunday and that was too much for his parents to take, so they fled. They fled from their living son to avoid memories of their dead one and left Brandon to privately deal with his personal pain; forced solitude offered no solace.

He walked into the kitchen and opened the refrigerator, pulled out a Coke, and popped the top. He then moved over to the cabinet, pulled out a glass, and poured the beverage into the container and began to drink quickly. He loved the perfect pain from the burn of a nice, cold Coca-Cola. As he drank, he caught a glimpse of a note on the counter by the phone. He didn't have to read it to know what it said; there had always been pastel notes written in delicate handwriting left all over the house for him to discover. Still, he moved over to the counter and picked the note written on his mother's lovely purple and green floral stationery and read it out loud:

Brandon,

Your father and I have gone to Los Angeles for business. We hope to be back in a few days, but we will let you know. We left you some money on your bed and paid your credit card bill, so you should be fine. If you need us, please call.

Love,

Mother

Brandon crumpled up the decorative paper and threw it angrily against the wall. Even though he expected as much, the simple words stabbed at him without mercy. He fought hard to keep his tears at bay because tears were a sign of weakness, according to his father. He thought about his brother and his parents and his loneliness and wanted to lash out. He threw the empty glass against the wall and watched it explode into a dazzling display. The empty words from her note rang in his head like the cackle of Macbeth's witches. The words he read were not the words she wanted to write. The message that he read between the lines of her pretty note packed a much stronger punch:

Brandon,

We still can't bear to look at you, especially so close to your brother's birthday. To avoid any awkward moments, we have decided to put a thousand miles between you and us. It is so very hard sharing a house

*with you, knowing that you are responsible for Patrick's death. We wish
we could love you the way we used to, but we simply don't feel the same
way anymore. And, the way you are makes us sick, so we ignore it.
We'll see you when we see you.*

With love,
Mother

*P.S.: Your father has made arrangements for you to attend college in
Europe when you graduate, though I think putting an ocean between
us still may not be enough.*

Brandon had a hard time understanding why his parents didn't
understand that he, too, was in pain. Why couldn't they see that
he grieved? Did it ever occur to them that he needed to talk
about what happened? Did they even know that he would gladly
take Patrick's death into himself if it meant that his brother could
live? Why did they refuse to even talk about Patrick? Why did
they treat him like the enemy instead of the drunk driver that
rammed into their car at seventy-miles an hour?

As thoughts and memories and pain and loneliness and heartache and images of Patrick overwhelmed him, he felt his knees
buckle and he collapsed slowly onto the floor. The emptiness of
the vast house offered no mercy; it was a living entity that fed off
his misery and reveled in his anguish. He pulled his knees into
his chest, resting his back against the wall. He was alone and left
to deal with haunting memories. Alone in the house, he was free
to cry without paternal retribution, but even in the midst of
solitude, he felt ashamed to let his tears flow. He looked around
fearfully, as if his father would suddenly emerge from the shadows
like a wraith and condemn his emotional outburst. He cried. No
matter how hard he tried, he couldn't stop the tears from falling;
he couldn't will the tears away or beg them to return to his eyes.
They flowed freely almost without pause.

CHAPTER 4

After some time spent sobbing in the kitchen, Brandon pulled himself together. He rose slowly from the floor and moved into the den, leaving his grief and his pain in a puddle on the kitchen floor. He felt suddenly renewed after his emotional purge. By now, it was close to seven in the evening, according to the clock on the wall, and Brandon had yet to confirm his plans for the night. He had a couple of options but decided to go with one of his regulars; he longed for the danger. As he passed his book bag and cell phone, which he had left on a table in the foyer, he stopped, pulled his phone from the bag, and finally replied to a text message that he had received earlier in the day. His laconic reply contained three simple words: I'LL BE THERE.

He moved over to the bar and took the top off a bottle of expensive brandy. He grabbed the bottle and poured more than a healthy shot down his throat. The burn of the dark liquid set him on fire, igniting in his throat and chest a fiery passion that could only be quenched by ritual. He took another swig, hoping to feel the full effects of the power of this magic potion sooner rather than later. He had cried enough for the night; now, it was playtime.

He picked up his bag, slid open one of the inside pockets, and pulled out the most perfectly rolled joint he had ever seen. He had rolled it in the bathroom at school earlier in the day and took pride in his handiwork. He wanted to blaze right there in the middle of the room, but feared the lingering scent of the weed. His mother had the sense of smell of an overwrought bloodhound. If she smelled any usual odors, she'd question him relentlessly until he confessed so he could get her to shut her mouth. Even though she was out of town, he didn't want to take the chance. If the scent lingered in the tiniest amount and she caught wind of his *special cigarette*, their uneasy peace would be breached.

Instead of smoking in the house, he walked out onto the patio and took a seat by the pool. The sun dipped right below the horizon, offering fleeting slivers of burnt orange light that jetted up like spikes in a colossal crown. He plopped down on one of the patio chairs and as he lit the marijuana cigarette he inhaled deeply, pulling the thick smoke into his lungs. Slowly, he exhaled. He closed his eyes and let euphoria wash over him.

Almost immediately, he felt the effect—this was high-quality marijuana. The Jamaican dude he had fucked on Tuesday always had the best weed. He repeated this action several times and finally opened his eyes. When the world came into view, he became intrigued by the picturesque scene. Something mysterious, almost magical, seemed to dance on rays of sun. For a few moments, he felt completely at peace as he watched glitter-like sparkles ping-pong their way on rays of hope. He wondered what lay beyond the horizon, right out of his reach. Were the dancing diamonds he viewed the manifestation of happiness or were they dancing fairies playing fairy games? He nervously extended his arm in the direction of the setting sun, hoping he could capture one of those fairies and place it in a jar for his exclusive use; yet, he remained fearful that whatever shone in the light would always be just out of his reach. His reach became more desperate and he grabbed futilely in the air, trying to snatch a piece of joy out of the sky before night fell. Helplessly, he watched the shine from the glittery dots fade and, right before his eyes, they lost their luster and faded into nothingness.

He inhaled again and again and again as the light vanished and gave way to a growing darkness.

✪ ✪ ✪

Brandon arrived in the designated neighborhood at the designated time and found the correct house. This was the usual meeting place for one of his usual tricks. The white two-story edifice sat on the corner and looked like the typical American house with the two-car garage and the white picket fence, but when he got inside it would be nothing like Mayberry. Tonight, he needed to walk on the wild side.

He slowly approached the house, fully aware of the routine.

He slowly opened the door and crept inside the dimly lit structure. There were no sounds or signs of life, but they were watching. They were always watching.

On the coffee table, he saw the white envelope that contained the $1,000 he'd get for his services. He picked it up, thumbed through the stiff bills, and stuffed them into the pocket of the jeans he wore.

In the envelope there also was a note on white paper written in blood red ink that instructed him on the next steps he should follow. The note commanded him to put on the costume he'd find in the black bag that was draped over the couch and proceed to the basement.

Brandon opened the bag and found a strap-on pair of white angel wings, a white mask that fit across his eyes, and a white jock strap.

"Interesting," he said to himself. Before he began removing his clothing, he noticed the customary tray of drugs provided by his client. Of all his clients, Brandon enjoyed this one the most. He took a seat on the couch and leaned his face close to the silver tray on the coffee table. He took a bump of cocaine and waited for the quick high to hit him.

Brandon had participated in several of this client's secret sex games over the last few months, but he had never seen his face. Usually, the client sat back in a dark corner and watched. He loved watching. He sometimes masturbated while Brandon performed whatever act he was instructed to by similar pieces of white paper with red lettering. Sometimes, he only wanted Brandon to strip. Other times, he wanted Brandon to masturbate or pleasure himself with some newfound sex toy. Brandon was eager to please. Sometimes, his benefactor would hire another man so that he could watch the two fuck. Brandon never knew what to expect, but he was always up for the challenge.

After he was dressed in costume—wings strapped to his broad back, mask on his face, and a thin cloth covering his unmentionables—he took a look at himself in the full-length mirror propped unnaturally between a small table and the wall. Indeed, he had the face of an angel and the body of a god. He turned from side to side to get a view of himself at every angle.

And Brandon saw that it was good.

Once he finished admiring his form, he made his way over to the door leading to the basement. He paused, just long enough to get himself together. He didn't know what he was about to walk into but based on the costume alone, it was sure to be an interesting night. This client was known for his bizarre fantasies.

He placed his hand on the knob and pushed the door open. Immediately, he was greeted by the thick smell of marijuana and funk. With extreme caution and care, he took his first step and the old wooden staircase leading to the bowels of hell creaked with agony beneath his heavy feet. He took a few more steps. His pulse quickened, as did his breathing, as he slowly descended into a maddening darkness. Moans and sighs rose from the depths and beckoned to him like the nefarious sirens that he had learned about in class whose sweet music enticed mariners to their ultimate demise.

He reached the bottom of the staircase in almost complete darkness and gave praise that the staircase didn't collapse and send him hurling to the bottom. He stood motionless for a moment, in order to acclimate himself to this brave new environment. A thick, dry heat immediately wrapped itself around him and he could feel beads of sweat already forming on his forehead. He looked to his left and saw a crimson glow sneaking out from the edges of another room—the room from which he heard deepening moans. Like Carol Anne, he too, went toward the light.

He opened the door and stepped boldly into the room, even as the warning in his heart told him to otherwise. He was excited and thrilled and scared and prayerful that this experience would give him the pleasure he sought. His purpose tonight was beyond rabid carnal desire; he sought to blunt out the force of artificial memories and to create his own existence. Drugs, alcohol, and extreme sex would anesthetize his imagined pain and joy would come in the morning.

His eyes took a moment to adjust to the pulsing red glow from the lights that hung from the ceiling. As he focused, writhing and slithering naked bodies came into full view. Men of all sizes and shapes were scattered throughout the room and were engaged in various sexual acts. Legs parted like church gates and heels pointed heavenward like steeples; mouths called out for forgiveness and the slapping sound of flesh upon flesh rang in Brandon's ears.

He continued to survey the room, which was sparsely furnished, except for a tattered loveseat in the corner and a leather swing that was in use by a wild pair who did not pause or slow their rough grind. They simply looked up at Brandon as he moved slowly about the carnivorous space. Various devices and sexual gadgets were strewn about, as if there had been little time to return the articles to their proper place. Brandon looked to his right and noticed an oversized wheel with velvet straps laying dormant in one of the more ominous corners of the cave. It waited, it beckoned; it waited to be used.

Brandon stepped deeper into the room and almost as if on cue, all of the men—regardless of how *close* they were to release—stopped their sex games and surrounded him. Like Pavlov's dogs, they salivated at the sight of fresh meat. They, completely naked and some fully erect, circled him, trying to size up their prey; they sniffed him and eyed him up and down as if he was meat on a bone. They licked their lips and barked at him in deep, husky voices that fanned out in all directions in the pit. They, too, were masked but wore wings of a darker hue; pointed horns jetted out from the sides of their heads. A ghoulish grin formed on Brandon's face as these devils reached out to him and corrupted his pretty young flesh. Countless hands rubbed his body and poked and prodded him. Their hands were moist and their bodies sweaty and they rubbed his body with a peculiar kind of flesh worship. His breathing quickened as he felt a wet mouth latch onto each of his hardened nipples. They sucked and pulled and bit and licked on him and their efforts gave rise to Brandon's massive erection.

Soon, he felt a mouth toying with the head of his dick as another one licked at his low-hanging balls. He felt aggressive tongues and sharp teeth and wet lips on each side of his neck and another forked tongue darted between his cheeks. Brandon had never known such ecstasy. He eagerly embraced the righteous pleasure, mixed with a divine pain, which forced him to scream out. Weakened by the intense sensations that spread across every inch of his body, he struggled to stand. Never before had he buckled under the weight of pleasure, but he felt weak and wobbly and his groupies, sensing his plight, supported his weight as they continued their nonstop sexual assault. They ravaged his body and devoured everything he had to offer; they tore at his flesh with tongues, teeth, fingers, lips and dicks while Brandon cried out... with pleasure.

Out of the corner of his eye, he saw a menacing presence approaching him, dressed in what appeared to be a shiny black robe. Based on the way he walked and his sizeable build, Brandon surmised that it was his benefactor. Brandon closed his eyes and bit down hard on his lip as the pleasure he felt built up inside of him and threatened to burst. The masked benefactor stepped with authority to Brandon and put a drink to the youngster's lips. The strong taste of an even stronger alcoholic beverage filled Brandon's mouth. He tried to drink the potion like a shot, but he couldn't take it all into his mouth and much of the brown liquid spilled down his chin and raced down his now sweaty body. The devils, eager with their tongues, frantically licked up the spilling liquid that poured from Brandon's mouth and raced down his chin, neck, and torso. Their desire to taste him prevented even the slightest drop from going to waste. Greedily, they licked his body and coated him with their sticky saliva. Their tongues fought each other for every drop!

Brandon watched the benefactor move back to his corner. He pushed open his robe and started to gratify himself at the perverse sight of this young angel being consumed by his hell hounds.

As the devils worshipped their fallen angel, a bell—as clear as day—rang out in the cramped space and the fiends parted from

Brandon and fell back into their respective corners; they waited. They waited for the main attraction. From behind a curtain in the far corner of the room, a behemoth emerged wearing nothing but a pair of thick utility boots on his heavy feet. He was the only one without a mask and his striking facial features looked to be carved from granite. His lips were curled in the corners in a permanent scowl to match the permanent scar that ran the length of the right side of his face. His dark eyes offered no emotion. They were simply black pools and the giant cast a dark shadow across the room. The Herculean figure suddenly stood before Brandon, erect and motionless. In two steps, he had conquered the distance of the room. He eyed Brandon from head to toe and licked his lips with a twisted delight. The beast reeked of cigarettes, gin, and sweaty sex funk. The man was all brawn and power, with muscles on top of muscles, and he heaved like each breath was a struggle. Brandon watched his muscles flex as his chest expanded with each deep inhalation. It sounded as if he was trying to suck all of the air out of the room and suffocate the whole lot of them in the underground chamber.

Brandon matched his stare—he was not one to yield. He smiled. This was just what he needed. He looked in the direction of his benefactor and saw his dark face in the shadows; he nodded his head in approval. Brandon smiled again, acquiescing to what was to come. High on weed, cocaine, and a strange beverage that lingered in his mouth, he displayed no fear, not even when the beast's dick engorged to the size of a small log.

"I am not afraid of you," he said defiantly. Brandon's voice emitted a fearlessness that contradicted the hesitation in his heart. In that moment, when he should have been deciding between fight or flight, he decided to give in to his base desires, even while the ball tightened in the pit of his stomach. He convinced himself that he was a man of steel, impervious to pain; yet, he swallowed hard. This hulk of a man may have been more than he bargained for, but he would certainly make the evening memorable, if Brandon survived his assault.

Brandon looked around the room and watched all of the imps slowly stroke themselves in anticipation of the main event. They cackled and cooed, calling out for their own satisfaction.

Brandon stepped closer to the monster, looked directly into his eyes, and spoke clearly.

"Fuck me like you own me."

CHAPTER 5

After the effects of drugs, sex, and alcohol wore off, Brandon was left with the dried memories of dangerous dicks dancing around his body. He drove recklessly and furiously down the dark highways, weaving erratically down the road, trying to get home as soon as he could. His skin burned and ached for a long, hot shower to wash away the residue of an evening that had already burned itself into the darkest place in his soul. Regardless of how hard he pressed his heavy foot on the accelerator, he could not go fast enough, or arrive soon enough to suit him.

When he finally did arrive, he wasted little time. He pulled into the garage and tore through the house like a track star, tearing clothes off as he ran down long corridors, leaving behind a trail composed of socks, his underwear, and his soiled T-shirt. He jetted up the staircase and down the hall until he reached his room. By the time he entered his room, he was completely naked and sped headfirst into the bathroom like a sprinter. He leapt into the walk-in shower and turned on the water, not caring if the first blast caused his skin to freeze or melt. He grabbed his favorite scented soap and lathered it onto his loofah sponge. As the water warmed and the steam rose high, he scrubbed. He scrubbed like he hadn't showered in days. He scrubbed his face and neck and chest and legs with force and vigor, but he couldn't wash away the feel of the grubby hands of faceless fiends clawing at him, nor could he cleanse the smell of sweaty sex funk, gin, and musty balls from the giant who had delivered such exquisite pain. A part of him wanted to forget.

Yet, a part of him wanted to remember it all.

He leaned against the shower wall and slid down to the floor, letting the water pour over his beautifully brutalized body. As he pulled his knees into his chest and let the warm water wash over him, he came to an understanding and a decision; an irrefutable truth remained after the dirt and grime and sweat and spit and cum stains washed down the drain. It was a truth he had always known in his heart. He sometimes tried to deny it, tried to protest and fight against it, but his anemic attempts at denial had no force or weight. He tilted his head up and let the water cover his face and thought back to his sexual experience.

The smell of the basement.

The hounds.

The monster.

The benefactor.

The money.

He thought about the filth and the grime and the hard grind and the perversion and the pleasure.

And, he smiled.

He had enjoyed it.

In that cleansing moment in the shower, he decided to stop pretending. He decided to stop acting as if he was bothered by his depraved nature. As the water washed away that thin covering, he decided to embrace the trueness of his nature. He no longer would pretend that he didn't enjoy his tricks. He would not pretend to feel unclean as he left the beds many of them shared with their husbands or wives or lovers or partners. His newfound truth gave him power. From now on, he would revel in his *gifts* and continue to build his bank account. He never whored himself solely for the money, but for the feeling he received; there was something delightfully wicked about the exchange of cash for sex. Now, he could stop pretending the money he received from being a rent boy meant nothing.

He thought about the first online ad he had placed on a popular escort site. He had done it for fun, to see what kind of response he would get. He remembered setting his digital camera to automatic and taking highly sexual and provocative photos that gave glimpses of his best assets. He was careful not to show his face in any of the online images, but he showed enough muscle and skin that within the first hour of the posting, he had received twenty-five inquiries, all of whom claimed to be ready and willing to meet his initial asking price of $500—a price he considered exorbitant— to be fucked by Brandon. He had been fucking for free for years and now he had taken his father's advice to heart: always know your worth. He remembered giggling at the thought of fulfilling some rich man's Mandingo fantasy and making some quick and easy cash. Soon, he doubled his asking price and went on a fucking spree that quickly became legendary on the site.

Sitting in the shower, he claimed his narcissism. He loved the hands and the lips and the erections he caused. He loved being paid for his services. He loved naming his price. He loved giving pleasure. He loved being pleasured. He loved the look on the faces of the tricks that he serviced. He loved the anticipation of that first meeting with them. He loved the butterflies that fluttered wildly in his stomach right before he got the first glimpse of their glorious cocks. He loved when he was close enough to their pricks that their man-scent filled his nostrils. He loved seeing the twisted faces they made when he first tasted them or delivered orgasm after orgasm to them. He loved having that power. And, he loved the feel of the money in his hands. *Money that he earned.*

After he finished showering and basking in his newfound self-appreciation, he dried off and wrapped a towel around his body and then stepped into his room. He was about to light up a joint when the sound of the ringing house phone startled him. He moved over to the nightstand and looked at the caller ID. It was his mother. He curled his lip in disgust, lit his joint, and inhaled.

CHAPTER 6

"Brandon, could I see you after class?" Cross asked as the bell sounded, signaling the end of yet another class and another week. Friday had once again arrived, bringing an excitement to the students as they left the room. Brandon followed the rest of the class and moved slowly between the rows of desks before plopping down in an empty seat on the front row. Cross's words may have formed a question, but the command in his voice did not go unnoticed, so Brandon sat and waited. *Eagerly.* His classmates moved slowly and leisurely out of the room, as if it wasn't the last class of the day. Brandon mumbled something under his breath and shifted his weight uneasily in his seat.

"I asked you to stay after class so that we can talk," he said after the last student had left the room. The concern in Cross's voice peppered his words and an unusual scowl crinkled his brow. He moved from behind his desk and took his place on the edge of the desk so that he could look directly into Brandon's wide eyes. "What's going on with you? All this week you've been somewhere else. I'm concerned. Are you okay? "

"I'm fine."

"Brandon, you failed my quiz. You're not fine. This score shows you didn't even try." Brandon, leaning back in the desk on the front row, stared blankly into space as if Cross's words didn't warrant a response. "Do you hear me talking to you?"

"Yeah, man, I just don't have an answer. I don't know what to tell you."

Cross looked at the loopy expression on Brandon's face and the drag in his eyes. "Brandon, are you high?" he asked with sudden astonishment.

"What? Nah. I'm just really tired. I haven't gotten much sleep this week; it's been rough. You know; dead brother and all."

"I can imagine," Cross said, trying to soften his tone. "How have your parents been?'

"Don't know. They haven't come back."

"Really? They've been gone more than a week."

Brandon snickered. "A week is nothing for them. I'll be lucky if they came back before my graduation."

"I think you should talk to someone. Maybe the counselor?"

"Cross, have you seen Ms. Stewart? She wouldn't know her head from a hole in a wall." Cross let the slip of his first name go without mention in light of the weight of their subject.

"Look, Brandon. I'm worried about you. You have a full scholarship, but you still have to pass my class. I don't want you messing up your future. I know you were going through some things—"

"You have no idea."

"I know, I know, but as I told you on last Friday, I'm here for you. If you don't want to talk to the counselor, you can always talk to me. Let me help you."

"You can't help me, Mr. Jones. I'm beyond help."

"What makes you say that?"

"I just know it. I'm not who you think I am. I'm the bad seed," Brandon said with a sneer.

Cross moved closer to Brandon and took a seat in the desk right next to him. "You're too young to be this cynical. I know this past weekend and week must've been rough for you, but I don't want you throwing away your life and your future. I know you loved your brother, but you can't keep living in the past."

Brandon turned and faced Cross and looked into his eyes.

"Do you really care about me? I mean, what happens to me?" Brandon's eyes widened and he leaned in closer to Cross, almost as if he was afraid that Cross's words would be lost in the space between the desks.

"Yes, I do. You are a bright young man with a lot of potential. You can go on to do great things; you can't let what's going on in your life right screw up your future."

Brandon snickered like a little boy. "I've already been screwed." Brandon's double entendre wasn't lost on Cross.

"This isn't a joke, Brandon. I need you to get serious. I'm here if you ever wanna talk." Cross reached across the aisle and placed a comforting hand on Brandon's shoulder.

"Hey, Cross," a voice called out from the front of the room. Standing near the door at the front of the room was Raul Walker, the teacher next door. "Oh, I'm sorry, I didn't realize you were… busy."

"I gotta go," Brandon blurted out.

He suddenly stood up, grabbed his bag, and bolted out of the room, passing quickly by Raul. Cross didn't protest, but sighed at Mr. Walker's timing.

"Are you okay, Cross?"

"Yeah, I'm just worried about him." Cross got up and moved over to his desk. "What's going on?"

"I stopped by to see if you had spoken to Ms. Gil about chaperoning the dance next weekend, but I see you have something else going on here."

Cross paused and pondered his words; they didn't sit well in his spirit.

"What does that mean?"

"It's nothing."

"It didn't sound like nothing."

Mr. Walker stepped into the room and closed the door behind him. "I'm just saying you have to be careful with these students nowadays, if you know what I mean."

"I'm afraid I don't know. Why don't you enlighten me?"

"Look, Cross, I'm not trying to start anything, but this is your first year teaching and I'd hate to see you getting in over your head. I've noticed that Brandon spends an unusual amount of time with you after class. And, people talk. I've seen many a reputation ruined because a student makes an accusation."

"Are you accusing me of something?"

"No, not all. Don't get defensive. I know you better than that. I'm simply cautioning you. Be careful with that one. He has a history."

"A history of what?"

"Of being…a little…unstable."

"Unstable?"

"Yes, unstable."

"Raul, I don't have a lot of time for riddles. What the hell are you talking about?"

"Cross, this is a high school. There are all kinds of rumors flying around here all the time. A rumor can travel halfway around the world before the truth has time to lace its shoes. Just be careful. Once things are said, they can never be unsaid."

"I have no control over any lie that anyone might come up with because I'm helping a student. If Brandon is a little unstable, then don't you think it is up to us to provide him, or any other student, with a foundation for support?"

"Ahhh, spoken like a novice teacher. Cross, I like you. You're an excellent teacher, but you need to learn that you can't get caught up in the personal lives of these kids."

"I'm not getting caught up. I have only the best intentions for Brandon."

"The road to hell is paved with good intentions. Just be careful." With those cryptic words, Raul smiled and walked out of the room.

✪ ✪ ✪

Hours later, Brandon stood outside on the porch for a few moments, trying to pull his act together. He planned on a legendary performance tonight that would get what he needed from Cross. Tonight was the night he'd make his move. He rubbed his eyes with his hands in an effort to redden them, even though the powerful Jamaican weed that he smoked earlier had already done the job. Standing on the porch with his shoulders slumped, he prepared himself. The way he looked down at the ground, the lack of confidence in his posture, and the sullen expression engraved across his face gave the impression that he was going through some deep-seated emotional issues. And, that's exactly the impression he wanted to give. He wanted Cross's sympathy and his support.

He looked at his watch. It was almost midnight, close to the bewitching hour. The air outside was still and the night was silent. No cars. No crickets. Just silence. He felt emboldened by the night, as if there wasn't anything he couldn't do. He was supernatural, able to fly and bend objects with his mind; he could command fire and earth and conquer any friend or foe; he could turn day into night and steal stars from the heavens, but could he cast the right spell tonight to claim his prize?

He inhaled deeply and rang the doorbell.

No answer.

He rang it again. Still, no answer or sound.

His hands began to sweat.

He rang the doorbell again and tried to subdue the anxiety that was rising within him. He put his hand on the doorknob and was surprised when it turned. Slowly, he pushed it open and stepped inside the room, his heart beating a mile a minute. He closed the door behind him and stood still, afraid to move. *Why hadn't Cross answered the door?* he asked himself. As he stood in the foyer completely motionless and barely breathing, it dawned on him that Cross may not be alone. What if some dude was here? What if they were upstairs doing *it* right now? The thought of Cross wrapped in another's arms felt like a hard slap against his face and anger suddenly swelled his chest. He needed to get out of there, get some air before he did something crazy. Just as he turned and opened the door to flee, he heard his name being called out.

"Brandon? Is that you?" He froze, hoping his superpowers would make him invisible, but he had no such luck. "What are you doing here?" Cross asked in a voice far stronger than Brandon had known from him.

Brandon had lost his nerves and now felt the pressure of his transgression weighing heavily upon his chest. Gone was the bravado that colored his thoughts and made him feel like Superman. No longer did he have the strength of a dozen men or the courage of a battalion. Slowly, Brandon turned around, as if in slow motion, but when his eyes landed on Cross, he wasn't quite prepared for the image that stood before him. Cross stood before him, chest heaving and dripping wet, wearing nothing but a blue towel wrapped around his waist. The moisture on his body caused his skin to glisten and shine, giving him a sleek and seductive look. Brandon eyed the spider tattooed on the left side of his chest and the silver ring that adorned his right nipple. As his eyes made their way down his taut body, he salivated at the tattoo of the pistol on the lower right side of his waist, the barrel pointing at his crotch.

Brandon prayed the towel would fall to the floor and leave Cross standing before him in all his naked glory. He suspected the man had a great body, but never in his wildest dreams did he imagine that he was flawless.

"Brandon," he said with more concern than anger, "what's going on? How did you get in here? How did you know where I live?"

"I'm...sorry. I Googled you," he said as his head hung low. "And, the door...was open. I...I mean, I rang the bell. I'll go; I shouldn't have come." Brandon turned and pretended as if he was leaving. *Please stop me.*

"Brandon, wait," he said as he leapt forward to intercept. "What's wrong? You look terrible. What's going on?" Cross took Brandon by the arm as he closed the door. "For real, what's going on?"

"I was at home, alone, and I started hearing...things...like my brother's voice. I thought I saw him a couple of times in the house. I know it sounds crazy; he's dead but it felt like he was in the house. It freaked me out. I couldn't be alone. I didn't know where else to go. I shouldn't have come here. I'm sorry; I'll leave now." Brandon turned around dramatically and faced the door as if he was about to leave.

"Brandon, sit down. I'm glad you came. I told you that you can always talk to me. Tell you what, let me go upstairs and put some clothes on. Then, we can talk."

"You sure? I mean, I don't want to interrupt your evening."

"You're not interrupting, but the next time you need to talk, you definitely should call first."

Brandon smiled secretly and then turned away from the door. "Okay."

Cross moved toward the staircase and Brandon watched as his glistening body faded out of view.

Playing the dead brother card works every time.

Brandon moved over to the couch, took a seat and stretched his long arms along the edge of the couch possessively, smiling wildly, as he eyed the room. The deep wood, blooming plants and small figurines of exotic animals placed decoratively around the open space made the room feel like the Serengeti; mysterious, magical—dangerous. Brandon felt in the zone, in his element, and he was ready to claim the spoils of victory. He had been here before, but this time it felt like he belonged.

He stood up and eyed the lay of the land while admiring Cross's decorating talents. Oddly, Brandon took a sense of pride in the décor, as if it he had something to do with the design of the interior. He began to strut regally around the room, with his head held high as he carefully took notice of the details. He moved over to the bookshelf and read off a couple titles—something about a learned man turned him on. He ran his fingers along the spine of several books before moving over to the table and slowly perusing the DVDs that lay across the coffee table. He picked up and leisurely leafed through a magazine that was strewn on the couch. He looked around the room and felt a sense of belonging, of ownership, and envisioned what it would feel like to share this castle; he wanted to take his rightful place at the side of his prince; he wanted dominion over this castle and together they could rule the land, side by side.

"Brandon?" Cross's voice fluttered delicately across Brandon's ears. When he focused, he saw Cross standing before him in a pair of sweatpants and a white T-shirt, looking as edible as a piece of Godiva chocolate. He could see his nipples poking through the cotton shirt. "Why don't you take a seat? Let me get you something to drink."

Cross disappeared and returned quickly with a glass of orange juice.

"Any vodka in this?" Brandon asked with an impish grin. Cross twisted his lips and took a seat in the chair across from where Brandon sat. "I'll take that as a no."

"You're a little young for vodka."

"I'm not a baby. I'm eighteen now."

"And the drinking age is twenty-one, the last time I checked." Cross leaned back in his chair and sipped on his cup of orange juice. "Why don't you tell me what's going on?"

Brandon sipped his cup of juice and began the delicate task of spinning haunting stories of loneliness and fear. His voice quaked and small beads of sweat formed on his forehead as he recalled his imaginary paranormal experience by his phantom sibling. Brandon's story, full of hyperbole, floated across the room and he watched Cross, who listened intently to him as he spun his tall tales. Speaking through his forked tongue, Brandon spoke with such deceptive conviction that he could have coaxed that man to eat forbidden fruit from the tree in the garden. He sensed the concern in Cross's voice and hoped his fake outpouring of emotion would engender a tender response from Cross. More than anything, he wanted Cross to take a seat on the couch next to him and comfort him with his manly ways; instead, Cross remained in his chair, sipping his drink and offering words of compassion. Brandon leaned back deep into the folds of the couch and closed his eyes, pretending that the pain had become too great to continue. He spread his long, sinewy legs wide. The pair of shorts he wore revealed the stone-like features of his powerful trunks. His thighs, golden brown and virtually hairless, seemed to stretch endlessly into the depths of the night. He hoped his not-so-subtle invitation would be well-received. He wasn't wearing any underwear and could feel a cool air creeping its way up his crotch. When he opened his eyes, he caught Cross staring—or so he thought—

his eyes following the path from Brandon's calves to his thighs to the pleasure zone.

Got him.

Cross suddenly looked away and stood up. He moved behind Brandon and over into the kitchen area.

"Brandon, you really need to talk to your parents about how you're feeling. They can't help you, or get you some help, if they don't know what you're going through."

"Don't you get it?" he said as he rose quickly in mock indignation. "They don't care about me. I am not my brother. They loved him; they don't give a fuck about me."

"You can't be sure of that."

"Yes, I can. I can *feel* it. They ain't never around and when they are, they never talk to me. When they look at me, it's like they're looking right through me. Trust me; I get no love from them. Fuck Julia and William."

Suddenly, tears began to flow down Brandon's face; it was as if his emotions had breached a great levee and his pain had spilled out. Gone were the crocodile tears that he used as a ploy to lure Cross into his web. The tears that streamed down his face were the result of an imagined pain so perfectly envisioned that it had become almost a permanent part of Brandon's disposition. The severity of his tears shocked him. He didn't know he could cry so hard on cue.

And so, the greatest pretender of them all put forth his greatest performance. He, who had grown masterful at pretense and sub-terfuge, found himself weeping. This perfect chameleon, who had convinced himself that he could always hide his true nature in plain sight, worked this moment. His machinations would win the night, or so he hoped.

Alone.

Cross took a seat next to him and pulled him into his arms, but his sheltering arms couldn't stop the pain.

Cross held the shaking child in his arms, with his head planted firmly on his shoulder. Brandon's entire body, usually as firm and strong as aged oak, was hobbled in concert with the ploy.

"I'm so sorry. There I go again, crying like a little girl," he said as he pulled away. "You must think I'm a freak. All I've done the last two weeks is cry."

"It's okay for a man to cry. We have pain, too. Crying doesn't make you weak."

Brandon wiped the tears from his face. "Tell that to my father."

"Your father ain't here."

Brandon found something comforting in the brown eyes of Cross as he stared into them; he felt mesmerized by their purity and beauty. The air they shared became charged with something more than grief and empathy. Brandon felt it; it was like fire in his bones and he hoped Cross felt it, too. No, he was sure that Cross felt it. He could see it in his eyes. This man cared for him—maybe even loved him. Then, Brandon went for it. He leaned in quickly and planted his moist lips on Cross, causing a reaction from Cross that he hadn't anticipated. Cross leapt up from the couch as if he had touched something so hot that it burned more than his skin.

"Brandon! What the hell do you think you're doing?" he exclaimed.

"Cross, I'm sorry. I didn't mean to—"

"You need to leave…now!" Cross's eyes tightened into hardened beads and his whole face sunk into itself.

"Mr. Jones, please—"

"Brandon, what have you done?" The hurt in Cross's voice stung Brandon's ears. "First, you show up at my house unannounced when I invited you only to call if you needed someone to talk to. Then, you pull this shit. This is not okay!"

"I know, I know. I made a mistake. It's just you were being so kind to me I thought…most men who are nice to me want to…and I thought you wanted to…"

"To what? To have sex with you? Have you lost your damn mind?"

"You told me that you cared about me."

"And I do; just not in that way. Brandon, you need some help."

"Are you going to call my parents? Please, don't do that. You don't know my dad. You don't know what he'll do to me."

Cross paused. "What are you saying?" Brandon pointed at a small, circular dark scar on his right forearm. "What is that?"

"A cigar burn. I got that on Christmas two years ago and what a merry Christmas it was."

Cross took a deep breath and eyed the mark.

"Brandon, if what you're saying is true, then we need to get you some help."

Brandon's tone changed from frantic to solemn. "I don't need help. I can handle it, but if you tell anyone about this, I'll have to run away because my dad will kill me. You can't protect me. The school can't protect me. I swear to God, if you tell, I'll leave and no one will ever see me again." Brandon's words latched onto Cross like a noose around the neck. "I am sorry for what I did. I really am." Before Cross could utter another word, Brandon had moved to the front door and had his hand on the knob. He paused, with his back to the Cross. "I'll die if you tell anyone. I'll die."

✪ ✪ ✪

Brandon stepped out and closed the door behind him. His quest to conquer had ended abruptly and badly. He stood on the porch and contemplated his next move. He was sure that Cross would not tell anyone about their kiss; he could see that much in Cross's eyes. He could tell that Cross believed his lies about his father and his threat to run away or die and he knew that Cross wouldn't risk that, but he didn't know what Cross would do next. The burn mark played perfectly into his story of abuse. On the Christmas in question, he had purposely burned himself with a cigarette just to see if he could withstand the pain.

In spite of this major setback, Brandon remained undeterred in his quest. He still had to have Cross. It may take a little longer and he'd have to be a bit more clever, but it would be done. Besides, he had gotten his first taste of Cross and it was sweet; the night was not a complete loss.

And, in that brief moment when lips met lips, he had *felt* something in Cross stir.

"It's just a matter of time," he said to himself as he opened his car door and stepped into his black Dodge Charger with the big rims and dark, tinted windows. He popped the key in the ignition and shuffled the CDs around in the changer. He needed to hear something pounding—something hard-hitting to take the edge off. He pressed "play" and soon the beat pumped through his sound system and he bobbed his head back and forth in rhythm.

He loved Cross's fiery display of righteous indignation and, *when* the time came that they would be naked together, that same fire would fuel their ecstasy and take them both to new heights. Brandon's desire and determination remained undeterred and through Cross's pretend protests, he could see that Cross was attracted to him, even if he was afraid to admit it. The constant desire in Cross's eyes betrayed the protest on his lips. *He would have Cross.* He was ready to pay any price, bear any burden, and make any sacrifice to conquer him.

CHAPTER 7

Cross stood in the middle room, stunned into immobility and watched Brandon dart out of his house. This bizarre evening had ended even more bizarrely. First, Brandon shows up at his house unexpectedly and then tries to seduce him—Cross hadn't seen this coming. Even in his wildest dreams, he couldn't imagine that Brandon would step so boldly across the line. Sure, in the recesses of his mind, he had always suspected that Brandon had a small, harmless crush on him; it was not uncommon for students to connect with a teacher. Cross wondered was there something in his behavior that had elicited this reaction from Brandon? Had he done something, said something that was inappropriate?

When he was finally able to move, he walked over to the door and bolted the lock, hoping to keep out any more interlopers. Cross had a careless habit of locking the door but not arming his alarm system. This time, however, he armed it as a precaution and walked over to the kitchen. He picked up the phone and dialed.

"'Sup, Cross? What's going on?" Lorenzo said when he picked up after a few rings.

"Not much. Just sitting at home bored," he lied.

"Geesh, when are you going to get out and live a little? You're gonna look up one day and find that life has passed you by."

"Can you just back off a bit? Every time we talk, you say the same shit. Give it a rest. Damn—"

Cross's words punched with the force of a man who had reached his limit. He took umbrage at Lorenzo's incessant needling and criticisms of his life. Tonight was certainly not the night for Lorenzo's jabs.

"My bad, Cross. I was only joking. Shit."

"Your joke is getting old." An awkward silence settled on the line, forcing both men to retreat a bit. Finally, Lorenzo broke the silence.

"Okay, something is going on; I haven't heard you sound so pissed off in months. Instead of biting my head off, why don't you tell me what's wrong?"

Cross inhaled deeply and tried to gather his thoughts. There was a part of him that leaned toward full disclosure, but his cautious nature suspected that, instead of support, he'd only get judgment and condemnation. Somehow, Lorenzo would twist the scenario around and make Cross feel as if he was the one that had erred.

"It's been a rough day; that's all."

"The kids are driving you crazy, aren't they? See, I knew this teaching shit would get on your nerves sooner or later. What happened? Did one of them cuss you out? Threaten you? Steal from you?"

"No, no, and no. It's nothing like that."

"One of those country boys roll up on you?" he said with a laugh. Then, there was silence again on the phone. "Cross...Cross? You there?"

"Yeah, I'm here."

"Shit. You didn't answer my last question. Did some little girl try to run up on you? Or, was it some little boy?"

"He's far from a little boy; trust me."

"Oh fuck, what happened?"

Cross wanted to hold his tongue out of fear of censure, but the sound of a familiar voice began to coax the truth out of him.

"Well," he began softly, "one of my students has been having some serious issues with his parents and dealing with the death of his brother. I've noticed lately that he's distracted and his grades have been falling. I gave him my number to call me over the weekend, in case he needed to talk. I mean, this kid has a lot of potential, and I'm really worried about him. It would be a shame if he messed up so close to graduation. I wanted to make sure that he knew that he had someone who would listen when he needed to talk."

"What's wrong with his parents? Why can't he talk to them?"

"He said they've been out of town for a long time and even when they're home, they don't listen to him. Anyway, tonight I was upstairs in the shower when I heard my doorbell ring. I came downstairs and found him standing in the foyer."

"What, he showed up at your house? How did he get in? How the hell did he know where you live?" The shock in Lorenzo's voice rang out like an alarm in the still of night.

"I left the door unlocked and it's not hard to find out an address nowadays. When I came downstairs, he was standing there. He looked a mess. Something was wrong so I told him to come in."

"Pleaaaase, tell me you didn't invite that child into your house!"

"Stop screaming. He needed help. You should have seen the look on his face. His eyes were wild, kinda like he was high. What was I supposed to do?"

"You were supposed to call somebody. Isn't there a protocol for shit like this?"

"If there is, I don't know what it is. I only wanted to help the boy; find out what was wrong."

"And did you?"

"Did I what?"

"Did you find out what was wrong with him?"

"Yeah, while he was telling me the story, he kinda…kissed me."

"Oh. My. God! He did what?"

"He kissed me, but he was confused. He was looking for someone to love him and he got his feelings mixed up."

"Oh, hell no. You stop acting like some therapist. You are a writer; not a doctor. You don't know what that boy was thinking. For all you know, he could've planned the entire thing. You need to get on the phone right now and call somebody, his parents, the principal...somebody...now!"

"I'm not sure I can do that."

"Why the hell not?"

"He said that if his dad found out what happened, he'd kill him or he'd run away. I can't have that on my conscience."

"Are you serious? That boy is probably playing you like a fucking fiddle. Cross, you are smarter than this. Don't fall for this game."

"You didn't see the fear in his eyes, or the sound of his voice. He was truly scared. And, don't you think I recognize when I'm being played. I'm not as naïve as you think I am."

"You are not responsible for this boy; this child. If you think there is some merit to what he said, then clearly he doesn't need to be in the house with this father. You need to call social services or something. You can't handle this yourself."

Cross closed his eyes and began tuning out the hysteria that had taken full control of Lorenzo. Just as he suspected in the beginning, he regretted this conversation. He shouldn't have confessed his secret. Lorenzo's speaking had gone from 0 to 60 in 5.5 seconds and he barked out an endless chain of *you-need-tos* and *you-should've-known-betters*. Now, not only did he have to deal with Brandon, but he had to deal with Lorenzo's tirades.

"Cross! Cross! Do you hear me?"

"Yeah; it's kinda hard not to, with you screaming in my ear."

"Don't be an ass. I'm trying to save you. I'm not the one having an affair with a child."

"We're not having an affair!"

"That may be true, but wait until the rumors start. If you don't handle this and the word gets out, not only will it ruin your little teaching career, but your writing career will be over, too! Your face will be plastered across every newspaper from here to Timbuktu. I can see the headlines now: Bestselling author Cross Jones caught in illicit affair with a male high school student. Your book sales will sink faster than the Titanic."

"Don't you think you're being a bit dramatic?"

"Not at all. Don't you think you're being too calm? You write books for teenagers. What do you think will happen to your career when the book-buying public gets word that you're using your status to seduce teenaged boys?

"That's not what happened."

"Doesn't matter. That's what the story will be. The media will crucify you. Cross, you need to handle this and don't try to be Superman and save the world. You need to save yourself."

"Whatever. I'll talk to you later."

Cross hung up the phone without giving Lorenzo a second to respond. Before he could put the phone back on its base, it rang again. Lorenzo was calling back, but Cross had had enough of him for one night. His ears could not take one more jab.

Cross rubbed his hands with his face. In his heart, he realized that Lorenzo was right. It was all about CYA—covering your ass. This incendiary situation certainly had the potential to burn down the entire house and his career. Then, he thought about Brandon's haunting words: "I'll die if you tell anyone." Cross was at a complete loss. Part of him wanted to help—to protect this boy from whatever demons haunted him—but another part of him agreed fully with Lorenzo. It wasn't his responsibility.

But, doesn't it take the whole village to raise a child?

CHAPTER 8

Cross was awakened by the brightness of the room. The night had passed, giving way to a beautiful spring morning. The sun's glimmering rays filled the room and caused him to stir. He followed his usual Saturday morning routine. He got up, turned on the television to crack open the silence that enveloped the house, and scrambled downstairs for a cup of orange juice. After about half an hour, the soles of his Nikes hit the pavement as he started his three-mile run. He didn't feel like going to the gym so he decided to change up his routine and jog instead. After the run, he came home, showered, ate a bowl of oatmeal with blueberries, and ran some errands, which included picking up fresh fruits and vegetables from the open air market right in the center of town. He returned, cooked lunch, and rested a bit before catching the latest movie at the Cineplex. He busied himself so that he wouldn't have to think about his troubles. He wanted all thoughts of Brandon out of his head.

Later that evening, after he finished staring at his computer trying to finish his novel, Cross settled in for the long, quiet evening at home. He readied himself for a *True Blood* marathon on HBO as the phone rang. He reached over and grabbed the phone off the hook before checking the caller ID.

"It's Saturday night and something tells me that you are stretched out across the couch. I want you to get your ass up and get out of the damn house. Go out and have a drink, meet a man, and have wild sex!"

"Lorenzo? What do you want now? Why are you harassing me...again?"

"I am calling because I am your savior, arriving just in time to resurrect your social life. And, I wanted to apologize. Maybe I was a bit hard on you last night. I know you have this S on your chest and you feel like you can save the world. Maybe you can help this boy; you just have to be careful how you do it. You're my best friend and I worry about you; that's all."

"I appreciate your thoughts and your apology. I'm sorry, too."

"Cool. Now that we got all that shit out of the way, what are you doing?"

"Having a glass of wine and watching TV." The sound of the doorbell ringing broke up their conversation.

"Hold on, Lorenzo; somebody's at my door."

"Oooooh, you have company. I hope it's a fine man." Cross tossed the phone onto the couch and dashed over to the door. When he looked through the peephole, he didn't see anyone, but he opened the door anyway.

As soon as the door swung open, Lorenzo jumped out and grabbed him playfully.

"Lorenzo, what the fuck are you doing? You scared the hell out of me!" Cross pushed him away hard, but his anger quickly gave way to happiness. "What the hell are you doing here, besides trying to give me a heart attack?"

Lorenzo draped his arms around Cross's shoulder and led him back into the house, suitcase in tow.

"Have you lost all of your New York instincts living down here in the country? Never open your door unless you know who's on the other side. I could have been a serial killer."

"Yeah, yeah, yeah; that still doesn't explain what you're doing here."

"Do I have to have a reason to visit my best friend?" He dropped his luggage.

Cross eyed the bag and then looked back up at Lorenzo. "No, but a little notice would be nice."

"Why? You ain't doing shit. After our conversation last night, I figured I'd come down here and help you out, or at least take you out for some fun." Lorenzo moved deeper into the house, looking around as if it were the first time he'd been there. "Wow, I like what you did to the place. I see you got rid of the carpet and added hardwood floors." Cross walked behind Lorenzo, who moved about the room like an inspector, scrutinizing every inch of the area, looking for the one piece of evidence that would solve his case. "You've redone the entire place and you didn't tell me."

"I needed a project."

"You need a life, but you've done good, little one; you've done good with the redecoration," Lorenzo said with laughter.

They moved into the den where Cross had previously set up camp.

"Why don't you pour me a glass of whatever you're drinking?"

Cross pulled a glass from the cabinet and poured a glass.

"You've been checking out my house, now it's my turn to check you out. Look at you, with all your designer duds." Cross playfully circled him, looking him up and down, taking inventory of Lorenzo's expensive shoes, diamond-studded watch, and designer shirt. "You're all blinged out. New York must be treating you well."

"I'm doing okay. Besides you, I've landed a couple other high-profile clients, so my agency is doing well, very well, and since my name is on the marquee, *I'm* doing well," he said boastfully.

"I'm so proud of you; the small town boy has made it big."

"Don't act like we don't share the same story. Shit, we went to high school together. And, if you hadn't written your first book while we were in college, I wouldn't be this extraordinary agent you see standing before you."

"Well, if you hadn't secretly read it and decided, on your own, that it needed to be published and hustled it to every publisher in New York City, while pretending to be a legitimate agent, then I wouldn't be the world renowned author you see before you." They both did a silly curtsy to each other and burst out into laughter. "You are so silly."

"My silly ass got you your first big book deal, didn't I?"

"That you did, my friend." Cross raised his glass in celebration. "Here's to a bright and shiny future, for both of us."

They tapped their glasses together and took a celebratory sip. Indeed, they both had come a long way from their humble beginnings.

"I know you have a lot going on, but one of my boys in Atlanta told me about this new restaurant and I made reservations for us at nine-thirty," Lorenzo interjected. "We're going to go out, have a good time, and not think about…unpleasant things."

"But—"

"But, nothing. I don't care if you've already eaten or what kind of excuse you have. I'm getting you into the city for a boy's night out. We're going to party and bullshit and party and bullshit," Lorenzo sang as he threw his hands above his head and started rocking his lean body to his own beat. "Now, while you are getting ready, I'll move my stuff into the guest room."

"You aren't gonna take no for an answer, huh?" Cross asked with folded arms.

"You know me so well."

"You know what? After the drama I had last night, I deserve some fun. So, what is this fabulous restaurant that we're going to?"

"Now, that's the Cross I know and love. My boy is back!" Lorenzo did a little dance in mock celebration. "I think it's called Misty Blues; it's supposed to be the new trendy spot."

✪ ✪ ✪

After a few cocktails and a light dinner at Misty Blues, Lorenzo instructed Cross that they'd be venturing to a new club—PuRE—located across the street from the restaurant. They ate and drank and laughed and reminisced about the days gone by. They talked of their times when they were in New York City, drinking at the Hangar on Christopher Street or chilling at Splash in Chelsea. Back then they were young, gay, and carefree and they consumed life voraciously. Cross missed those days but was happy that he had settled into a more stable position in life.

By the time they paid their dinner check, the drinks they had consumed were working on their systems. Cross hadn't felt so free in many months. They dodged traffic on Peachtree Street and made it safely to the club. As the dynamic duo approached the door of the club, the line had already begun to form and patrons anxiously awaited their turn to go through the perfunctory ID check and pat down. When they approached the line, Cross couldn't help but notice a tall, dark-skinned man lingering behind the blue, velvet rope, whispering into the ear of one of the bouncers. His face demanded attention and Cross obliged subtly as he gently tucked at Lorenzo's arm to get his attention. The gentleman, dressed in all black, stood proudly, even while he conversed. As he chatted, he lifted his head and his eyes met Cross's, who promptly looked away, not wanting to appear eager or even interested.

"Shit, he saw me," he murmured to Lorenzo.

"Who?"

"Him; *him*."

"Oh my God," Lorenzo exclaimed in mockery, "I knew my old friend was still in there somewhere. Guess you just needed the proper *stimulus*."

"Oh, shut up. Anyone can see that man is fine."

"And, he's still looking at you."

Cross looked up as they reached the barricade and smiled at the man. He suddenly felt awkward and unsteady, not sure why he was smiling at the man and not sure how to react if the man spoke to him.

"Good evening, gentlemen," he said with a smile that sparkled up the darkened night. "I hope you have a good time at the club tonight. We have drink specials all night and for your viewing entertainment, we have some of the hottest dancers in Atlanta later on in the evening. If you need anything, find me and I'll get it for you," he said, looking directly at Cross. "*Anything*." He winked.

Cross blushed and proceeded into the club without comment. *Whew.*

Once inside the club, blue lights and blue velvet couches positioned along the walls gave the entire split-level space the appearance of some swanky lounge that was bathed in swirling light. Some of the lights flickered, adding a strobe-light effect to the room, coating the room with a psychedelic pulse. It was still relatively early, so the place wasn't packed yet, but there were enough people inside for Cross to feel the vibe. He looked around at the faces of his peers—they were certainly in their element, dancing with freedom and enjoying the company of other like-minded folks. Even though he was roughly the same age as many of the clubbers, he felt out of place, as if the club experience was foreign to him.

Lorenzo took him by the hand and led him to the bar in the far corner of the room. The placement of the bar allowed them to get a good view of the men who entered the room. Before he knew it, Cross had a drink in his hand, compliments of Lorenzo, and was sipping a strong concoction that he couldn't name, but he definitely tasted rum. He sipped and watched people pile into the club, leaving all of their troubles at the door and surrendering to the night.

"So, what do you think? Are you having a good time?" Lorenzo yelled over the music.

"So far, so good."

"The night is young and I expect you to take full advantage of it. It's been a long time since we've been out together, so let's have some fun." Lorenzo suddenly raised his drink into the air, closed his eyes and, as if he had been overcome by a spirit, started swaying his body back and forth in rhythm with the beat. The beat seemed to grow as if it were a sentient being that survived on energy; it became louder and louder with each thump; vibrations rose slowly from the floor, like a spirit resurrected. Cross soon found himself enchanted and overcome with energy. The stimulating atmosphere revived his dormant spirit and he didn't protest when Lorenzo led him onto the dance floor. The two dipped, popped, twerked, dropped, wiggled and shook everything that could be shaken—careful not to spill their cocktails—as an energy shot through the room like lightning, infusing the growing crowd with vitality and a vivacity that Cross hadn't seemed in many, many months.

After about thirty minutes of dancing, Cross abandoned Lorenzo on the dance floor and moved back over to the bar. He grabbed a napkin and wiped the sweat from his brow.

"You look like you were having a good time out there," a deep voice from behind said to him. Cross turned around and was met with the intoxicating smile of the gentleman who had smiled at him on the way into the club.

Cross wasn't sure how to respond. "Yeah, it was fun. I don't get out that often." He blushed.

"Why is that? Your man keeping you tied down, huh?" he said with a hint of flirtation.

"Nah, nothing like that. I'm not a club person. I mean, not that there's anything wrong with that." Cross tried to keep the butterflies in his stomach at bay, but the flurry of their wings gave him that old feeling.

"Let me refresh your drink."

"That's okay. I'm fine, really."

"Yes, you are." Cross tried to stifle the smile on his face, but the smooth words of his suitor were music to his ears. He had almost forgotten what a compliment sounded like. He drank the remainder of his drink and placed the empty cup on the bar.

"Thank you."

"Oh, how rude of me. My name is Zeric."

"Zeric?"

"Yes, it's like Eric, but with a Z. Don't ask," he said with a chuckle.

"Zeric, I'm Cross."

"Cross," he repeated. "Now, that's an interesting name. Let me get you that drink." He leaned across the bar and said something to the bartender that Cross failed to decipher. He watched the bartender as he poured various liquids into a shaker and poured it into a blue martini glass. "Here ya go. It's a bluetini, a specialty of the house."

"Thank you. What do you do here at the club? You a bouncer?"

Zeric took a sip of his drink and smiled. "Nah, I don't really work here. I help out from time to time when they need me. My cousin owns the joint, though. "

Cross suddenly felt self-conscious and awkward, as if he had insulted the man.

"I'm sorry. I didn't mean to imply—"

"No need to apologize."

"Well, the club is…impressive."

"Not half as impressive as you. I've read all of your books," he said with a sly smile. "I love vampire stories and your novels are so refreshing."

Cross almost spit out his drink at Zeric's confession. Even though he enjoyed some literary stardom, he was always taken aback when he was recognized by the public.

"Are you serious? I can't believe you've read my stuff and know who I am."

"How could I not? The picture of you on the back of your last book is wonderful, but it doesn't do you justice. You are far more… *impressive* in person."

Cross took a sip of his cocktail to divert the attention. As much as he tried to deny it, that old familiar feeling of falling—falling for the charms, falling for the looks, falling for the swagger of a man—flooded his whole body. He felt a slight buckle in his knees, but managed to brace himself with the bar so that his nervous twitch was imperceptible to anyone else. It had been such a long time since a man had flirted with him—at least a man his own age.

Cross smiled and looked directly into his face; it carried a dark brilliance that was tantamount to staring into the sun. Even though it made him uncomfortable, he couldn't look away, even as the fear of being burned made its way into his thoughts.

"Are you always this charming?"

Zeric chuckled. "Charming? Nah. I'm trying hard to not act like a total goof in front of my favorite author."

Cross smiled and turned his head toward the dance floor. Lorenzo was grinding on some pretty, young thing—just the kind he liked—and seemed to be having the time of his life. Cross watched him and remembered what it felt like to be young, vibrant, and full of energy. He had always admired Lorenzo's youthful energy and spirit; regardless of what was going on in his life, he could still find time for celebration.

"So, is he your man?" Zeric asked.

"Who? Lorenzo? Nah, that's my best friend. We go way back."

"Aight, that's what's up; cool. So, the next question is, do you have a man?"

Cross took a deep breath and smiled. "Nah, I'm completely single," he said as he held up his hand and wiggled his left ring finger. "If he liked it, then he should've put a ring on it."

They both burst out into a silly laugh at his very corny pop culture reference. Cross immediately regretted saying it, but their laughter filled the awkward space between what they said and what was left unsaid. This flirtation thing felt good to Cross and it was something he didn't even realize he had missed during his self-imposed exile.

"Listen, it's about time for me to get this show started. Promise not to leave before we speak again."

"I promise."

Zeric winked at him and moved from the bar, disappearing into a door off to the side.

A few moments later, sirens could be heard throughout the club as the pace of the flashing lights sped up dramatically. The music quieted and a booming voice that Cross immediately recognized as belonging Zeric poured from the speakers.

"Gentlemen, welcome to the hottest Saturday night party in the A-T-L! Welcome to Hot Chocolate Saturdays!" His voice screamed throughout the club and was joined by the raucous and joyous noise of the crowd. They cheered and yelled and hollered and clapped and jumped up and down as if Oprah had promised them a new car. "We have the finest selection of men this city has to offer. Now, let's welcome to the stage our headliner for the night; that's right, no waiting to see the man you've come to know and love. Welcome the one you know as Seduction!"

People pushed and shoved their way closer, all hoping to get a better view of this highly prized dancer.

The lights in the club dimmed and an erotically charged hip-hop beat blared from the speakers. Slowly, a figure clad in an all-black body suit and a black mask slinked from behind the curtains. He moved slowly and seductively, making each movement of his body count. The suit he wore left little for the imagination. Even from his distance, Cross could see that every muscle in this man's body was highly developed and the protruding part of his lower anatomy bulged through the thin suit. Seduction certainly understood the art of seduction as he coiled and rolled his body in ways that made Cross want to reach deep into his pockets and make it rain.

"Damn, he is fine," Lorenzo said as he snuck up on Cross from behind, startling his old friend.

Seduction stood on stage, slowly pulled his arms out of the tight sleeves of the suit, and rolled the whole suit midway down his torso, revealing his perfectly sculpted chest and strong biceps. The crowd begged and pleaded for him to remove the rest of his clothing as dollars began to rain from the crowd. After a few more minutes of tempting his fans, he yanked the suit off and stood on stage in nothing but a red G-string. Money rained down on the stage, but the dancer didn't bother to pick the bills up; he was too busy having money stuffed into the front of his G-string by an eager fan who looked as if he was doing more than stuffing money in his sacred spot.

"Damn," Cross said out loud.

"Exactly. I wish I was that G-string."

"You so *ignant*."

They laughed and sipped their drinks and continued enjoying the show. Seduction took a seat on the stage and stepped completely out of his G-string, revealing every inch of his naked and glistening body. The crowd went wild as he grabbed his dick and began to stroke himself.

"Damn!!" Lorenzo exclaimed.

Seduction hopped back up onto the stage and continued to titillate the crowd with his sensual moves.

Taut flesh everywhere.

Smooth skin.

Chocolate nipples.

Sculpted abs.

Thick thighs.

A raging bulge in his G-string.

Tribal tattoos etched around solid arms.

He danced as if his life depended on it and moved for the crowd. He turned his back to the crowd so that they could get an eyeful of his spectacular ass. He flexed and shook his body so that every muscle came to life. Finally, he turned to face the crowd, grabbed his penis, bent forward, and kissed his own dick, sending the crowd into a frenzy for his final display. He took a bow and quickly exited the stage as the stagehand ran out and collected his dollars.

"Who was that masked man?" Cross asked as if the dancer was the Lone Ranger.

"When I find out, I'll let you know. You need another drink?"

"Yeah, but let me pee first. Where is the restroom?" Lorenzo pointed to a set of double black doors on the other side of the bar behind the dance floor.

When he returned to the bar, Lorenzo had his drink waiting

for him and passed it to him without words. Cross took a sip, leaned back on the bar, and turned his attention to the other stripper that was on stage.

After about an hour and a half, the show officially ended and the strippers climbed down from the stage and mingled with the crowd, continuing to work their bodies. Smaller stages were set up throughout the club so patrons could get a better view or they could go down to the VIP section for a lap dance.

Cross watched as Lorenzo danced his way back onto the floor. When Lorenzo tried to entice him to join him, he decided against the dance, opting instead to continue his cool pose against the bar. Then, without warning, Zeric appeared, as if by magic, and took his hand and led him to the dance floor before Cross could protest. Not a single word was uttered.

As they slid their way through the crowd to the center of the floor, Cross tried to locate Lorenzo, who had no doubt scurried into some dark corner with a new man of the hour or had made his way downstairs for a private show. Cross put thoughts of Lorenzo out of his head and focused singularly on the beautiful man who danced seductively in front of him. As the music enchanted them, the distance between them disappeared and Cross soon felt his suitor's hands around his waist, pulling him closer and closer until no distance remained. They were pressed against each other and Zeric grinded his hips against Cross, who caught his thrust and threw it right back to him in a move so sexual they each felt the pangs of lust in their groins. Cross could feel Zeric's heated breath on the back of his sensitive neck and he felt fire shoot through his entire body, weakening his knees. He pulled away, pretending to dance; in actuality, he had to break free before his body completely betrayed him.

The music and the flashing lights and the atmosphere and the sweaty bodies and the drinks blended together so sweetly. He suddenly felt young and free again—and more than a bit intoxicated, too. He closed his eyes and let the music control his motion. He was dancing and swaying and smiling seductively when Zeric grabbed him by the waist from the back. Cross took his hands and placed them on top of the hands until they interlocked. He was delighted that his dream lover had returned to him so quickly. Cross continued dancing with his eyes closed, enjoying the feel of the strong erection that was pressed up against his buttocks. He wanted to give in to temptation, to throw caution to the wind, and invite this man back to his place for a passionate session of powerful lovemaking. He wanted to let this man know what he was feeling; he wanted to confess his desire. He conveyed his deepest yearning without the clumsy use of words; his body, fully versed in the art of communication, could tell the story far better than his lips. He pressed himself harder and harder against the force that knocked at his back door and grinded into him so that any doubt about his desire was removed. He felt the softest lips press firmly against his neck as he released his final reservations about the rest of the evening. The kisses on his neck sent him into a sexual frenzy; he could feel his erection beating against his zipper, wanting—needing to be set free and given attention; he imagined himself ripping off Zeric's clothes and going down on him right there on the dance floor, in front of a hundred voyeurs.

A few hours later, Cross had danced away his blues and had found the much-needed comfort of a man. Club dalliances usually didn't lead anywhere, but tonight he was reconnecting with life and not looking for anything from anyone.

"Zeric, I have had a wonderful time tonight, but it's time for me to go home."

Zeric smiled. "So soon?"

"I haven't been out this late in a long time."

"I really don't want you to go."

Cross smiled.

"I know, but you see my friend over there?" Cross motioned toward Lorenzo, who was standing near the exit door playing with his phone. "He's ready to go and I have to go with him."

"How about I drive you home?" Cross raised one eyebrow. "I'm serious and I promise not to try anything. I just wanna keep talking to you."

Cross decided to throw caution to the wind and take Zeric up on his offer.

CHAPTER 9

A pair of enraged eyes cut through the room like daggers. His snarl twisted his face, making it almost unrecognizable.

Carefully hidden amongst the thick crowd, Brandon had been watching Cross all night. He was always watching.

And, what he saw tonight made his blood boil.

The same man who only last night had thoroughly rebuffed Brandon's attempt at seduction had left the dance floor where he had been caring on like a common whore with some man he had just met. Brandon held Cross in much higher esteem. Cross was a man of virtue, a man of pride, and as far as Brandon knew, Cross wasn't one for Internet games, one-night stands or easy sex. He was above all that. If he was of loose sexual character, Brandon was certain he would have bedded him by now. Many, many times.

Yet, Cross was all up in some dude's face, smiling as if the stranger possessed joy itself.

The rage that mushroomed inside Brandon was nuclear.

Brandon watched them leave the club together. Surely, Cross wasn't going home with this dude, Brandon thought to himself; or worse still, Cross could be taking him back to his house so they could fuck in the bed in which Brandon had already spread his seed to lay claim.

Brandon continued to watch, just off in the distance, cloaked by shadows and hidden by the night. Cross and Zeric moved easily down the sidewalk with the dude Cross had arrived at the club with. Cross and his suitor were much too close and far too into each other for Brandon's taste and for them to notice anyone watching them. Brandon picked up a brick that lay on the ground near him and fought the urge to run up to them and bash the dude in the back of the head and throw Cross into his car, but he decided against it. Too many people around.

But he remained determined and desperate to stop them from leaving together; he had to stop them from doing what men who met late at night in clubs did together when they went home together.

The thought of Cross in bed with another man drove Brandon to madness.

He crept over to his car just in time to follow them. He started his car, put it in drive, and was able to follow Cross, who got in a white Toyota with the dude, leaving the other dude behind.

While turning the corner to begin chase, Brandon had a horrible thought: what if they were going to have a threesome? The thought of that sent Brandon's emotions into a tailspin. He had never seen the dude that Cross had spent most of the night with before Casanova arrived; he and Cross could be friends, ex-lovers, potential new lovers or friends with benefit—they could be anything. At this point, Brandon had no way of knowing.

As they drove into the night, more than anything Brandon hoped and prayed that Cross wouldn't do something that would force Brandon to do something he *might* regret.

Brandon stayed far back enough to get a clear picture of where they were going and he didn't make any aggressive moves to draw attention to his car.

They winded down Peachtree and headed toward the interstate. Traffic snarled along and a sea of red lights lit up the night. Anxiously, Brandon moved his head side to side, trying to see through and around the car in front of him, so he could keep his eye on the car. Soon enough, the traffic broke and cars resumed a normal speed and before he knew it, the Toyota had increased speed and burst onto the freeway in a blaze of glory. Not to be outdone, Brandon shifted gears in his muscle car and gave chase.

Exactly thirty-three minutes later, Brandon had his answer. They arrived on Cross's street. Brandon's anger had not subsided; in fact, it was growing. Brandon parked down the street and nervously stretched his neck to see what could be seen. As he peeped, he saw the car pull into the driveway and stop. Seconds later, he saw them step onto the pavement and walk to the front door.

Brandon yelled so loud in his car that it hurt his throat.

Now, he didn't know what to do. He was determined not to let them get too comfortable and intimate, but he wasn't sure how to stop them; he only knew that he had to do something.

He drove his car around to the side street and parked. He quietly got out of the car. He then raced down the street, being careful that his feet didn't make too much noise when they hit the pavement. He darted between parked cars and hid behind bushes and finally made it to Cross's backyard. He hoped he could get into the house the same way he did before. When in the yard, he moved stealthily to avoid detection. He was more than thrilled to find the window unlocked. Slowly, he raised the window so that he could slip inside. He wasn't sure what he was going to do when he got inside. The only clear thought he had was to prevent them from having sex.

The room was dark.

As he peered inside, he could see the faint glow of light from the hallway. Brandon panicked. If they hadn't turned on the lights, they might *already* be doing it. He prayed that he wouldn't catch them in the act because, if he did, he could not be responsible for the outcome of the evening.

He slipped inside.

He had barely enough light to see the shapes of objects in the room, but he remembered where items were placed.

He crept slowly like a predator.

He moved closer to the door and stopped when he heard voices—they were in the den laughing and talking. Brandon peeped around the corner and saw them hugged up on the sofa. Then, he watched this stranger lean in and kiss *his man*. Brandon wanted to scream but suppressed the sound before it came out. He wanted to burst into the room and throw some blows upside the dude's head.

He held in his horror and watched.

The kiss lingered.

It wasn't a simple peck on the lips, but a full-lipped, deep-throated kiss designed to ignite the loins. There was no way in hell Brandon was going to let them consummate their young relationship.

Then, he heard Cross's voice. He couldn't make out all of the words, but it sounded like Cross was sending him home.

Yes! Cross told him that he had had a great time, but he was really tired and needed to rest. The man asked if he could stay but, after some hesitation, Cross said no. Then, he heard Cross making a date with the man for the next evening.

Hell. Fucking. No.

Brandon continued to listen, to be certain Cross didn't change his mind and invite the man to *their* bed. When Brandon was convinced that Cross would hold firm in his decision to send the man away, he slipped out of the house the same way that he had entered.

Even though nothing had happened between Cross and this mystery dude, Brandon remained incensed that this man had the audacity to step in and try to claim what had already been claimed.

And, just because they didn't go all the way, that didn't mean they wouldn't tomorrow. Or the next night. Or the night after that. Sooner or later, Cross might give up something that Brandon believed belonged exclusively to him.

Brandon raced back to his car and drove around the block. He had to be certain that the dude was going to leave. When he came around the corner, the car was still in the driveway. He hoped that in the five minutes it had taken for him to sneak out of the house and get to his car that Cross hadn't changed his mind.

After an uneasy ten minutes in the car, Brandon saw the man practically skip to his car. He snarled again; he guessed that the bounce in his walk was due to stealing another kiss from Cross. The man got into his car and pulled out of the driveway.

Brandon followed.

He had to end this before it even started.

The first rule of love is to eliminate the competition.

His heart pounded as he watched the red brake lights on the Toyota.

The Toyota was the only other car on the road, so it wasn't too difficult to follow the crimson brake lights in the dark of night. Brandon didn't turn his lights on, but used the light from his prey to guide him. He hung in the background and navigated the narrow and curvy streets of Cross's neighborhood. He followed the car down a steep hill, around a sharp corner and up an even steeper hill. As he drove, he felt powerful under the cover of darkness. The immutable grasp of the darkness seemed to swallow everything in its entirety. Trees, houses, cars, and even the road itself, were all devoured by the night. The man's headlights managed to cut small slices into the night, but his beams could not compete with the vastness of the darkness.

He followed the car until it turned suddenly into the parking lot of a 24-hour convenience store. Brandon slowed down and watched his competition pull into a parking spot and step out of the car as if he was the shit.

Brandon had never been one to shy away from a little competition.

Brandon turned into the parking lot from a different entrance and parked near the air machine. He left his engine running and shifted his body so that he could view the man through the windows. He kept an attentive eye on the man as he moved throughout the store. Brandon stretched his neck and tilted his head, trying to maneuver himself into a position to ensure that he didn't miss a single move that the man made.

He watched the man approach the register and drop some items onto the counter. As he waited for the man to leave, his anger grew again. He thought about him touching Cross.

Flesh against flesh.

Lips against lips.

Tongues snaking around each other.

Hands exploring peaks and valleys.

By the time he snapped out of his trance, the man had gotten back into the car and was backing out of the spot. Red brake lights signaled his imminent departure as Brandon lay in wait. Once the man maneuvered into the street, Brandon resumed his slow pursuit. As he followed, Brandon was consumed by thoughts and visions of lust and became enraged. In his mind's eye, he could see *that* man and Cross going at it like old lovers.

As the man followed the sharp contours of the darkened road, Brandon squeezed his steering wheel so tightly that the veins in his hands throbbed. As he turned around the next bend in the road, Brandon's nostrils flared and he pressed harder and harder onto the accelerator until he was within inches of his prey. He turned his high beams on so as to cloak his dark intentions with light. He could see the man shifting his head and looking into the rearview mirror in an attempt to get a glimpse of the driver behind him. The man tapped his brake lights a few times as a warning to Brandon, but he did not relent. He could not allow—*would not allow*—any man to lay claim to what was already his, in his head.

Brandon rammed his car into the back of the man's vehicle with such force that he saw the man's head snap forward. He could still see the man peering into the mirror as he accelerated. Brandon stayed hot on his trail as they rounded the next bend. When they rounded the curve, Brandon clipped the side of the man's car hard enough for him to lose control and careen over the embankment and down a steep ravine. The sound of the car crashing and rolling over several times filled Brandon with joy.

In the dark Georgia night, there was no one around to hear Zeric scream.

CHAPTER 10

O n Monday morning, when Cross arrived at the high
school, he still felt unsettled and slightly on edge due to a
highly unusual weekend. He had hoped to spend a nice
Sunday afternoon with Zeric, but Zeric had never called or
returned his call. Cross wanted to get angry but didn't; being
stood up simply played into his distrust of men and Zeric's
behavior was typical of many men Cross had met before. He
surmised that because they hadn't had sex the night before that
Zeric had quickly moved on. He couldn't deny that he was somewhat disappointed; it wasn't that he was looking for anything
long-lasting from Zeric, but he did like the emotional excitement
he felt and hoped that it would last a bit longer. Clearly, it was
not meant to be.

Without the distraction of Zeric on Sunday, Cross was forced
to confront his thoughts about Brandon. He had spent much of
the weekend wrestling with himself over the proper course of action
to take in regards to Brandon. In part, he wanted to pretend as if
nothing had happened and to go on with his normal routine, but
another part of him needed to have a conversation with Brandon.
He didn't want to further inflame the situation by making it an
even bigger deal, yet he knew that he couldn't simply ignore
what had happened. Cross understood how difficult it was being
a teen; especially a gay teen, and how feelings can become blurred.
He wasn't quite ready to go to the school authorities, out of fear
that Brandon would do something extreme. He felt he owed it to

Brandon—and gay kids like him—to provide some support; he knew the pain of struggling with sexuality identity at a young age.

As he made his way down the hallway, he saw Brandon standing off in the distance, leaning against the row of lockers as Sheila, his ex-girlfriend, smiled in his face. As if they could sense each other's presence through the roaring sounds of high school, Brandon immediately looked up toward Cross. Their eyes connected quickly and uncomfortably and Brandon looked away awkwardly, opting to focus on the girl in front of him.

Cross continued down the hall, passing Brandon but not daring to look directly at him, and moved into his classroom. He immediately walked over to his desk and dropped his bags into his chair. He exhaled. His energy level was scattered, almost manic, as he tried to calm himself. This situation had taken him far out of his element and that was an uncomfortable place for Cross, who prided himself on always being in control of his life and his emotions. Suddenly, his carefully crafted world seemed to unravel under the weight of this terrible burden he carried.

Cross was far from naïve. He realized the explosive nature of this volatile situation. If it was handled wrong, it could blow up in his face; yet, he wasn't terribly concerned about losing his job since he was financially secure. He was concerned about what effect a scandal would have on Brandon. If word got out, the rumor mill would start grinding out stories of how they were involved in an illicit homosexual affair and someone so delicate might crack under the pressure.

He simply did not know what to do.

No sooner than he had taken a seat at his desk and had taken a sip of his Chai tea did he hear a knock at his door. He looked up and saw Brandon standing in the doorway, smiling nervously like a little orphan abandoned by the world.

"Mr. Jones," he called out in a voice that was much meeker than his usual tone.

"What do you want, Brandon?"

"May I speak with you, just for a second?" He stepped timidly into the room and closed the door behind him, not giving Cross a chance to respond. He took a few steps closer, but stopped midway to Cross as if he didn't want to cross the invisible line in the sand. Cross stood up and faced him. Brandon took a few seconds to gather his thoughts. He cleared his throat and began to speak. "I just wanted to really apologize for what happened. I don't know what got into me. I feel so bad about it. I couldn't sleep all weekend; I was scared that you would hate me. Please, don't hate me, Mr. Jones. I am so sorry. And, please, don't tell my parents," he begged. "They don't really know about me, if you know what I mean."

Cross took a deep breath and chewed on Brandon's words. He looked into the eyes of this child. Brandon, usually a bastion of self-assuredness, shifted his eyes away from Cross's gaze.

Cross sighed. "I don't hate you, Brandon. I hate what you did, but I don't hate you."

"Oh, thank God. I just knew you'd never want to see me again," he exclaimed with sudden relief.

"Brandon, I want you to understand something. What you're feeling can be confusing, but you have to understand that, in this world, we have lines that you can't cross. You have to understand that there is nothing between us besides a student-teacher relationship. What you did by showing up at my house uninvited and unannounced, and kissing me, will never happen again. Do you understand me?" Cross's voice was stern and absolute. He looked directly at Brandon when he spoke.

"I understand, Mr. Jones. I am so sorry."

"I spent most of the weekend trying to decide how to handle this situation."

"What are you going to do? You aren't going to tell anyone, are you?" Brandon's voice sounded panicky.

"Well," Cross said with a deep breath, "I haven't decided yet."

"What do you mean, you haven't decided? You can't tell anyone, Mr. Jones. You just can't!"

"You really need to talk to someone; someone who can help you process everything that you're feeling."

"You said I could always talk to you."

"Yeah, I did say that, but in light of what has happened, it would be more appropriate if you talked to a counselor."

"I wanna talk to you. You're the only one that I can trust."

"Funny thing about trust, Brandon; it's a two-way street. I'm not sure if I can trust you." Brandon held his head low and shifted his weight nervously from side-to-side. "And, I'm not a therapist. You are dealing with some serious things and you deserve someone that can provide you with the guidance and support you need before you do something that can't be fixed with an apology."

"You act like I'm crazy or something."

"I didn't say you were crazy. I said you were dealing with some serious issues. At your age, there is so much that you have to learn, and sometimes things can happen that you aren't fully capable of dealing with. High school is tough enough as it is, let alone dealing with family tragedy and your sexual orientation."

"I can handle it."

"I don't think you can. You're struggling, Brandon. Your grades are slipping and you're making provocative actions toward me; that doesn't sound like you're handling it. I should talk to your parents. Let them help you."

"You can't do that, Cross," Brandon said with force. "If my father found out about me, he'd beat the shit out of me and throw me out of the house. My uncle came out six years ago and my dad hasn't spoken to him since." Brandon moved in a bit closer. "My father can never know. Never!"

"Brandon, I want you to take a deep breath and calm down, okay. Now, listen to me. I get it. You can't talk to your parents, but if that's not an option, then you have to talk to someone about what you're feeling."

Brandon remained quiet for a second. Cross paid careful attention to his body language, which had suddenly taken on a more defiant stance. Then, Brandon exploded into a rambling and almost incomprehensible diatribe about his parents, his life, and the school.

As Cross listened to his growing protests, something amazing happened.

Brandon transformed right before his very eyes.

No longer did Cross see a scared child hiding from monsters; gone was the innocent teen that lashed out dangerously at the world. Finally, Cross's instincts kicked into high gear. Something didn't *feel* right and he watched Brandon's face with careful detail as the young student continued to speak. Cross felt a measured warning in his spirit; it wasn't strong enough for him to shut Brandon down, but it carried enough force for Cross to doubt everything that Brandon said and everything that he was. Brandon continued his ranting while Cross pretended to listen. Instead of listening to the words, he listened through them. In Brandon's gruff voice, he heard a lack of sincerity that rang out with crystal clarity. Even though the change in Brandon's tone was minute, an uneasy feeling settled deep down in his bones.

He no longer saw fear in Brandon's face.

What he saw was something insidious—deception.

What kind of game is this boy playing? Cross asked himself. *Maybe Lorenzo's warnings were right all along.*

✪ ✪ ✪

The very next afternoon, Brandon walked into the locker room and was instantly assaulted with the tangy smell of teenage sweat, funky socks, and testosterone. It was time for track practice and he wasn't in the mood for the immature antics of his classmates. He had other things on his mind. Cross still occupied a prominent space in his thoughts and Brandon found it difficult to let go, even after his attempts at seduction ended in a fiasco. He realized the error of his ways: he had come on too strong. He should have known that a man like Cross wouldn't fall for his high school tricks. A man like Cross needed to be slowly caressed and eased into submission. Brandon knew that he'd need to be cleverer with his game if he were to ever claim his prize.

As he slid quietly into the room, he hoped to remain unnoticed by the rowdy bunch. The space was abuzz with laughter and energy, boldness, and bravado. Heavy voices called out vulgar names and rolled-up socks were tossed across the room as if they were base-balls. He looked over at his friend, Marvin, who was demonstrating his oral skills by wiggling his long tongue between his index and middle fingers in a crude simulation of oral sex as he boasted of his conquests to a captivated audience of pubescent males. *I got something you can do with that tongue*, Brandon thought to himself as he eased on by over to his locker, not stopping for a front row seat of the spectacle. The lack of maturity of his peers was one of the reasons he was so infatuated with Cross; high school boys wouldn't be able to handle the fire that he brought.

Brandon opened his locker and took a seat on the cold bench while half-listening as Marvin continued to work the crowd up into a frenzy. Marvin was a marvelous storyteller, but Brandon was not in the mood for his fables. He had more important things on his mind, like how he was going to win over his prince.

Then, Marvin dropped to the floor, wearing only his tight, white underwear, and began moving his body as if he were having sex. Brandon subtly eyed the boy's tight set of buttocks as they contracted underneath the thin cotton material. Marvin continued to roll his body like a snake as the boys cheered him on.

"Oh, Sheila, this is for you, baby," he called out in jest as he thrust even harder. "Oh, oh, oh, Sheila."

"Damn, Brandon, you don't care that Marvin be running up in yo' ex like that?" one of boys called out.

"Shit nah. I don't give a damn about that girl. For all I care, y'all can all run a train up her, but just remember, I hit that first," Brandon said with a sense of pride. He smiled and leaned over to untie his shoe when a gruff voice called out from the corner.

"Marvin, get yo' ass up on that damned floor and quit acting like an idiot. You couldn't get laid in a damn whorehouse!" Coach Thomas called out in a voice that boomed like drums. Marvin hopped off the floor as if he was on fire and the crowd quickly fanned out in various directions. "I want your asses out on the field in five minutes. Not six minutes, not seven minutes, but five, and if you are one second late, then your lazy asses will regret it. Got it?" The boys started scurrying around the room in an effort to gather their belongings and to meet the deadline. "Brandon, they need you in the principal's office."

"Now?"

"Yes, right now."

"For what?"

"Do I look like the damned secretary? Just get your ass up there."

The coach turned around and walked toward the door. "Four minutes and thirty seconds!"

Brandon closed his locker, picked up his backpack, slung it across his shoulder, and headed for the door. As he made his way out of the gym and into the hallway, he wondered what could be so urgent that Principal Harris needed to see him right that minute. Maybe he had gotten another scholarship. Principal Harris took great pride in Brandon, often calling him his model student because he excelled in sports and academics and whenever Brandon received an accolade, Principal Harris delighted in being the bearer of good news.

As Brandon rounded the hallway and entered the administrative offices, he casually approached the information desk, told the school secretary working behind the counter that he had been summoned, and she pointed him down the hall to the office, as if Brandon needed directions. He bounced around the corner, speaking to every staff member and teacher that he encountered, and smiled as they all spoke to him by name. He had gone out of his way to get to know—almost befriend—teachers, assistant principals, and other staffers. It paid to have as many allies as possible.

As he approached Principal Harris's office, he glanced through the window and saw a woman from the back that was speaking to the principal. A woman in a big black hat and a beige dress.

He knew that hat.

He knew that dress.

He froze in place.

"What the fuck is my mother doing here?" he asked the space around him, half-expecting a cogent answer. Brandon had taken one step backward when the principal looked up, saw him in the window, and waved him into the office. His hand gesture was animated, too excited. *He can't be that excited to see me.*

"Fuck," Brandon whispered to himself. He took a breath and propelled himself forward. Having his mother in the principal's office was never a harbinger of good news, so he tried to prepare himself for whatever was going on.

Sometimes, he wished someone would drop a house on her.

He nervously placed his hand on the doorknob, then slowly turned and pushed the door open. The door emitted an odd creaking sound that grew louder the further it was extended.

"Come on in, Brandon, and have a seat," Principal Harris said without delay as he moved from behind the colossal desk and met Brandon near the door. He placed his hand on Brandon's arm and guided him deeper into the interior of the room as if he were afraid that Brandon would turn and make a run for it. Principal Harris then moved over to the window and pulled down the metal blinds, which fell to the windowsill with a bang, startling Brandon.

"Mother. What's going on?" She was poised almost to perfection.

"Just have a seat, Brandon," she said as she stood and gave her son a lukewarm hug. Brandon rapidly tried to process the scene and failed to notice another figure looming over in a corner to his right. Out of his periphery, he saw the figure move and he turned his head quickly.

"Hey, Brandon," Cross said flatly.

"Cross...Mr. Jones...what are you doing here? Would someone please tell me what's going on?"

"Just have a seat and we'll talk."

"No, I wanna know what's going on."

"Brandon, don't cause a scene. Just sit down." His mother looked directly at him as she smiled. Her haughty voice sounded strained and Brandon obeyed her commands.

Oh, fuck. This isn't good. He recognized that tone and it always meant trouble.

Brandon lowered himself into the middle seat directly in front of the principal's desk. Cross moved over and took a seat to Brandon's left while his mother, with her legs neatly crossed and her well-manicured hands laid delicately on her lap, sat on the right. Principal Harris moved back behind his desk and slowly lowered himself. He shifted his weight uncomfortably in the leather chair and took time to make eye contact with the three people who sat before him.

"Is someone going to tell me what this is about? I have track practice right now and coach says I have a good chance—"

"Calm down, Brandon. I've been called away from an important appointment and I'd like to get to the bottom of this."

"Bottom of what?" He turned his head to face Cross. "Why are you here?" he hissed.

"We're getting to that, Brandon," Principal Harris interjected.

"Well, can we get to it? I don't have all day to be here," he said with much attitude.

"I hardly know where to begin," Principal Harris said. He locked his fingers together and placed his extremely large hands on his very organized desk. He sighed and looked at Brandon through the thin spectacles that sat atop his even thinner nose. His cheeks reddened slightly, bringing a bit of color to his usually pale face; he blushed even before the story was told.

Brandon's mother spoke. "How about you start at the beginning?" She leaned back in her chair and looked at Brandon. "Shall we begin?"

"Yes, let's begin." Principal Harris cleared his throat. "Brandon, it has been brought to our attention that you may need some… counseling."

"Counseling? For what?"

"To deal with the feelings you might be having."

"Feelings I'm having? What are you talking about?" He sneered at Cross. "I *feel* just fine."

"Brandon, Mr. Jones is really concerned about you. He said

you two have had some conversations that alarmed him. He thinks that you may be experiencing some things that you are not able to fully understand at your young age. Do you understand what I am saying?" Brandon cut a quick look toward Cross that conveyed his message without words. "Brandon, what you're feeling is okay."

"With all that you're going through, it's important to find healthy ways to deal with it," Cross said. "I don't want you to get overwhelmed trying to figure it out."

His mother let out a snide chuckle. "Oh, I get it now. You're talking about the fact that my son is gay, right?" Her words were blunt.

"Well, uhh, yes." The principal looked around the room uncomfortably.

She looked at Brandon. "What have you done?"

"Nothing. I don't know what this is about," Brandon protested.

"So, you're aware of your son's—"

"There's not much about my son that I don't know, Mr. Harris. Is this it? Is this why you called me, to tell me that my son is a homosexual?"

"Does his father know?" Cross asked. "Brandon told me—"

"Yes, his father knows. We are his parents, after all."

Cross looked at Brandon, but Brandon looked away, not daring to meet his gaze.

"Wow. That's not the story I was told," Cross said, while shaking his head.

Brandon felt like running, screaming from the room, but he could not will his feet to move; they felt like heavy stones, even heavier than the truth he had worked hard to conceal. Slowly, Brandon's web of lies was unraveling and he was powerless to do anything about it.

"Mr. Jones, please don't do this. I thought we had an understanding?"

"An understanding about what?" Cross asked quickly.

"An understanding about *us*," Brandon said. His voice shook a bit, causing his words to slur.

"Brandon, you keep speaking of *us* as if there was something more between us. This is exactly why we're here."

"Cross—"

"Brandon, let him speak. I'd like to hear what he has to say."

Brandon turned his head away and looked off into the distance. He could feel his anger growing inside. Hot flashes lit up his skin, causing his palms to become moist and little beads of sweat to gather on the tip of his nose.

Cross cleared his throat and looked him directly in the eye.

"I think Brandon has some serious emotional issues and has been acting out in unhealthy ways."

"What do you mean?" his mother asked.

"Mr. Jones, please don't do this. Please—"

"Someone better tell us," Principal Harris interjected.

"I'm only trying to help you," Cross continued.

"Has my son done something or do you think simply being gay warrants special counseling?"

Brandon sat back in his chair and stared directly ahead above Mr. Harris's balding scalp. He peered out of the window as Cross began to lay out details of their conversations and interactions. Every detail of their conversations was laid out like evidence before a jury. Brandon knew that with his history, his mother would believe every word from Cross's suddenly sanctified mouth. He sounded so pious in his recriminations of Brandon's behavior that the question of guilt was no longer a question.

While Cross spoke, a quiet fury slowly boiled underneath

Brandon's skin. He continued to look forward and did not speak. He barely breathed. A part of him was afraid of what he'd do if he were forced to participate in this charade. Brandon knew that Cross wanted him. The eyes don't lie; that kiss didn't lie, but his holier than thou attitude stood in the way and all of this mess was his attempt to cover his ass, in case they were discovered. Brandon had the game all figured out. He closed his eyes and pretended that he was somewhere far away. He imagined dazzling strangers on the streets of Paris or bewitching Londoners on the Tube. He pretended to entertain patrons in a quaint café on a cobbled street of Amsterdam; yet, as much as he tried to tune out the conversation that was taking place in his presence, he couldn't. He felt the sting of every accusation and the lash of every detail.

"All of this behavior can probably be explained by the death of his brother. I don't think Brandon has properly grieved."

Brandon gasped.

"Brother? What are you talking about? Brandon doesn't have a brother." She turned her head slowly and looked at Brandon, who avoided eye contact with anyone.

"I'm talking about your other son, Brandon's brother," Cross said with confusion.

His mother shook her head from side to side and looked down for a second. "I apologize for what my son has been telling you, but he has never had a sibling. He's an only child."

Even while looking directly ahead, Brandon could see three heads turn in his direction and he felt the weight of six eyes glaring at him. He could see Cross staring at him, dumbfounded, his mouth open with astonishment. Even while the harsh truth circled around the room, all Brandon could think about was how he could get Cross to forgive him.

"Brandon, baby," his mother said with a peculiar calm, "wait in the hallway for me." She patted his leg with her hand and smiled at him. "And close the door on your way out."

Brandon got up slowly, but he couldn't let it go.

"Why don't you ask him what else we did that night at his house?"

The room froze. Heads slowly turned toward Cross.

"Mr. Jones, is there something you need to tell us?"

"Not at all. I told you what happened at my house. He kissed me and I put him out; that's what happened."

"Cross, that's what he likes me to call him when we're not in school," Brandon said casually. "Why didn't you mention the vodka you gave me? Why don't you tell them about the things we did together?"

"Brandon, stop the lies. You know that nothing happened."

"It's okay, Cross. They know. You don't have to lie about our relationship anymore." Brandon reached down for his backpack, unzipped a pocket, and pulled out the pair of underwear he had stolen from Cross's house. He threw them at Cross. "Those are a pair of his underwear that he gave me to remember him by. He said if I got lonely or horny I could smell them and think of him. If you're gonna tell our story, then tell the whole story."

"That's a damned lie and you know it, Brandon. I never gave you this underwear!"

"So, they do belong to you?" Principal Harris asked.

Cross looked at the underwear closely. "As far as I can tell, but—"

"That's enough, Brandon, I told you to go into the hallway. Now." She didn't raise her voice but the force of her words was strong.

"He said he loves me and we'll be together after I graduate," he said before storming out of the room and slamming the door. The force of the slam caused the door to bounce open slightly and Brandon stayed within earshot of the conversation. Brandon believed in going down swinging.

"Mr. Jones, I apologize for my son," his mother began, "but I don't need to hear what he has to say. I love him very much but I can't believe a word that comes out of his mouth; I never could. He's been making up stories and lying since he could speak. He tells lies so often that he believes them. I'm not sure he even knows what the truth is. You seem like a nice teacher who is genuinely concerned about Brandon, but don't waste any more of your time. Brandon will be okay; he always is."

"I don't understand. Why would he make up a story about having a dead brother?"

Mrs. Heart looked at Cross from head to toe. "When Brandon fixates on something he likes," she said, "he'll do just about anything to get it, and I mean anything. Lying is his second nature. He's always been like that, even as a little boy. I'm sure his story was to get closer to you; so that he could get into your good graces."

✪ ✪ ✪

Brandon wanted to race back into the room and slap her mouth shut, but he restrained himself, for now. His lips quivered on top of clenched teeth. His hands were balled into angry fists. He continued to listen as she painted him in the worst possible light and revealed things a mother should never reveal about her son to strangers, even if they were true. She was supposed to defend him at all costs, but she sold him out. As far as Brandon was concerned, this was the final betrayal.

Her truths complicated his plans of conquest. How on earth would he ever get into Cross's bed now? Once again she had swooped in on her broomstick and swept clean his carefully laid plans.

Incredulously, Cross spoke again. "He told me that his father would beat him, almost kill him, if he found out that Brandon was gay. Why would he lie to me?"

"Mr. Jones, Brandon's father is one of the gentlest men in the world and he adores Brandon, in spite of his behavior. Brandon came out to him when he was eleven. We don't have a problem with him being gay. He is who he is."

"He's been lying to me, all this time?"

"Mr. Jones, Brandon has always been…difficult," she said with carefully chosen words, "and we have done everything humanly possible to help him. We've taken him to therapy and he passed every test they gave him; we had him meet with our minister, who agreed that there's nothing wrong with Brandon. We've loved him in every way we know how and we have supported him in everything he does. Brandon has a good life, a good home, and a good family, but he's always been the bad seed, if you know what I mean. He makes up these outrageous stories in his head and he gets confused on what's real and what's not. We have been cleaning up his messes for years now and I suspect we'll continue to do so. He's my son, so what is a mother to do?"

Cross remained speechless.

"Don't be too hard on yourself," she said as she stood up and starting gathering her belongings. "You're not the first person to fall for my son's charms or his lies and I'm certain you won't be the last."

Brandon stood up and gazed through the window into the office. His eyes met Cross's and Brandon felt like scurrying away. The look in Cross's eyes was almost too much for Brandon to bear. It reflected hurt, disappointment, pity, anger, shame, and confusion. It was a look that tore through Brandon like a jagged blade.

It was a stare he would never forget.

Those eyes would never gaze upon Brandon again with any kind of fondness.

He would never again feel a comforting hand from Cross on his shoulder.

And, it was her fault.

CHAPTER 11

On the ride home, Brandon and his mother didn't speak. Instead of voices, the car was filled with the sound of the air rushing in from the windows. His mother drove with purpose, but not with attitude. Anger didn't separate them, but the truth had always gotten in the way. Every so often Brandon would eye her to see if her facial expression had changed; it didn't. She looked pleasant, given the circumstances.

Brandon wasn't surprised that she wasn't surprised; after all, she had been down this road with him many, many times. Over the years, she had been called to so many meetings in the principal's office that the school district should have put her on the payroll. Time and time again she had arrived to clean up Brandon's messes, as a mother should. But this time, she had gone too far. She had no right to confess his sins to them. With her loose tongue and careless words, she had taken away the only thing that mattered.

Brandon wanted nothing more than to jump out of the car at the next red light and run back to Cross to offer an explanation. If he could find the right words to confess his love, maybe, just maybe, Cross would listen. He would throw himself at his feet and beg forgiveness. He'd do whatever he had to do to make it right between them. He'd sacrifice a thousand virgins or slaughter a field full of animals if a blood offering would make things right. Maybe that's what he needed; a sacrifice.

In his heart, he knew nothing would make this right, but he had to try. Nothing was more important than Cross.

Once they arrived at their house, they walked in together as if everything was okay. No words had been exchanged until they crossed the threshold to their home.

"Your father says hello. He'll be back Thursday evening," she said casually. "How about I make your favorite dinner tonight, steak and mashed potatoes? How does that sound?"

"Fine."

"Now, Brandon, don't be mad. We've been through this before." She moved about the house the same way she did every day. Today was no different. "Why don't you go listen to some music while I cook? I'll let you know when it's ready."

Brandon turned away, then headed toward his room. He could hear his mother humming a song in the kitchen, as if she didn't have a care in the world. He stopped in place and listened to her melody. Her humming sounds quickly became song. He instantly recognized the song: "God Bless the Child."

He turned and walked into the kitchen toward her, as if called by the soothing sound of her voice. Her back was to him as she stood at the sink and sang lightly. He saw what he needed on the counter and approached her.

"I thought you were going upstairs?" She felt his presence and turned. He pulled her into him as if he was going to hug her.

With a determined stroke, he stuck the long knife into her belly.

She made an odd gasping sound.

He felt her warm blood on his hands.

He pressed the knife deeper.

He listened to the gurgling sound as she spit up blood. She looked as if she wanted to ask the proverbial question of *why*, but the blade silenced her.

The look of shock on her face burned itself into Brandon's mind. He always wanted to remember that look; the look of a mother who had betrayed her son for the last time.

He continued to hold her close to his body.

He pressed the knife deeper and deeper into his mother's womb until the light in her eyes faded to black.

"God bless the child that's got his own," he sang in perfect harmony.

CHAPTER 12

Cross let out a deep breath when he got to the end of the story. Lorenzo sat on the couch absolutely mesmerized by the details.

"Please don't say I told you so, Lorenzo. That really is the last thing I need to hear. I feel like such a fool."

"I wasn't going to say that, but I did tell you to be careful and to leave that boy alone," he said mockingly.

"I don't even know why I bother to talk to you." Cross jumped from the couch.

"Wait, I'm sorry. I was only kidding. I was trying to make you laugh."

"This isn't a laughing matter. This is serious."

"I know, I know. My bad. But, just be thankful that it's over and the truth came out before some real damage was done. Can you imagine what would've happened if his mother hadn't come forward?"

"He was setting me up the whole time. I still don't know how he got my underwear."

"These kids today are some sneaky bastards; you can't put anything past them."

"I still can't help feeling a bit sad. That boy is trouble. Who knows what he'll do next?"

"They moved him out of your class, right?"

"Yeah, but if they don't get him some real help, the next time there'll be some real trouble."

"Okay, enough about that boy. I have an idea."

Cross looked at him cynically.

"What's that look for?"

"Your ideas usually involve a man and some vodka."

"See, that's where you're wrong. I was gonna suggest we get some margaritas; that's tequila," he said, laughing. "We could go to Atlantic Station and then go out. I mean, this is my last night in town. I have to go back to New York tomorrow evening."

"Man, I don't think so. I'm exhausted. I want to take a long bath and drink some wine."

"What you need to do is find a man to take your mind off your troubles. Did you ever hear from Zeric?"

"Nope. He never called and I'm not calling him again. It's cool, though, because tonight I wouldn't be good company for anyone."

"Are you sure? I wanted to catch the Stars of the Century drag show at The Jungle tonight. *RuPaul's Drag Race* ain't got nothing on them."

"I love a good drag show as much as anyone," he said sarcastically, "but I'm tired. You go and have a good time. If you're sleep when I leave for work tomorrow, I'll wake you up to say good-bye."

"The hell you will. You better let my ass sleep." They hugged in the event that they didn't see each other in the morning. Cross lugged himself up the stairs, into his bedroom, and closed the door.

✪ ✪ ✪

Brandon's plans changed when he saw the strange man leave Cross's house. It was the same man that Cross was at the club with the other night. He had already eliminated one man, but this one continued to be a thorn in his side. He didn't know who he was, but he was suddenly determined to find out.

The car pulled out of the driveway and Brandon followed its red lights all the way into the city to The Jungle.

✪ ✪ ✪

At 2:15 in the morning, Cross was awakened by sounds that he hadn't heard in a long time. At first he thought he was dreaming, but the headboard pounding against the wall was far too loud to be in his dreams. As annoyed as he was that Lorenzo had met some trick and brought him back to his house, and as annoyed as he was that he had to listen to his best friend having sex in the next room, he found himself oddly turned on. The banging against the walls and the muffled sounds of ecstasy warmed him up. He felt his dick stiffening. He could hear the bed squeak against their frantic rhythm. He touched himself. They were going at it full force and it sounded wonderful! In that moment, Cross wished he had fucked Zeric that night. At least then the hunger he now felt wouldn't be so strong.

He imagined Zeric's strong hands on his ass.

He imagined kissing those very lovely lips.

He remembered his intoxicating scent.

Cross decided that tomorrow he'd start living again. He missed the pleasures of the world and he longed for human touch, for companionship.

As he masturbated, he imagined being loved; it wasn't solely a physical need that he envisioned, but an endless, undying love. The more he thought about what it would be like, the more he jerked. He loved himself so many times that night, dreaming of love and listening to sex, that his dick became sore. When he was done dreaming of love and releasing his pent-up frustrations, he thought of Brandon.

In the morning, things were clearer. He decided not to make a big deal about Lorenzo bringing a stranger to his home. After all, he had enjoyed it, too.

Before he left for work, he lightly tapped on the guest room door. It opened slowly.

Cross stepped into the room and moved over to the bed. He saw a single silhouette in the silk sheets; his boy toy must've found his way home. He was probably doing the walk of shame in front of his house right now.

"Lorenzo, wake up. I'm leaving. I wanted to say good-bye." He pulled the sheet back enough to reveal Lorenzo's face. Lorenzo rolled over and wiped the sleep out of his eyes.

"Damn it, Cross. I told you not to wake me up. I'm tired as hell."

"You are always so cranky in the morning. You can at least say *I'm sorry* for waking me up last night when you were doing the nasty."

"Oh, you heard that?" he said playfully. "Ol' boy was wild. Speaking of which, where is he?" Lorenzo sat up and looked around the room.

"Good morning, Cross."

Cross turned his head slowly and saw Brandon standing in the doorway of the bathroom, completely naked.

"What the fuck is going on here?" Cross looked at Brandon and then at Lorenzo. "What the fuck is this shit?"

Lorenzo sat up in the bed. "You two know each other?"

"This is Brandon, the student I told you about last night—"

"The crazy one?" Lorenzo asked with shock.

"Crazy one? The only thing I am is crazy in love with you, Cross." He stepped out of the door and into the room.

Lorenzo leapt out of the bed and slid into a pair of boxers. "Cross, I didn't know this was him, I swear. He told me his name was Travis."

"I know you didn't know, Lorenzo. Brandon, get your shit and get the hell out of my house!"

Brandon's face lit up. "See, I knew you loved me. If you didn't love me, you wouldn't be so upset. Now, I am sorry I had to fuck your best friend, but it was the only way. Don't you see?"

"Brandon, get outta here before this gets ugly."

"Are…are you threatening me?"

"Boy, if you don't get outta of here, you're gonna catch one old country-ass whopping!" Lorenzo yelled.

"Why don't you shut yo' little dick ass up before I bust you in the face!"

Lorenzo lunged at Brandon, but Cross held him back. "Yeah, that's right, you better hold your little dog back before he gets cut down like that other fool you had over here the other night."

"What? Who are you talking about?"

"That muthafucka you met at the club. What? You think I didn't know about that shit, huh? You think I was just gonna let you bring his ass up in here so he could fuck you? You must be out of yo' damn mind!"

"Did you do something to Zeric?"

"Oh, how you gonna throw his name up in my face like that? See, you trippin'."

"Brandon, what did you do to Zeric?"

"Let's just say he shouldn't drink and drive. These roads around here are a bitch and sometimes the bitch bites back. But, it's okay now, baby. I'm here with you and nothing will stand in our way."

Cross looked at Brandon's wild eyes and could see his detachment from reality. Brandon's voice alternated between highs and lows and his mood swings ran the gamut of emotions. One moment he spoke with lucidity, but other times his words were as complex as a riddle. All the while he spoke he remained naked, completely unashamed of his nudity.

Cross wasn't sure what to do. He didn't want this situation to turn violent, out of fear that someone would get hurt.

"Okay, Brandon, why don't you put some clothes on so we can talk?"

"I talk much better without my clothes; ask your friend. Baby, all I've ever wanted was you. Everything I've done was for you. You love me and I understand how hard it is for you to admit it because of this situation, but no one can stop our love."

"This boy is crazy as shit," Lorenzo said. "And I've had enough. I'm calling the police. Where the fuck is my cell phone?" Lorenzo looked around the room and disappeared into the hallway.

"Are you going to let him do that, baby? You gonna let him turn me in for some shit I did for us?" Brandon's voice became elevated.

"Brandon, you need to calm down."

"I know, I know. I just get so excited when I'm around you. See, look." Brandon smiled sexily and looked down. Cross couldn't help but notice Brandon's growing erection. "You see what you do to me? I can't help it." Brandon stepped closer to Cross, who pushed him back.

"Brandon," Cross began with a heavy voice, "you need to listen to me and listen to me good. I don't love you. I will never love you. You and I will never, ever be together. Do you hear me, you stupid boy?"

Brandon flinched as if he had been slapped across the face; the words stung.

"Stupid? Baby, why are you talking to me like that, huh? Is this foreplay? Ahhh, I get it. You're trying to upset me because you like it rough, huh? That's cool. I like it rough sometimes, too."

Cross shook his head, almost in disgust. He couldn't figure out how to get through to Brandon, so he decided on being direct.

"You are fucking delusional. I don't know what else I can say to you to get you to understand that if you were the last man on earth, I still wouldn't fuck you. You see, I like my men much more sophisticated than you. You're just a boy who doesn't know his head from his asshole. You wanna play grown-up games but you're too much of a child to know when the game is over."

"I ain't no fuckin' child!"

Cross was intentionally pushing his buttons in the hopes that it would shock him back into reality, but he wasn't sure it was working. Brandon looked confused, as if he couldn't decide what his next move would be. Cross felt a tingling sensation in the pit of his stomach and he felt like running away, but he didn't. He wanted to talk Brandon off the ledge.

"Why don't you take your little backpack and go to the playground with the rest of the children?" He pushed again.

"What the fuck is wrong with you? I thought we had something, Cross?"

"Why the hell would you think that? You don't know this, but when I first started teaching, I tried to have you removed from my class, but no other teacher would accept you, so I got stuck with you. I didn't want you then and I don't want you now."

Brandon froze in place.

As Cross looked into his eyes, he saw tears form in the corners and then fall down his face. Brandon remained still as the tears fell. His eyes were fixated upon Cross. Cross heard Brandon's heart break but it was necessary to end this.

Then, Brandon spoke. "Do you have any idea what I've sacrificed to be with you? My mother tried to keep us apart, but you don't have to worry about her anymore."

Cross suddenly felt a sense of dread like he had never felt before. "Brandon, what does that mean?"

"You think I'm crazy, but I'm not. I know what I'm doing. I'm going to leave now. Is that okay?"

"Did you do something to your mother?" he asked with concern.

Brandon didn't speak.

Cross was torn between pursuing this line of questioning and letting Brandon go. He decided to let him go; if Brandon had done something to his mother, there was no guarantee that he wouldn't lash out at him.

Brandon bent over and picked up his backpack and the clothing surrounding it. Brandon slid into a pair of jeans and threw on a blue shirt. Cross looked toward the door for a second, hoping Lorenzo was nearby. He didn't see Brandon lunge toward him and plunge the knife into his stomach.

It took him a few seconds to realize what had happened. Cross felt his own blood ooze out of his body and stain his shirt. It wasn't until he tasted blood in his mouth that he truly understood what had happened.

Brandon held him against the wall and pushed the knife in deeper.

Brandon whispered in his ear. "If I can't have you, then no one will." Brandon kissed him hard, in spite of the blood in Cross's mouth. The kiss was deep and full of youthful passion. As he kissed him, he pulled the knife out.

Cross managed to let out one loud scream for Lorenzo before he collapsed to the floor. When Lorenzo raced into the room, Brandon stabbed him, too.

Lorenzo went down swiftly.

EPILOGUE

Brandon, clad only in a pair of tiny bikini underwear and an oversized pair of expensive sunglasses, lounged at the pool of the beautiful mansion of his benefactor on Grand Turk Island in the Turks and Caicos Islands. The sun bathed this island paradise with a magnificent splendor and Brandon couldn't resist soaking up some rays. He was enjoying a second tropical drink brought by one of the servants; he didn't know what the drink was nor did he care to find out. It suited his palate well.

It was here on Grand Turk Island that he found peace.

On Grand Turk Island, the bluest water he had ever seen sparkled with a brilliance he did not understand; it cleansed his hands of blood.

With all the brouhaha sounding the attacks, Brandon had fled. Once he had left Cross's house that morning, he had slipped out of town unnoticed, with the assistance of his benefactor.

He could never go back to the United States, at least not as Brandon Heart. His benefactor had promised to use his considerable wealth to buy him a new identity, but Brandon was in no hurry to leave this island paradise.

Here, the warm breezes blew away unpleasant thoughts.

Here, the troubles of the world were a thousand miles away.

Here he found peace, even if it was without Cross.

When he thought about the sacrifices he had made for love, he felt no remorse. Love always required sacrifice and great love always required great risk; love is a gamble and you win some, you lose some. In hindsight, Brandon saw the error of his ways. If he had played the game differently, had been a little more subtle and patient, then maybe he would be in paradise now with Cross instead of his benefactor. Lesson learned: patience is a virtue.

He wished Cross hadn't forced his hand and driven him to commit the ultimate act. When Cross mocked him and cast him aside, Brandon felt his hands had been tied and that he had no other choice. He couldn't let the blood sacrifice of his mother be in vain. He offered his mother for slaughter, yet Cross scorned his love.

If he wouldn't give his love to Brandon, then Brandon wouldn't let him give it to another.

"Brandon, why don't you come inside? We need to get ready for dinner," his benefactor called out. Brandon smiled. He wasn't being called for dinner; he was being called for something more carnal. He had grown particularly fond of Blues Carmichael and he thought if you can't have the one you love, then love the one you're with.

"Alright, Blues, I'll be there in a second, baby." He looked up and saw Blues blow him a kiss. Now, more than ever, he was happy he had met Blues.

They were kindred spirits, cut from the same cloth.

Brandon grabbed his phone and logged onto the Internet. He read a story about a dead mother, a crying father, a wounded lover, and a remarkably strong-willed teacher who had survived a vicious stabbing by a "deranged student" as described in the *Atlanta Journal-Constitution*.

Deranged.

Brandon didn't like that word. He wasn't deranged. He was just crazy in love.

Some monsters, like Blues are made; others, like Brandon are born bad, rotting from the inside out.

Once a monster, always a monster.

ABOUT THE AUTHOR

Lee Hayes is the author of the novels *Passion Marks*, *A Deeper Blue*, *The Messiah* and the editor of *Flesh to Flesh: An Erotic Anthology*. He currently resides in the Washington, D.C. metropolitan area. He can be reached at lee@leehayes.info or via Facebook at www.facebook.com/leehayeswriter. Please visit his website at: www.leehayes.info